CARMEN LOUP

ONE
QUOTE

* * * * *

"Only you exist, you and you alone. Truly, you are contained in everything. Again, you are indeed That Itself, in all infinity is He and no other. I alone am." - Anandamayi Ma

TWO
PROLOGUE

* * * * *

Far from Earth in the system of Flotluex resides the Yenuket Municipal Space Port, abandoned by all except its robotic staff, several strains of chartreuse cave skrum, and a single Tuhntian scientist who rather enjoyed having the place and all its failing electronics to herself.

Typically, she worked in the storeroom of a deserted trinket shop. The corroded metal sign in front of the shop used to read 'Bezalbum's Baubles,' but time had worn away most of the letters and re-dubbed it 'EZ Lab,' so that's what Mazelmez called it. Her latest invention, however, could not be completed in the EZ Lab, as there was absolutely nothing in the old trinket shop shiny enough to use as a mirror.

The old Moonshine Cafe, a short walk away from the EZ Lab, had an enormous mirror installed behind the bar. A mirror originally intended to alert the bargoer to dangers lurking behind them, its purpose for the last several eons had been to double the feeling of emptiness. It reflected nothing but the unused chairs caught in dim rays of yellow light and the back of the bartending robot.

For several decades, the robotic bartender's only action had been rhythmically opening and closing the till. Press a button to open it; it opened. Press a button to close it; it closed. Occasionally, it would fail to do one or the other so the robot would have something interesting to occupy himself for a bloop or two. Then it was back to testing. Open? Open. Close? Close.

"Hey, barkeep!" Mazelmez announced herself as she blundered into the cafe.

She carried two baskets overrunning with tools, scrap, and wires, one in each hand. Her outstandingly pink hair tumbled down her pale blue face in messy waterfalls. "I need to use your mirror, buddy."

"It's not my mirror," replied the robot. The till opened; the till closed.

"Right, well, I'm using it anyway." Mazelmez climbed onto the counter and sat crosslegged, leaning forward to get a good look at herself. She leaned slightly too far; her long Carmnian nose bumped into the mirror, and she twitched it in surprise. "I'm inventing something big, barkeep. Want to guess?" She pulled a thin, kinked wire from one of the baskets and held it aloft.

"Not particularly," he said.

"It's a universe-hopping tongue ring!" She stuck her tongue out to show him the small metal ball embedded in it, but the robot remained focused on his task. Till open, till closed, till open. "Iths gonna de dig!" said Mazelmez, attempting to confer to the robot that this invention would be "big."

Open.

Closed.

She put her tongue away. "Not literally, of course. Metaphorically big. Literally, it's quite small. And once it's working, I'm gonna collect every version of myself in the multi-verse and form the most single-minded research team! I just need to fine tune a few things with it installed, but there isn't a mirror in the EZ Lab—"

The robot sighed cavernously at her.

Taking the hint, she shut up and returned her attention to the mirror image of herself, gently twisting the tiny ball in her tongue until it popped open, revealing a network of micro-cables and nano-gears.

She began to tinker.

And she continued to tinker as hours slipped by, so lost in the minutia of her task that Time just plumb forgot about her. The robot had nearly opened and closed the register a thousand times when she finally popped the metal ball closed and smiled, her tongue still hanging out. At last, it was ready for a test drive.

Her first alternate reality. A momentous occasion, and she had no-one but the ornery lump of metal at the till to share it with. Rather than bother him again, she touched the back of the ring to her front teeth and, after a brief feeling which could only be described as the sound and texture of a cherries jubilee, the robot was a foot to the right of the till and rubbing away at the bar top with a thread-bare rag.

He paused for a nano-blip to eye her suspiciously. "Oh, you again," he said, then carried on. Nothing could surprise him at this point in his long life.

"Excuse me, but is this another reality?" Mazelmez asked.

"How should I know?"

She frowned, hopped off the counter (from which her baskets had disappeared) and ran out of the bar, the rubber souls of her shoes crushing familiarly on the rusted concourse floor.

"EZ Lab?" she asked herself, staring up at the sign above her beloved laboratory. It now quite clearly read 'Bezalbum's Baubles,' though the paint was chipped.

She threw open the door and was met by hesteculix music wafting from a radio she knew she had disassembled seasons ago.

The door to the storeroom opened slowly, carefully, and Mazelmez prepared to come face-to-face with herself. Would her other-self be evil or good? she wondered. Then, just as suddenly, she wondered if she was the evil one. And then she put the whole silly idea of evil versus good aside, knowing that everyone is everything. Besides, there was very little evidence that evil and good even existed objectively at all.

The door opened fully, and Mazelmez gasped. "I'm invisible in this dimension," she whispered, delighted.

"What's that Bretsy?" asked the invisible Mazelmez, though her voice was weak and rough. This version of me, thought Mazelmez, must be a smoker. Good thing I gave all that up in the name of science. Are there invisible cigarettes?

"I'm not Bretsy," she said. "I'm you! But visible. And from another reality." Mazelmez held up her hand, awaiting the tender high-five which everyone in her reality, universally, understood as a respectful greeting.

A wrinkled old Udonian woman topped with a puff of white hair slowly appeared from behind the counter, climbing a small set of stairs to lift herself up to customer-level.

"Oh, dearie, you're not Bretsy!" She squinted large, watery eyes at Mazelmez's tall, thin frame. "You've dyed your hair pink, I see! Trying to trick old Bezalbum are you?"

"No, not at all," Mazelmez said, realizing her mistake now. She wasn't invisible, and this was the original owner of the EZ Lab, some ancient Udonian woman with bad eyesight.

"Now stop trying to confuse old Bezalbum. You're all the same to me, anyway, you are. These kids and their variety of hair colors and silly words and emergent species..." And then, somehow, Bezalbum squinted more. She shook her head. "You don't belong here, dearie. Did you get into my invilitex?!" she shrieked. "Get!" Bezalbum shooed Mazelmez with a quick flick of her wrists and, suddenly, though Mazelmez hadn't touched the tongue ring again and the essence of cherries jubilee didn't assault her, Mazelmez was back in the EZ Lab's foyer, alone.

THREE

AN OSTENTATIOUS START

* * * * *

Every successful rocketship racer becomes successful because they believe, truly and deeply in their hearts, that they cannot die. That a horrible, fiery crash might happen to someone else but not to them. Never to them.

May fully, absolutely believed that she would never be in a horrible, fiery crash, and this was why, over the past four years, she had become outstandingly successful in the field of rocketship racing. Money had amassed along with her courage. Every win netted her a few hundred thousand more crystals and another affirmation that she would be just fine.

The misplaced Earthling who found her calling in space, the underdog.

"Everyone loves an underdog," May thought out loud to Xan, her co-pilot, as they prepared the ship for another race. She had taken a break from fidgeting with the fin alignment, which she was convinced would simply never be perfect, to check their bank account. A figure she couldn't have dreamed of earning back on Earth flashed cheerfully on the screen. "Maybe even God," she added, a mystical part of her habitually turning back to the old Earth myth.

Xan had been repairing a ripped seam along the arm of his chair with an old-fashioned needle and thread, a seam which had ripped because even after hundreds of races, he had enough sense to be utterly terrified by what they were doing and spent the majority of the races trying to physically merge with the seat. His eyebrows pulled together in concern just as he tugged on the string, pulling together the upholstery.

"You've met a god, May. They don't love anyone, especially not an underdog. Immortality does funny things to your sense of empathy…"

"Right, no, I meant in like a…bigger sense."

"Bigger?"

"Like…THE God? I don't know. Fate, maybe."

"Fate's the cruelest of them all!"

A hollow, distant beep from outside the ship alerted them to get ready, and Xan dutifully plopped into the seat he had just repaired and strapped in, then watched May sit down. She didn't bother with the safety precautions anymore.

"May," he reached a hand out to her, touching her hand gently. She tensed. He always did this when he got serious. She didn't want him psyching her out. "May, don't get all Propopolactic on me."

It was her turn to scrunch her eyebrows at him. "Propopolactic? Doesn't translate."

"Greg Propopolactic was a famous Tuhntian physician. His clients were the wealthiest of the wealthy. Claimed he could bring people back from the dead. Actually DID do that—a few times, apparently. He got smacked with a huge fine for it, too."

"From whom?"

"Fate."

"No way. There's no god of fate."

"No…just…fate," Xan said.

"We can pay fines," May said, grinning as she prepared the rocket to launch. "Any fine they can throw at us! Besides, I'm not bringing people back from the dead; I'm just destroying everyone by being really, really fast. Who knew the fastest being in the universe would come out of a planet that hasn't even made contact with interstellar life yet?"

Xan sighed. "He didn't pay the fine with money."

May clicked on the viewscreen, displaying the field of obstacles they were about to hurl themselves through, which hovered ominously in the emptiness surrounding them. "Then what's the big deal?"

"He paid with his life," Xan said.

"Five..." said the muffled voice of the Manager outside.

May turned to him now, leaning forward, emphasizing the lack of strapping in she had done. "Hey, relax, Xan. We've done this hundreds of times now. I know what I'm doing. It's going to be okay."

Xan nodded, though instead of his characteristic easy smile, he gave her a long, flat, tight-lipped line. He didn't believe her.

"Four..."

"Let's take a break after this one," she suggested, trying desperately to lighten the mood. Usually, he was the one doing that. "Get some ice cream, maybe."

"Three..."

Xan very much had the feeling they would not be getting ice cream after this. This was something he'd heard about but never experienced... The Ness was speaking to him in a still, quiet voice. Something was about to come to a disastrous end, and he knew it. All A'Viltrials, even Tuhntians like Xan, got glimpses of the Ness when they dreamed, but most could never interpret it.

"Two..."

"Xan?" she leaned in closer, genuinely concerned about his wellbeing. He'd never been this resistant to race before. Well, he had, but never like this. It was always a goofy, overblown sort of terror he showed. Nerves. This was different. He didn't answer her.

"Go!!" The Manager's voice seemed even farther away now, and it took May an extra moment to recognize it was time.

"Shit!!" She grabbed the control and plowed away from the starting line, four little points of light representing her competitor's thrusters already far too small ahead of them.

"Xan, uninstall the Collision Cushion, now!" she shouted, spinning them around an asteroid twice their size and scraping past another one that had been hiding behind it.

"Illegal!!" he said, exasperated.

"It's the only way," she said. "We'll be fine, they won't notice. Just take it out and pop it back in as soon as we land."

"I really don't think that's—"

"Don't think, just do it!!" And, taking her own advice, May squeezed the rocket through an obstacle that appeared to be an enormous purple sphincter, thinking that going through it would be faster than going around. It was not. The sphincter caught them and squelched them onwards painfully slowly, popping them out the other side to find an even larger distance between them and their competitors.

"Please, Xan! I need you to do this for me."

Resigned, Xan released the safety belts with a click and woosh and crawled under the console.

"Don't hit anything, okay?" He popped out the disc that controlled the Collision Cushion, and the ship responded by redirecting the energy used to maintain the cushion into the thrusters.

"We're gaining!" May said, bouncing in her seat. "It worked!"

Xan didn't get up; he just braced for impact.

"Shit!" he heard. "No, no, no," he heard.

He didn't have to ask.

The rocket dove nose-first into the side of a derelict starship.

"You hit my zuxing starship, you blighters!" The Race Manager's robotic voice sizzled, echoing around the inside of the starship from the rocket's combox, which sparked on the floor a few meters away from the rocket's twisted hull.

A few meters beyond that, at the end of two streaks of blood, one red and the other blueish green, May and Xan moaned to prove to themselves and each other that they were still alive.

"I swear on O'Zeno's pink thong, if you're not dead, I'll kill you," said the combox. "Do you have any idea how much that starship cost?" it continued. "A zuxing lot! A zuxing zuxing lot!" it went on like this for some time before shifting back to the race momentarily to congratulate the winners.

After a few bloops to recover a sense of up versus down, Xan dragged his aching body over to the combox and shut it off.

They had landed inside an abandoned starship. Its oxygen field had held despite their intrusion, but it was ancient, weak, and cold. It would be enough to sustain him for awhile, but May needed lots of oxygen and warmth and...he hadn't had the willpower to go check on her yet.

Earthlings were fragile.

He knew it wouldn't be good.

She hadn't done much more than moan since the crash. He crawled over to her on hands and knees, then carefully turned her over. The light from a guttering hover orb down the hall was so faint, he couldn't distinguish what bits were blood and what bits were sweat on her dark skin.

"You alright, starshine?"

She didn't open her eyes, but she did roll her head to the side and coughed out a mouthful of blood, so she was alive.

"Blitheon's galaxy, that looks bad. I mean, you don't look bad. The uh...the blood looks bad. You look great. Really very healthy and well."

The black eye only enhanced the hopelessness in May's squinted glare. "Call Mazelmez," she said in a horse whisper.

"Won't the Manager be sending some sort of Medic?"

May laughed callously, but that sent her into a coughing fit that went on far too long and deposited far too much blood on the cheap metal tiles. "No. Waste of money."

"Zuut, alright, I'll call her. You rest."

"How's the *Ostentatious*?" May asked, trying to turn her head to see what was left of her gorgeous, bright blue ship.

Xan peered back at the wreckage of their ship, the top of it had peeled back like a banana, exposing a mess of crackling wiring and bent girders.

"It's fine, I'm more worried about you." Only the last part was true, but Xan hadn't ever been known for his perfect honesty.

Fortunately, May knew this about him. She knew it was not fine, but she let him comfort her anyway. She didn't have the energy to argue.

FOUR

AN AUDACIOUS START

* * * * *

"What in Blitheon's soiled trousers is that?" was not the crudest thing that had ever been said regarding the rocket ship called the *Audacity*, but it was the crudest that had ever been said regarding the *Audacity* to a stadium full of all-ages race enthusiasts. For that, Yistalapoog of Morpas would be flogged, and he knew it.

Yistalapoog was quickly replaced with a younger, less jaded announcer named Yistalapag who had this to say: "Well, folks, it's certainly shaping up to be an interesting run, isn't it? Two camera persons down with sudden onset acute photic retinopathy and several hundred thousand spectators shielding their eyes from the hideous sheen on that rocket, which, I'm told, is sporting an outlawed enamel hue called Obtrusive Orange.

"Folks, if I were a cleverer being, I'd have already bought stock in sunglasses. Whoo-eee, that is one ugly ship! Let's see how she moves."

May smiled a self-satisfied smile, listening to Yistalapag over the tinny speaker in the *Audacity*. There was nothing more entertaining to her than being utterly despised at the start of a run only to swoop up a well-earned win and a prize of a few billion crystals.

"It's not ugly," Xan said beside May, patting the console consolingly. "Just causes irreversible eye damage. Why does everyone think it's ugly?"

"Love is blind." May enjoyed throwing idioms at her Tuhntian companion. "In this case, blinding."

May swiped the screen to show a view of outside; she wanted to suss out her competition. To their left, a sleek white number with no defining characteristics apart from the word "Valiant" in looping script. To their right, a classic red racer. Just beyond it, another white rocket and then a black one.

It was the mundane-looking rockets she had learned to watch out for. Designed to be underestimated.

The viewscreen guttered and flashed, then cut out all together, leaving them in the dark.

"What happened? Does it need a reboot?" Xan asked, worried. May was already under the console, prying off the plastic siding.

"Naw, reboots are too much work, and no one's ever happy with the results." She poked around in the wiring for a moment. "Looks like the plasma arc blew out. I'm just going to create a new arc." May carefully twisted together two stripped wires and flicked the view screen's breaker back on. A brilliant arc of blue current bridged two metal rods under the control panel, and the screen lit up.

"That's it! But will that affect the continuity? Of the screen? The screen's continuity?"

"Nope. I didn't take anything out, just twisted some loose ends together, and there you have it: brand new arc." May popped the siding back onto the console and crawled out from under it, standing to be sure everything was online, and they wouldn't be parking as a fiery blaze.

"This is it, folks, the final blip before our race begins, and the tension out there is... Well, I'd say it's been broken by that hideous orange number, don't you think? Just cut right through. What is that, anyway? Who would ruin a gorgeous Class 20 Racer like that? Worried it would get lost in a docking bay, eh?"

"No, but that is a perk!" Xan chirped over the outercom.

The audience let forth a confusing mixture of jeers, boos, and good-natured chortles.

"Alright, alright," the announcer spoke over the uproarious laughter of the crowd. "May the best ship win!"

"You wish!" May had leaned over Xan to shout into the speaker.

Xan quickly shut the speaker off. "Isn't that implying that our ship isn't the best?" he whispered at her.

"Oh, it definitely isn't," May said.

"Fair point," Xan said as he scooted over to regain control of the speaker. May had been known to start unnecessary rivalries when she had the speaker.

"Remember to keep those fins inside the light-grid track, watch the language when you trash-talk each other, and buy Giant Jan's Diet Jams for the tastiest breakfast this side of the civilized universe. Giant Jan's— If Jan Can't Can It, It Can't Be Canned. And we've got the green light in ten...!" shouted Yistalapag.

The "green light" was neither, strictly speaking, green nor a light. It was, in fact, an enormous metal ring strung round with tiny thrusters that allowed it to hold its position in front of the racers. A thin plastic sheet spanned its center. The sheet, at the moment the race was to begin, was programmed to vibrate itself to pieces to let the ships through. Still, it was traditional to say "green light" instead of "vibrational destruction of the massive plastic diaphragm" because it was quicker.

"Nine," continued the announcer, as if there hadn't just been a wordy aside about racing tradition jammed into the narrative. "Eight...seven..." he continued on in this manner, winding the audience up, creating a palpable anticipation until, at last, he got to "one" and the plastic withered away.

The *Audacity* shot off the platform first, taking a clear lead. May knew the ship started strong and ended strong...it just had a lag in the middle, which was fine by her because the middle was where all the obstacles were anyway.

Though May was certain they had left their competition far behind, three ships were suddenly plummeting ahead of her, piercing the steady darkness of space with their silver noses. All three of them. There hadn't been three silver rockets at the starting line, thought May. Then she thought, Holy shit, what is that thing?

That thing was the first obstacle.

The size of a small planetoid, bulbous and organic in shape, glowing with blue light and spurting tails of white-hot flame at random intervals right in the middle of the light-grid track. If she flew around it, she'd be flying far outside of the race parameters. If she flew through it, she'd be dead.

A flash of light, and the silver rocket in the lead became a smattering of grungy debris. May searched for a way through. Another flash of light, and the second rocket ahead of her met the same fate. A third flash of light, May continued at full speed toward it.

"You're going to go around it, right?" Xan asked, eyes flicking between May and the bursting flame thing.

She shook her head, barely, so focused she didn't have the capacity to respond to him.

"No?" Xan clarified. "No, you're not going to avoid the flame ball? Because, as your co-pilot, I really think we ought to avoid that thing."

"Can't, no room." She pushed the *Audacity* to go faster.

Xan had always hoped he wouldn't be burned to death if he were being honest. He always imagined he would leave a beautiful corpse, not a cloud of ash, but he didn't have enough time to explain his reasoning for not wanting to die like this to May. The ship whizzed straight through the flame ball and out the other side unscathed.

Xan pulled up the rearview screen to watch the flame ball recede behind them. "We're...alive?"

"Yeah, we're alive, blue. That thing was a hologram. I knew no one was ahead of us," said May with a smug grin.

"Psychological obstacles now...huh," Xan mused, shutting off the rearview.

Ahead, a school of spike-nosed spacefish swam in

circles. They were contained by a ring of buoys that produced a disorienting light pattern. It was a digital net full of very real fish, and this is how May knew that they were, indeed, real this time: The classic red racer had gained on them, and May eased up just enough to allow it to enter the fish-field first.

Each glistening creature was twice the length of the ship, and hundreds of them swarmed the rocket, obscuring its red hull beneath silver scales. The red racer fought back. A brief burst of light from the ship's blaster, and a dozen of the creatures were flung away from the dented ship, lifeless. More fish attacked it, revenge fish. The red racer slowed.

May angled both of the *Audacity*'s Ultra-Ray-Super-Destroyers at one of the digital buoys and blasted it, taking out the entire net. The remaining fish, delighted to be free, scattered in all directions, clearing the way for May to zoom ahead of the ailing red racer.

The attack on the red rocket had left it damaged, its flight path a disorienting wiggle toward the finish hub. May gave a crooked grin at the other rocket's misfortune, keeping them up in the rear-view mirror as she overtook them.

"Xan, you're good at ethical quandaries; is it wrong of me to enjoy watching them struggle back there?"

"Eh, well, Percipitus, the only philosopher to come out of Tuhnt's five-century-long hedonistic age, says, 'That which pleasures thee, pleasures me,' but the context was vastly different. Seeing as they've consensually entered into friendly, if deadly, competition with us prior to—"

"Short version?"

"You saved all those fish, I think it balances out." Xan shrugged.

"We have a winner!" Yistalapag shouted. May sat back, satisfied. Xan had been so busy philosophizing he hadn't noticed the race was over. It was better that way, though. The less he noticed that they were hurling themselves at absurd speeds through an obstacle course filled with deadly traps, the more he enjoyed racing. He particularly enjoyed watching May win a race. She never cheered or jumped out of her seat or raised her arms in victory. She just seemed to be, for a few blips, absolutely at peace with the universe.

"Sorry, go on?" May said, noticing that Xan had stopped talking.

"Oh, uh...don't worry about it. Best not to think about your competition's misfortune at all, right? Then you can't feel good about it accidentally."

May nodded, the crinkle of thought returning to her forehead. "Yeah, I guess. Feels like an ethical cop-out, though."

"Cop-out? What's that?"

"Eh, probably better that you don't know that one." May stood and stretched tall, a habit she'd intentionally worked into her routine after realizing that racing got her more tense than rival astrophysicists arguing the rate of universal expansion.

Standing with her, Xan pulled a comb from his pocket and leaned into the chrome lining of the viewscreen, which was just reflective enough for him to tell that his orange pompadour had become disheveled but not enough for him to satisfactorily fix it. "You want to go down to the Morpas station and bask in the warmth of the audience's hard-earned adoration?" he asked, giving up on his hair for now.

"I'll sit this one out." She flicked on the old TV and flopped onto the couch, accepting whatever fizzy TV signal happened to be nearby. An ad for discount gorpop insurance assaulted her senses, delightfully enumerating all the things that could possibly go horrifically wrong with a gorpop. May had learned not to ask Xan what mysterious alien objects were. The ones he could explain all involved sexual gratification, and the ones he couldn't, May suspected, were a sex thing, too.

Xan paused to watch the commercial with her, leaning casually on the couch. "Eugh, can you imagine being that incompetent with a gorpop?"

"I sure can," May said.

"Not an Earth thing?" Xan asked, and she shook her head.

Counting the three years of interstellar travel she'd un-lived thanks to The Seam resetting their universe, May had lived off Earth for almost five years and was still frequently mystified by alien cultures.

"Don't take too long out there. I want to head off to the orbital race at the Huuloorian track after this. It's almost two parsecs from here, and the warp drive's been laggy lately."

Complaints and concerns scrambled for attention in Xan's mind with the ferocity of the error codes that tended to clog the *Audacity*'s viewscreen. He was quickly approaching his lifetime limit of death-defying rocket ship races. He held them all back, though. Again.

"I'll be back before you can miss me," he said cheerily and teleported down to the afterparty below to get a dose of the only thing he enjoyed about racing: the attention.

A sound like the very fabric of the universe tearing open, followed by the unmistakable scent of cherries jubilee, made May jump off the couch and look back, startled, thinking something had gone wrong with the teleporter.

She saw nothing, but a feeling of dread twisted like a scalpel in her core.

Slowly, she turned back around to find what appeared to be a literal scalpel sticking out of her, just below the ribs, and Xan's face inches from hers, wincing apologetically.

FIVE

SUSPICIOUS METAPHYSICS

✳ ✳ ✳ ✳ ✳

Typically, in a crisis, May took charge. Typically, in a crisis, May either knew what to do or was outstandingly good at pretending like she did. Typically, however, May wasn't on the verge of death, bleeding out in a corridor of an abandoned starship after a terrible, high-speed rocket ship crash.

Xan needed a higher power. May had suggested Mazelmez. Of course she had. For some Blitheon-cursed reason, May trusted his erstwhile sister.

He didn't trust her. He had grown up with her.

Any wandering space-medic would've been better, but May had asked for Mazelmez, and Xan was nothing if not amicable. He called his horrible sister, whom he did love, but mostly from a distance.

Her cheesy grin filled the screen of the PALM device embedded in his left hand.

"Quaxlagon! How's the vibe, mun?"

"Bad, Mazelmez. The vibe is very, very bad. Look," he turned his PALM out to May, hoping that would dowse her cheery attitude. "We crashed, and May's... I mean, she's—"

"Ah, Blitheon, she's dying!" said Mazelmez. "What did you do?"

"Me?!"

"Xan, Earthlings are fragile! Send me your coordinates —I'll see what I can do. And don't just leave her there while you wait for me! Isn't there a medibay on the *Ostentatious*?"

"Well, yes, but—"

"Take her there! Get her in the Diagn-O-Scan and do whatever it tells you to do. I've got an idea. Honestly, this is a fortunate mistake; I get to test my latest experiment!"

Xan groaned. "Blitheon, please don't tell me that. Don't experiment with May's life."

"Hey! She's going to be okay, alright? Confirm to me that you're going to take her to the Diagn-O-Scan."

"What's left of it..." he mumbled.

"Huh?"

"Yeah...yeah. Confirm to me you're going to be here soon, though."

"I'm already in the taxi, mun!" the video clicked off, and Xan was thrust into a deep, chilling silence. He didn't trust the *Ostentatious*'s teleporter to disintegrate and re-integrate their atoms correctly with the ship so outrageously zuxed, so he would have to somehow haul May into the partially crushed manual access hatch and crawl down (or was it sideways now?) into the medibay with her.

"Can you get up?" he asked her pointlessly. She could barely flutter her eyes at him. He was sure the look she'd been going for would've been scathing.

Stooping beside her, he slipped his arms gently under her back and knees, and, whispering an ancient Tuhntian prayer for strength, he lifted her up and brought her to the ship.

The rocket had been sliced open like a can of soup, and he slipped in through the gouge in the living room. The relative gravity was still online, and the moment he entered its field, he fell sideways to the metal floor. Cursing, he stood again and took the manual access hatch down to the infirmary. The lights were still on down there and oxygen plentiful.

He set her down on the Diagn-O-Scan and flicked on the diagnostic system.

It whirred to life. It scanned. It got excited.

This wasn't some sprained ankle or paper cut; this was the kind of life-threatening mutilation the Diagn-O-Scan had been programmed for! If it had been afforded a religious processor, it would've kicked in just about now, but this was a cheaper, secular model.

Xan watched the screen flash red across a map of May's body, hemorrhaging there, shrapnel here, broken bones galore. He had felt a sense of general worry for her health before, but now he had a list of specific injuries to worry about, which somehow made him feel better.

The Diagn-O-Scan flashed several courses of action that could be taken to save her life. Flashed them quite urgently and with a great deal of exclamation points and then expletives as he slowly read them through.

"Stop the bleeding?!" he whispered. "It doesn't stop on its own?"

The Diagn-O-Scan went blank for a second, trying to find a program it could run that would allow it to insult his intelligence. There was none, so it resorted to cryo-stasis mode, dropping a plastic pod over May and piping in some viscous blue vapor that would keep her from dipping below the point of no return, hopefully long enough for someone more competent to arrive.

"Ah, cryo-stasis. Probably for the best," he said to the Diagn-O-Scan, trying to catch a final glimpse of May through the blue fog. "You're going to be alright, mun," he said out loud to himself. "You too, May. If you can hear me." He put a helpless hand to the glass and willed her to get better.

"Zuut, you look like you've been in a rocket crash!" Mazelmez said through a gaping hole in the side of the ship.

"So do you!" Xan retorted.

It wasn't entirely unwarranted, either. Mazelmez's thick pink hair was tied in a messy bun, crowned with a pair of massive goggles, wefts of hair sticking out, waving in the weak draft. Under her stained and wrinkled lab coat, she wore a shirt that used to be white but was now the color of rust and sturdy cargo pants packed with supplies.

"Thanks." She dragged herself and two shopping baskets full of supplies from the small Startaxi and tapped the Diagn-O-Scan until it freed May from the bubble of cryo-stasis.

"O'Zeno's toes, you really zuxed this one." Mazelmez gently lifted one of May's eyelids to little response. She checked the Diagn-O-Scan's readout and began plucking the larger bits of glass out of May and peeling back her shredded suit.

"You can fix her, right?"

Mazelmez shrugged, focused on her task. "She needs blood."

"Take mine! I've got plenty left!" Xan tore off what was left of his own sleeve and presented his pale blue arm to Mazelmez, who looked at it with a raised eyebrow.

"You're paler than the Cream Sea, mun. You keep what you've got. It wouldn't work in her, anyway." Mazelmez dug in her satchel and produced a device that looked like a staple gun. "Stick out your tongue."

"Why?"

She lifted the device to eye level, and the light glinted off something in its jaws. "This is a universe jumping tongue-ring. You're going to find her body double in another universe and drain her."

"Drain her?!"

"It's not really her. It's a body double. They aren't sentient. Look, there's only one you, right?"

"Well--"

"Your consciousness can't exist in two places at once. The other universes are like backups. You die in this one, your consciousness wakes up in another, and life goes on."

"That doesn't..."

"On Carmnia's honor," Mazelmez said, exasperated. "I've talked to myself in other universes. Soulless, unaware puppets, all of them! Fleam." She handed Xan a ghastly-looking spring-loaded lance. "And here's a bucket." She bent to dig in one of the two baskets she had brought and thrust a head-sized tin bucket at him, which he grudgingly took.

"Alright, but consider: how do you know for certain these other versions of us aren't just as conscious as we are? You're not the most warm-hearted Tuhntian in Trilly!"

"You really want May to die, huh?"

"No! I just don't want to 'drain' another version of her!"

Mazelmez dug again in her basket and produced a multicolored ring, which she slipped on her finger to show him, along with a little card that depicted five different colored dots. The ring went from a blotchy rainbow to solid red on her finger, and she tapped the card.

"This is a consciousness meter," she said, then flipped the card around to reference it. "See? Red for lusty. Black, down here at the bottom of the card." She showed him again, pointing to the black dot. "Soulless Zombie. Every version of me in another universe has come out as a Soulless Zombie. Does that satisfy? Stick one on your target, it will turn black, guaranteed. The body doubles are not conscious!"

"Why are you lusty at a time like this?!"

"I don't know, I'm usually lusty. Danger turns me on, I guess. Now go on. I've got a lot of work to do here."

The Diagn-O-Scan, which had been throwing gentle alerts as to May's declining wellbeing, was now beeping rather urgently, a development that distracted Xan. He leaned over her, picking blood-encrusted chunks of hair off her face. "Zuut, May," he whispered. "Alright," he said at last. "I'll do it." He stuck his tongue out at Mazelmez and shut his eyes tight. The tongue ring pinched going in, but the pain was minor compared to his own injuries from the crash.

Mazelmez grabbed the tip of his tongue and held it out with one hand, rubbing some of May's blood on the bauble with the other. "DNA matching," she explained at his look of disgust. "Okay, bite it! That should take you to within four feet of her. Hopefully, it won't manifest you inside another object...or outside habitable space."

"Hopefully?!"

"Probably it won't! I calculated for that!"

"Who checked your figures?"

Mazelmez winked. "I've been absorbed in the sciences, mun! I'm the only one checking my figure lately. Now go on! Fill it up!"

Resigned, he flicked the tongue ring on his teeth and crackled away into an unreality.

SIX

BLOOD BATH

* * * * *

Instantaneous teleportation via tongue ring is far cooler than the average wrist or palm teleportation device, though notoriously imprecise.

This is why all tongue-teleporter manuals emphatically warn users not to teleport inebriated, naked, or holding sharp objects, such as a well-pointed pencil or a rusty fleam, such as the one Xan of the *Ostentatious* had just accidentally skewered May of the *Audacity* with.

This horrible realization quickly surmounted his shock at how unbelievably orange the interior of the otherwise identical ship was.

"Oh! Zuut, I'm sorry about that!" He tugged on the fleam, but it had lodged itself quite deeply between her lower left ribs, and the pained gasp she gave when he tried to extract it made him nervous.

"Fuck! What the hell, Xan?!" May sank to the couch and tried to see through the searing pain.

"I'm sorry! That was an accident. Listen, I know this is a lot, but I'm not your Xan ,and you're not... You aren't real. Because the real May—I mean, my May—was in a rocket crash, and she's going to die if I don't get her more blood right now immediately. Is that...okay?" he asked, wincing. He figured it wouldn't be.

Before she could tell him this, though, the shock took her, and she dropped to the floor like a flailing tube dancer when the air cut off.

Hesitantly, since the damage had already been done, Xan twisted the ring off his finger and slipped it on hers. It turned black. Soulless zombie, just as Mazelmez had said, relaxing a little now that she wasn't interacting with him, he retrieved the ring and then maneuvered the lip of the bucket underneath the protruding fleam, jiggled it to really get the blood flowing, and respectfully looked away.

"If you can hear me, I really am sorry about this. I know you aren't real, but even soulless zombies deserve respect, right? I think so. Mazelmez probably doesn't. But I think you do. It's just that the real you is going to die if I don't do this, and I...can't let that happen. You understand, right? Yeah. You'd understand, I'm sure. She's you! Do you... Zuut, maybe you don't even have a concept of you-ness." His mutterings became increasingly circuitous as he waited for the bucket to fill. He must've hit something important because every time he shifted the fleam, more liquid gushed forth into the bucket.

"Let's not tell May about this, yeah? The real one, I mean. She doesn't need to know," he said, retrieving the bucket. He checked the pulse in her neck and found that despite the bucket of blood he'd collected and the sizable puddle soaking the shag carpet, she was still alive. Maybe, he briefly thought, body doubles were hardier stock anyway. "Uh, thank you..." he clicked the tongue ring, tore open a seam in space and time, and slipped neatly back into the reality where he belonged.

✳ ✢ ✳ ✳ ✳

Xan, the *Audacity*'s Xan, resplendent in purple flower garlands, chunks of metallic confetti stuck to his skin, and a litany of admirers shouting overtly sexual questions at him, had just been handed a perception-altering drink as tall as his forearm when he got the distress call from May on his BEAPER.

He twisted his wrist to look at it, accidentally spilling some of the icy drink on himself, and, without sparing a moment to explain his departure, teleported back to the *Audacity*.

"May!!" he called as he was teleporting, the effect of which was always off-puttingly like underwater ventriloquism. "May!" he repeated, clearer, once he'd fully manifested. He took a frenzied gulp of the drink he still held, hoping whatever was in it would help him cope, before setting it down and catapulting himself over the back of the couch. "What happened?"

She was sitting up now on the floor against the front of the couch, trying not to touch the strange contraption protruding from her. She twisted slightly so he could see. "This...happened?"

"Blitheon! Blitheon, May. Blitheon," said Xan, examining the device. "Does that hurt?" he reached for it, but May jerked back.

"Agh! Obviously!"

"Come on, we've got to get you to the medical hub," he began to stand up, trying to scoop his arm under hers, but she refused.

"No, no, I don't want to cause a commotion. It's embarrassing."

"We'll be discrete!" he shouted in a whisper.

"Really, it's not that bad. And we've got the medibay on board. No one has to know! Just help me get it out," she said, but even looking down at the blood-splattered handle of the fleam made her feel woozy.

Again, he reached for it.

"Don't touch it!" May scooted back again, defensively.

"You just told me to get it out!"

"Well, yeah, but give me a minute. I need to...I need to calm down first. Get ready."

Xan bit his bottom lip, wondering if someone could actually be ready for such a thing. He took the winner's ribbon off from around his neck and draped it over May, hoping that would cheer her up. "How did it happen?" he asked as casually as his coursing adrenaline would allow.

"I think..." May held her head as if she could draw out and tidy up her memories that way. "You from another reality did it. He said I wasn't real? I'm real, though, right?"

"Yeah, mun, you're real." Avoiding the fleam, he slipped an arm around her shoulders and gave her a comforting squeeze. "You're uh...really cold, too. And kinda greyish."

She leaned into the crook of his neck and closed her eyes, leeching his warmth. "You're calling me pale?" she teased half-heartedly, comparing the back of her brown hand to his barely blue hand.

"Relative to how you normally look, yes! Mun, I think we should go to the medical hub. They have coupons! First traumatic injury is free."

"Fine. Just promise to make up a cool story about it to tell them."

"Promise." Xan shuffled his arm under hers and lifted her up, finding that he had to either stoop uncomfortably or carry her whole weight. He decided to stoop. It was easier on his back.

"You know, I'm starting to think he was right. If I were real, I'd be dead by now."

Xan chose to pretend he hadn't heard that.

SEVEN

OMINOUS WARNING

* * * * *

Alien hospitals were difficult for May to cope with. The only other time she'd been in need of a medical professional (after she caught an ancient space flu at the Adventure Hole), they'd found the only doctor living on Not Tuhnt was working out of the back of a scooter mechanic's shop and prescribed something for her which warned that uncontrollable engine sputtering was a possible symptom. Xan had taken her back to Largish Bronda and fixed her an old folk remedy involving a bottle of strong shermel instead.

The medical hub on Morpas included professionals in every conceivable division of medicine. Several of whom, according to the sprawling tele-directory, specialized in moltsopial glands. There was no map, only a directory full of private practices and a repositioner that would whisk you off to a waiting room. Most clients found the repositioners disorienting and mildly incapacitating, which would set them up nicely for the rest of their medical experience.

"Zuut, none of these mention Earthling biology," Xan

whispered, scrolling down the list as May hung on him. "Except the vet."

"The vet!?" she shouted, spouting more blood. Fortunately, the medical bay's floor was quick-wicking.

"Sorry, no, the shamanic vet. Says here you get one unrelated ominous warning per visit—that's neat! I feel like we haven't gotten one of those in a while. Probably due."

"You're taking me to a vet?"

"They have good reviews."

"Their patients can't complain; of course they have good reviews! Let's go back. I'm feeling better. I think I can leave it in," May said, then looked down at her soaked clothing and began to hear that characteristic ringing that would call her consciousness away.

Feeling her faltering, Xan shifted her weight on his arm and forced her to look away from the puddle of blood spreading at their feet.

"Whoa there," he said.

"Don't talk to me like I'm a horse!"

"I still don't know what a horse is," he mumbled, dragging her into the repositioner and pressing the button that would take the pod to the shamanic vet.

The waiting room was alive with soothing music and gently undulating colors. The occupants all rested on their haunches or lay on their fuzzy sides. Among them was only one other humanoid, and they were holding the leash of a sluggish-looking sluggy thing.

"Fuuuuck," May said.

"Hey, remember when you sliced your hand open and I had to wrap it up tight and it bled for beoops until it finally stopped? That's unusual out here. If we took you to a regular doctor, they'd just take the thing out and expect the wound to close up on its own. Clearly, obviously, that's not going to work for you. Right?" Xan whispered, partially to convince himself that this was the right choice.

A beaded curtain shimmered open, revealing a hunched prignette with greying fur, a substantial beard, and milky doe-eyes. They scanned the room calmly until they saw

May.

"My, my, sapling," they said, tottering over. "You've done quite a disservice to yourself, haven't you? Follow."

May obliged, but only because Xan was doing half her walking for her, and the shaman ushered them into the exam room, which was black-lit and lined with various tubes of glowing, colorful liquids.

In the middle of the small room squatted a tub of blue gel.

"Get in," said the shaman.

"What is it?" May asked.

"Oh, I'm not terribly sure, but it seems to calm my clients down a great deal."

"I'll skip it, then." Without realizing it, May had been pressing further and further into Xan, and he had to widen his stance to keep the two of them upright.

"She's not a biter or a scratcher, is she?" the shaman asked Xan, slipping on a delicate pair of spectacles.

She was, as Xan had found out the few times they'd tried wrestling to pass the time, but he figured in this context, she would probably be able to restrain herself.

"No! I'm a human, not an animal," May snarled at the shaman. Sorry, not snarled. Spoke forcefully at.

"Earthling?" the shaman asked.

May nodded.

"You shouldn't be alive, sapling," they said, smacking their soft, fuzzy lips as they pushed their spectacles up on their rounded goat-like nose and peered at the fleam still drizzling blood.

"You know how to fix Earthlings?" Xan asked.

"Oh, I know how. I know how. Don't rush me," said the old goat, turning to a chest of drawers from which they pulled a simple roll of gauze.

A sound like the fabric of the universe ripping announced the appearance of Mazelmez. "Oh! You survived that. Wow. You lost a lot of blood, you know? Well, maybe you don't know. I'll just...take that back, thanks!" Mazelmez grabbed the fleam, ripped it out of May's side, and then disappeared.

"Shit!" May pressed her hands to the open wound, but

nearly as soon as she moved to cover it, it had closed. She tore open her flight suit enough to get a good look at her side and discovered barely a scar where the fleam had been just a moment ago.

"How unusual," mused the shaman.

"Aimz!?" Xan asked the empty air where she had been. "Aimz did this?! May, you can't tell the difference between me and Aimz?"

"It was definitely you! You two don't look that similar."

Xan had already called Aimz on his BEAPER and was leaving a message. "What in O'Zeno's secret pornography collection was that for?! You stabbed May?! Tell Listay I said hello," he ended the call with an angry huff. "Zuut, May, I'm sorry about her."

"No, it's fine. I'm okay," she said. "Somehow. Look, if that Xan wasn't you, then that Aimz wasn't your Aimz, right? Maybe they were...time travelers?"

"But we've already established that time travel isn't possible," Xan said. "Not into the past, at least. Just, you know..."

"Yeah, into the future at a rate of one blip per blip," May said. "What else could they be, though? Clones?"

"Who would clone me? Aimz would clone herself, sure, but why me?"

"That's enough speculation!" said the shaman, waving their spindly fingers in the air. "Now, your body is healed, sapling. As for your spirit, would you like a prescription for psychotropics, psychedelics, or psychoballistics?"

"Psychoballistics?" May whispered at Xan.

"Oh, zuut, May you'd love those. Maybe too much. Probably shouldn't get you hooked on that," Xan replied. "We're good, thank you!" he told the shaman. "Can we have our ominous warning now?"

"Oh yes, of course. Don't sign any paperwork for the foreseeable future," said the prignette shaman, snacking on the gauze.

"Got it. No paperwork, thanks," Xan said, shifting May again, though it wasn't necessary. She stood up perfectly fine on her own now.

"We excel at skipping out on paperwork," May said,

smiling at Xan as she recalled the many race entry forms they had scribbled through. They'd eventually agreed to at least give the Race Manager the ship's actual name after a few dozen races run as "The Speedy Cheeto" (May's contribution to the tom-foolery) had landed them in some legal trouble with Frito-Lay.

As soon as they left the shaman's exam room, however, it became clear that getting out of this paperwork would be more difficult than they thought.

A pair of white-suited, sunglass-wearing, three-eyed lizardly humanoids awaited them, each wielding a clipboard stacked high with paperwork. "Alright, you two," the one on the left addressed them. "We are the Administrative Assistants. Come to our office; we have some paperwork for you to fill out."

Xan gasped. "The paperwork! Run, May!"

The pair bolted through the waiting room and slammed into the little repositioner pod, making it rock in its tube.

The Administrative Assistants did not run. The one on the left looked at the one on the right.

"I will never understand these emotional reactions to a few contracts and signatures."

"They have vulnerable skin. Papercuts."

"Ah. Yes, that makes sense now." The pair turned to look at May and Xan, who were both hurriedly pressing buttons, none of which were the "exit" button.

"Don't worry, delicate ones, I've brought a box of finger condoms," said the one on the right, holding out a small box that was, indeed, filled to the brim with finger condoms. It was unopened. "This should work," it whispered to its comrade.

"Jesus, paperwork and digital sex? That's just cruel," May said. Their button mashing had confused the pod, and it resolutely did nothing but beep at them until May located the EXIT button. "Stop, stop," May said to Xan, who was still pressing every button he could find on the teledirectory. "This one," she said, and once the pod stopped beeping angrily at them, she pressed it.

The pod sealed and scuttled them away towards the exit, which was, thankfully, within teleport distance of the parking lot.

They remerged, panting, on the teledisc in the *Audacity* at last.

"You're sure you're okay?" Xan asked.

May visually checked her side again. The wound had not re-opened. In fact, she couldn't tell where it had been. "Peachy keen."

Xan smiled. "Peachy keen!" he repeated. "Peachy keen?"

"All good," May clarified. No matter how many idioms she taught him, she always seemed to have more. That's what he loved about her. He grinned and picked up the enormous drink he'd set down beside the teledisc and handed it to her.

She drank it gratefully. "Let's skip Huuloorian. I need a vacation."

"Zuut, I'm glad to hear you say that," Xan sat in the co-pilot's chair. "The Andolonian Tree Museum is near here!" He held out a brochure to her.

"Tree museum?"

She read the pamphlet 'Eight zillion trees!' it read. 'Sit on their knees!' it continued. 'Learn the secrets of bygone civilizations once thought lost to the ceaselessly clawing fingers of time!' it finished.

"It rhymes in Andolonian," Xan noted. "Tree museums can be fun. Trees see everything, you know. When was the last time you had a larch comb your hair and recount in exacting detail the hilarious tale of how the Gorgatuines of Taeloo IIX invented wind turbines? Or the legendary Mortovinal tire heist of 1082?"

"I mean...it's been a while." May typed in the coordinates, and the ship shivered to life, launching easily off the low-grav parking space on Morpas. "I'm going to get cleaned up. You got this?"

"What, autopilot? Yeah, I think I can manage."

EIGHT

THE ADVENTURE ASTEROID

* * * * *

The *Audacity* approached Andolon, a micro-planet with such tall, ancient trees it looked like a Chia Pet. A billboard hovered just in front of the planet, haloed in a rakish green that drew the eye.

"Last chance! Save yourself from the boring old rustle of wizened trees. Right this way, through Pontoosa's Ludicrously Opportune Transdimensional Wormhole to Pontoosa's very own Adventure Asteroid!" And, as the sign had suggested, a small manned wormhole could be seen outlined by a red vapor vented into it by a little green kiosk hovering at its edge.

"Oh no," Xan said, reading along with May.

"Oh yes!" May switched the thrusters from starboard to port and brought them around to the kiosk that tractored the ship to keep it in place.

"Destination?" said the automated attendant, its robotic voice fizzling over the innercom.

"Adventure Asteroid!" May replied.

"Hold please," said the attendant. A popup appeared on the *Audacity*'s viewscreen. A little white square with a hastily scrawled map of the wormhole, just a crude cylinder with a little star at one end that said 'You Are Here' and about halfway through an arrow pointing to the right of the wormhole that read 'Adventure Asteroid.'

"You're gonna need to take a hard right exactly two blips into the wormhole, traveling at precisely nine hundred frackels per beoop. If you don't, you might end up just about anywhere in the multiverse. Here's your universal key in case you get lost." A string of numbers flashed across the screen, and May quickly screen-grabbed it. "Got that?"

"Got it," May said. And she did. For this, Xan was grateful. Despite a few decades as an intergalactic ambassador, he still didn't have a firm grasp on frackels or how to do a screen-grab.

"That'll be three hundred crystals," said the attendant, and the blue flash of the facescan was over before May had a chance to contest that outrageous fee.

The water vapor outlining the wormhole went green.

May prepped the thrusters to send them to nine hundred FPB in an instant, then peeled out, pushing them into a hard right turn seconds later and plowing straight out of Pontoosa's Ludicrously Opportune Transdimensional Wormhole (otherwise known as the PLOT hole).

Wormholes are highly disorienting.

Throwing a rocket ship into a hard right turn is highly disorienting.

Rocketing into a hard right turn through the edge of a wormhole is, thusly, absurdly disorienting. But May did it anyway.

Xan had had the presence of mind to tuck himself under the control panel and hang on, his fingers gripping under a seam in the paneling. May had cinched her legs under her hover chair and held onto the steering wheel as her mass was ripped sideways across the galaxy.

The same effect could be replicated, should you be brave enough to do so, by running yourself through a paper shredder zip-tied to an old truck doing 80 down a dirt road, then having a mangey coyote paste pieces of you back together with its tongue.

At the other end, Xan was quite sure a strip of his thigh two inches wide was now, while physically there, spiritually missing. May had a trendy new asymmetrical hairstyle and the sense that her brain was sitting just slightly to the left of where it ought to be.

"We spent five beoops exploring the wrench production facility because you wanted to learn about wrenches," Xan whined.

"The wrench plant was interesting."

"I bet they have a tree that knows all about wrenches," Xan said as he carefully returned himself to the co-pilot's seat. "They've got all kinds of trees. Each one specializes in some kind of esoteric knowledge."

"I like mundane knowledge. It's more useful. Besides, you 'had fun in the Pontoosa Adventure Hole,'" May said, Xan finishing the sentence with her. It was odd how often she was able to bring up the incident with the tiny novelty flag in the Pontoosa Adventure Hole gift shop.

"Alright, but by O'Zeno's thumbs, there better not be a flag that says 'I had fun in Pontoosa's Ludicrously Opportune Transdimensional Wormhole' because that blew," said Xan.

"Blew? You mean sucked?" May corrected.

"No, blew as in 'that blows,' right? But I suppose it also sucked. It both sucked and blew. Zuut, that cancels out, doesn't it? English is by far the most difficult language I've had to learn, and I can carry on a conversation in neo-Hooflatooan mind-meld."

"That's the language that consists primarily of synonyms for space plankton, isn't it?"

"The very same. A sentient Hooflatoo has a lot to say about space plankton. A lot to think about them, rather," Xan said.

"Sounds fascinating."

"It's not, if you can believe it."

"Oh, I can. Here we are!" May announced excitedly as the auto-parking tractor beam on the Adventure Asteroid caught the ship in its glittering pink grasp and began directing it into a parking spot. The auto-parking tractor beam had been such a huge hit with theme parks that the patent holder had been held at phaser-point until they signed over the patent to the public domain.

"Welcome," said the digital voice of the auto-parking technician. "To the Pontoosa Adventure Asteroid of Sector O9. No relation to the Pontoosa Adventure Asteroid of Sector O11. Bunch of name-stealing sods. You'd think there'd be a law about that, but allegedly, it's just different enough. Just enough, I ask you? It's the same bloody name! Anyway," the digital voice regained its composure. "Please enjoy your journey through the Perfect-Park terminal. For your pleasure, the tractor beam has been infused with the scent of freshly washed patio furniture." And a scent that could truly only be described as freshly washed patio furniture did seem to waft into the ship.

"Please remain seated until your vessel has come to a complete stop. Upon arrival, your teledisc will be loaded with the coordinates of our reception area. If you do not have a teledisc, you can get out and walk like the pauper you clearly are."

Xan clenched his teeth. "Eugh, bit classist, don't you think? A little rude."

"If you have a problem with it, please feel free to get out and walk," said the voice politely.

"Oh, no, I... No. No problem." Xan hated unnecessary walking.

"Good."

The voice stopped, and soon after, the rocket touched down on a pristine launchpad, surrounded by row upon orderly row of personal conveyance. May and Xan hopped onto the teledisc and fizzled into the reception area, pleased to find it bustling with joyful activity. This, clearly, was a popular place.

"This is mulch better than an arboretum," May said.

Xan made a tiny noise of grudging agreement, and they queued up for the ticket stand. Moments later, he gasped. "Blitheon's stars, May! You said 'mulch', didn't you? You made a pun!"

May smiled. "And you caught it! Eventually." He was

getting better and better at puns. A decade of sporadic English lessons and half an orbit spent without a functioning translation chip (more on that later. Or perhaps earlier.) had really polished his grasp of the language.

Enormous banners hung from the tall ceiling of the reception area, each boasting an experience more fantastical than the last.

"The Pontoosa theme park company has come a long way from 'Water Where There Ought Not Be,'" May remarked, remembering the dingy old Pontoosa Adventure Hole.

The Crennalto Experience boasted the ability to make it feel as if you were soaring through the air above a Crennaltian vista, dipping into the craggy cliffs and zooming around the massive ancient Crennaltian lewd carvings which depicted, it would seem, several varieties of Crennaltian genitalia.

Another poster simply read 'Very Small,' with an image of a family joyfully pointing at what appeared to be an enormous Q-tip. It was unclear if the experience was meant to make you feel very small, to showcase a very small family, or would actually reduce you to the size of a germ.

May figured it was better not to think about all the things alien technology could and couldn't do to a body. Something it could do, according to the next banner, was hurtle one at speeds faster than the fastest known racing rocket around and through the Adventure Asteroid in an aerodynamic car on a tractionless rail reassuringly dubbed the Murder Rail.

"Murder Rail," May whispered wistfully, pointing to the banner that portrayed a shrieking Udonian.

Xan had been expecting this, and he took it in stride. He breathed deeply, eyeing the banner with pure dread, and released a haggard sigh. "If we must," he said.

"I can ride it alone, you know."

He hadn't actually known that. The idea that they could go somewhere and do things as individuals was new to him, but the more he turned it over, the more he liked it.

At least in this instance. "Alright, you go ride that, and then we'll meet up at the virtual reality arcade and have some real faux fun?"

"Sure," she said, patting his arm.

They obtained tickets and bid farewell at the gate, May dashing off to the Murder Rail and Xan taking a more leisurely pace toward the arcade. Rather than a single gift shop, the Adventure Asteroid was lined with shops peddling everything from temporary rhinoplasty to the latest BEAPER tech to tiny novelty flags that read 'I had fun in Pontoosa's Ludicrously Opportune Transdimensional Wormhole.' Xan bought one for the irony of it. Besides, it would make May laugh, and that was his favorite pastime.

He tucked the small, triangular flag into his pocket and strode on towards the enormous marquee that crowned the arcade building. The nice, perfectly safe arcade. Entirely simulated thrills were more Xan's style. Simulated relaxing strolls along a beach were even more his style, and as such, he was pleased to find that the arcade had several rows of digital cabanas (complete with actual mixed drinks) in which he could lounge until May returned from her harrowing thrill ride.

This, Xan thought as he popped on the virtual reality electrodes and climbed into the cabana, hand held out to receive a strong, icy mixed drink, would do nicely. The cacophony of blips, dings, and other garish sound effects that permeated the rest of the arcade fell away as Xan chose the precise shade of green he wanted his virtual ocean to be.

NINE

DISINTEGRATION OF ALL THINGS

* * * * *

No one ever really believes that total universal disintegration could happen to them. Other universes, sure. But not theirs. This is why May and Xan were having such a hard time with the chilling unreality Mazelmez was trying to explain to them over dinner at the EZ Lab.

"Mazelmez, I'm too tired for this." May set down the can of forbinated moringarg she had been picking out of and leaned heavily on Xan's shoulder, disrupting his cautious unwrapping of a decades-old gorpal-pop. It crumbled into dust. "I just want to call up the race track and get the *Ostentatious* towed back here. I'll fix it up, and we'll be on our way."

"Oh, you can't fix that," Mazelmez said. "It was torn in half! Also, the universe is disintegrating, so there's really no guarantee the wreck even exists anymore. I feel like you haven't been listening to me. Have you been listening?"

Xan brushed the gropal dust off his pants and shifted position on the fainting couch. May's eyes were closed, and her breathing had already shifted; he needed to get comfortable before she fell asleep on him. "I've been listening," he whispered, trying to let May sleep. "But you aren't making any sense, Mazelmez! I wasn't particularly worried about that, on account of you never make much sense, but usually you're coming up with solutions, not problems. What makes you think the universe is disintegrating, anyway?"

Mazelmez held her PALM up to show Xan a three-dimensional hologram of the galaxy, with hundreds of stars pinpricking the air and labeled with their names. Mazelmez refreshed the hologram, and it appeared to zoom in, cutting out the stars closest to the edge. She refreshed it again, and it zoomed again. "The known universe is expanding like a slamahar in heat. I'm a little proud of myself, actually. Seems that the experiments I did with alternate realities busted ours! Distant galaxies are just disappearing, the intergalactic news is flooded with reports of outstandingly bad luck, and..." Mazelmez put her finger up, her eyes flicking about. "Do you feel that? Your atoms? You can feel them, right? If you really pay attention. It's like the moment before teleporting, right?" She smiled broadly, her eyes wide. "We're becoming more and more unreal by the blip!"

"I don't feel any such thing!" Xan insisted, though he had to admit he was buzzing more than he usually did.

"I feel it," May murmured, her eyes closed and face smooshed against Xan's chest. "Like the whole universe is falling apart." She sighed, seemingly becoming heavier on top of Xan.

"That's just depression, mun." He pet her hair softly, eyebrows furrowed.

"It's the universe disintegrating! I'm telling you, I busted it. It's like when you're at the beach, and you make a little moat and then the tide comes in, and kablam! Entire beachfront is in the ocean suddenly. My little inter-dimensional moat is collapsing, and we're on the sand bar!"

"Alright, fine, maybe you destroyed the universe. I can believe that, I guess," he told Mazelmez in a seething whisper. "What do you suggest we do about it?"

Mazelmez presented her hand to him. Three little metal barbells rested in the crux of her palm. "We go universe shopping! These zuxers will take us anywhere. If we die and our consciousness gets punted into another universe, our sense of continuity will be lost, and we'll take on whatever history our doubles had. If we take ourselves there, though, we survive as is!"

"And we'll be together," Xan added, looking down at May.

"Right. No guarantees you'll even know each other in your next life. It's the best option! Plus, added benefit, we get to murder our doubles. Free murder cards! No guilt!"

"Yes guilt! Lots of yes guilt! I can't murder someone!"

"Yourself? An unconscious body double of yourself? Sure you can do that! But, I mean, if you're offering him up, I'd be happy to do it for you."

"You'd be happy to murder me."

"Not you, zoup-nog! Just a body that looks exactly like you. You remember that time you got us lost in the filporthean weet fields back on Tuhnt, and I broke my leg so bad it took a whole day to heal, and we had to eat raw tribilite to survive? I'll consider this payback."

"Mazelmez, I don't know. Moving to a different universe...it's a little rash. What if it's really weird? Like we enter a universe where ice cream never existed."

"Then we invent it and make our fortune!" Mazelmez handed him two of the tongue rings and popped the third in her mouth before jumping up and running to an open wooden chest, where she began noisily pushing around the contents.

"What if our doubles kill us instead? Then what happens?"

Mazelmez hauled out a harpoon gun, which was just barely small enough to carry, and mounted it on her shoulder. "I don't think there's a chance of that happening," she said delightedly. "There's plenty of weapons lying around this place! Just pick the best ones. Put those in," Mazelmez nodded at the tongue rings.

"Now? You know, May taught me this Earth saying I

think is pertinent right now: we should 'sleep on it.' It means we should—"

"I get it. You want to delay the inevitable."

"No, it means--"

"Xan!" Mazelmez dropped the harpoon gun from her shoulder and became serious for a moment. She held up her right hand and then slowly passed her left hand directly through it. "We don't have time to sleep on it. Our reality is collapsing. Wake her up, grab some weapons, and let's go!"

TEN

MURDER RAIL

* * * * *

At the entrance to The Murder Rail queue, a kiosk advertised a free shawl to anyone who didn't scream on The Murder Rail and displayed a hideous strip of fabric printed with the word "Adventure!" in a miss-aligned pattern. May tilted her head curiously at it, and the Tuhntian behind the counter took that as a cue to interact.

"Reduces noise pollution!" they shouted at May, who smiled and nodded awkwardly before walking on. Small talk was Xan's forte; in the time she'd spent with him, she'd gotten even worse at it from lack of practice.

She was going to get that shawl, though. Ugly as it was, she couldn't refuse a challenge.

The line was long and gave her entirely too much undistracted time to think. What had otherXan meant... she wasn't real? Why had he stabbed her. and furthermore, why hadn't that been a bigger problem? Mostly, she wondered, why her? She actively avoided being too interesting. She wanted to go really fast, make lots of money, and generally do a little more than get by in the universe. Why did the universe keep throwing her detours?

May was lost in thought when the safety bar dropped and the ride countdown began. Fortunately, moments later, her body was going too fast for her mind to keep up with it, and she was free.

Everyone else screamed, but she remained as stony-faced as possible as the ride catapulted her in every legal direction at every legal orientation.

And then, May was somewhere else entirely.

✳ ✳ ✳ ✳ ✳

May found herself in front of a dirty griddle, the wind gone from her hair, utterly still. In her right hand, a spatula. Her left hand was tucked into the pocket of her apron. She looked down at herself. The sleek, breathable flight suit she usually wore was replaced with an itchy, over-starched polo that announced her name just under the logo of her captor: Sonic.

"Hey, mun, you alright? Your burgers are burning," said Xan's familiar voice in her ear, his hands on her shoulders. She jumped, not sure how to rectify Xan being in the kitchen at Sonic. He was wearing a Sonic visor and matching apron, giving her a tired smile.

"I'm...not sure," she said, flipping the burgers hesitantly. "Why, uh...why are we here? We were just at the Pontoosa Adventure Asteroid...right?"

He checked the incoming orders screen and began swiftly assembling a milkshake. Like he knew what he was doing. Like he had done this a million times before.

"Adventure Asteroid? You mean the Adventure Hole? That was years ago. I wouldn't say we were just there." He bagged the order and wiped his hands on a towel. "Burgers," he reminded her, helping by laying out some buns.

Her training kicked in, and she delivered the meat to the rounds of spongy bread automatically, unable to shake the feeling that she did not belong there.

"No chatting—it's lunch rush!" Kathy's voice crackled so

loudly in May's earpiece that it cut out at points.

That did it. The sound of her old manager's voice broke her. She threw the spatula down and ripped off her apron. "Xan! What the hell are we doing here? I was on the Murder Rail, and you went to the digital arcade. Why are we on Earth?! WORKING HERE?!"

Xan blinked, clearly torn between following orders and helping her cope with reality. "May, we'll get in trouble."

"We're already in trouble if we're working as fry cooks."

"Just for a while! Just until we save up some Earth money, and then we can fix the shuttle, and I'll go back to the Agency--"

"No. This isn't right."

"Back to work!!" Kathy shouted so loudly May could hear it rattling through Xan's earpiece. She hit the return call button.

"We're done. We quit," she said calmly. Far too calmly. She grabbed Xan's hand and led him out the back, emerging into a cool, sunny day that she couldn't have imagined in the dingy, hot kitchen.

"How're we going to afford rent?" Xan asked.

"I don't know, and I don't care. This isn't real. This can't be—" Across the street, she saw something even stranger. Aimz, along with two others who looked an awful lot like her and Xan stood watching them. Aimz held a harpoon gun, otherXan wielded a porcelain statue of a farmer attached to a lamp, and otherMay carried a classic, beautiful sci-fi plasma gun glowing with chaser lights and a bulbous plasma lamp. May had never gotten her hands on something like that but would've really liked to. She was jealous of herself.

"We're not staying here," said her double before flicking her tongue and promptly disappearing with the others.

"That was weird," May tried to say to the Xan she had just rescued from a life of working at Sonic, but he was gone. The whole street was gone. Replaced by the other side of the Murder Rail ride queue.

May had not screamed. She was too confused to do much of anything.

Someone draped a shawl around her neck.

* * * * *

The digital cabana had lulled Xan into a sleep-like trance, which is why the invisible hands shaking his arm had startled him so much. He ripped off the VR electrodes and found that, despite the sun being virtual, his pale blue arms were green with sunburn.

May had shaken him awake and was crawling urgently into the cabana beside him, wrapped in a fuzzy shawl.

"Xan, were you somewhere else just now?"

"Yeah, on the beach—" he pointed to the screen.

"No, literally. Just now, you and I were working at Sonic on Earth, and it was the lunch rush, and I made you quit and—" She blinked. "This is real, right?" May grabbed the edge of the cabana to confirm its reality. It didn't help, though. The spatula had felt very real. She was almost sure if she checked under the shawl, she'd be wearing that polo again.

"Probably some sort of perception filter, mun. You're real," he scooted farther into the cabana to let her settle in. "The shawl's new, though..."

"Oh, you get a free shawl if you don't scream on the Murder Rail."

"How was that?"

May shrugged. "It was alright. I wanted to scream, but I wanted to win the shawl more."

"I didn't know you liked shawls."

"I hate shawls. It was the principle."

"Ah." Xan wondered if he should bring up her brush with un-reality again or not.

He didn't have to.

"We need to find Aimz. She's got something to do with this, I know it," May muttered.

There had been no answer from Aimz over the BEAPER. She hadn't even seen the message. Though she hadn't seen the messages Xan had been sending for over two seasons ago, so he figured she'd broken her BEAPER yet again.

"You know, the trees see everything. If we went to the

Tree Museum, they might be able to help us."

"Are you just saying that because you want to go to the Tree Museum?"

"Well...I DO want to go to the Tree Museum. But also, I know where the trees are. I have no idea where Aimz is. She's a tough Tuhntian to track."

"Listay will know." She started to get out of the cabana, then noticed that something was poking into her thigh. She shifted over. "Jesus, Xan, what kind of beach was that?"

"Just a regular—" he noticed what she was staring at. "OH! You mean this?" Xan dug into his pants pocket and pulled out the novelty flag, holding it up so she could read it.

"So you did have fun in Pontoosa's Ludicrously Opportune Transdimensional Wormhole!" May said, taking the flag to marvel at how cheaply it had been made.

"Oh, yeah, ridiculously unbelievable amounts of fun. That's why I got the flag. As a sort of monument to the thrill. Every time I look at that tiny novelty flag, I'll recall fond memories of being flung across the galaxy, and it'll remind me to never do it again."

"It's probably the quickest way back to Flotluex. This place didn't even show up on our maps. We might be halfway across the galaxy. We might be in a different galaxy altogether."

"Eugh," Xan said, tucking the flag back into his pocket. "Wormholes should be outlawed."

"I think they're fun," May was already on her way out of the cabana, clutching the shawl around herself as if it could bind her to reality. She thumbed the cheap fabric of the shawl, trying to cement in her brain that the shawl was real. If she had it on, she was where she was supposed to be. Or...was she supposed to be back on Earth? At the Sonic? Was that reality? And she was so desperate for adventure that her consciousness had created this whole farce to entertain her?

May's body stepped out of the cabana, but her consciousness stepped out of reality.

ELEVEN

DUBIOUS DEITIES

* * * * *

For the hundredth time, Aimz stepped out of the gaudy gold saucer dripping in jewels and drowning in a glitter-infused white tunic. A hole had been tastefully cut out of it to reveal her entire mid-section, sternum to pubis.

For the hundredth time, Aimz raised her arms aloft, flicking a line of harmless crackling photons from two small devices lodged under her fingernails.

For the hundredth time, she announced that she was, in fact, a great and powerful Chaos goddess and suggested, yet again, that the confused and dirty life forms who had gathered around the ship should be very afraid, bow down, and lug as much food and precious resources as they could carry into the open ShuttleDisc.

This was the first time anyone spoke up to note that it would be difficult to bow down and carry goods into the ShuttleDisc at the same time.

"Oh," Aimz said, squinting at the dirty ground. "Yeah, I suppose that's true." She bit her bottom lip and crossed her godly arms. "Can you come out here? This group's being mouthy. I think they're more evolved than the last ones. We really should catch them right before the logic starts to develop," she muttered. "Why don't we just focus on the ones that are on the cusp of sentience, huh? Still a little gloopy."

A groan coiled slowly out from the open hatch, and Supreme Ultimate Ruler God, though we shall call him Surg, stumbled out, naked apart from the sheet he hastily tied over his muscular shoulder. He ducked out of the hatch, squinting into the bright sunlight of the nascent planet, the silver-white sun bouncing off blue skin, flowing golden hair, and coiling face horns which arced above his head creating an impressive halo of light.

"Mun-mun, the gloopy ones don't have jewelry. You want jewelry, right?" He slid his thick hands over Aimz's bare shoulders and gently cupped her face, going in for a kiss. "Shiny, bright little points of light for your pretty blue—"

"Save it, Surg, you know jewelry doesn't excite me. Look at them," Aimz gestured out to the surrounding crowd. Some of whom still lay prostrate in the dirt, impressed by the photon show, but others, the ones concerned about the mixed messages, shuffled awkwardly from foot to foot, feeling as if they were interrupting the alien lover's spat. "They're all symmetrical, weird slimes cleared up, organs tucked neatly away. Boring! I want to see some really freaky stages of evolution! Can't we intimidate some semi-conscious monstrosities?"

"Of course, my little bean-curd, but—" He lowered his voice to a threatening growl. "Let's keep the act up for the neophytes, huh? What were you going with, benevolent or wrathful?"

Aimz eyed the sorry-looking crowd of peasants gathered around them. An entire village, waiting to receive something from the heavens that they could believe in for millennia to come. "You know, I think the worshipers of an Indifferent O'Zeno had about the right idea."

Surg guffawed. "O'Zeno was a hack! Although, I have to admit indifference is a zipnite's toe easier than benevolence or wrath. Sort of a set-it-and-let-it-roll deal, isn't it? None of those pesky prophets to deal with every hundred or so years when people start to forget about you," he said, thinking out loud again. He had developed a minor telepathy over the past millennia, which often turned out to be more of a drawback than a power, as he could no longer really tell the difference between the words in his head and the words outside of it.

Immortality had made him slow, too. When one has all the time in the world, one tends to take it. Aimz crossed her arms, waiting for him to come to a conclusion, subconsciously comparing him with her previous lover, Listay. Listay had been a general in the Rhean military. Listay had had a mind as bright and quick as a photon. Listay had never insulted Aimz with a measly handful of precious gems and metals where a rotting carcass would do. It had been a long time since Aimz rummaged through a rotting carcass, and that was a damn shame.

Aimz's mind turned to that time Listay was a rotting carcass, re-animated, of course. Fond memories. That had been the initial attraction. Listay was just a beautiful zombie in a garbage pit and—

"Thus it is spake; thus it shall be written. Aaaahhhhmeeeehhhhnnn!"

Oh, thought Aimz, the speech was over already. She had been so lost in reverie she'd missed it. For good measure, she shot a photon bolt out of her middle finger into the sky, and it began to rain. The wretched crowd cheered and danced with each other, splashing mud up to their elbows.

Surg hurried Aimz back into the little ShuttleDisc and shut the hatch, leaving the fledgling civilization to work the rest out for itself, confidant that his appearance had made an impression.

Surg had a hearty never-ending feast, rivers of alcohol, and several well-attended orgy rooms to get back to on Crennalto, a planet in the Premerfherf system. Crennalto served as headquarters for many of the major pantheons that had sprung up after the whole Andolon debacle.

Fifty thousand years of immortal rule had turned the once verdant planet of Crennalto into Crennalto: Realm of the Gods, a veritable wasteland sustained only by the shipfuls of offerings the various minor deities who lived there stole from budding civilizations across the universe.

Yes, across the universe.

Fifty thousand years, it turns out, is plenty of time for a few clever, immortal scientists to figure out how to quickly fold space, pop down to a galaxy far, far away, and be back by brunch.

It was not, apparently, enough time to invent technology that would completely dispense of the need for a working class, however, so the native Crennaltians toiled away in the service of their many thousands of gods.

At least they got nice jewelry out of it.

Surg and Aimz popped (for this is the most accurate description of a vehicle that doesn't so much travel as it does bring the destination to you) directly into the sumptuous grand dining hall within Surg's own little slice of heaven, a gold-drenched acropolis.

Typically, the dining hall was alive with the laughter of lesser gods, all wearing white gowns, all in the process of hideously staining said white gowns with wine or other pleasurable fluids. But no longer. Now, instead, armies of grey-green scaly humanoids in white suits were boxing up candelabras, plates of food, chairs, and even, in some parts of the hall, groups of angry but well-accessorized Crennaltians.

Aimz emerged from the ShuttleDisc behind him and began stuffing the folds in her clothes with food from the trays that had not yet been packed up.

"What's going on?" Surg boomed across the hall. He liked to boom, there was a spot marked at the front of the hall where he could stand to ensure that the acoustics of the hall would promote a nice, earsplitting boom. He was careful not to discuss private matters in that spot, but on the rare occasion he forgot, the other gods were careful not to mention it.

"Please sign here," said someone behind him, holding out a clipboard and a pen.

"Notice of Acquisition," Surg read slowly. And then he read it again. There was other, finer print beneath the big block letters, but he had been so confused by the big ones that the little ones didn't seem all that crucial. Had he read the little ones, he would've likely not signed the paper.

"The Administration of Godhood and All Things Divine thanks you for your cooperation," said the Administrative Assistant. "The Coordinator will see you for onboarding in two to three business rotations."

"Please sign here," another assistant held out an identical clipboard to Aimz, and she recoiled, clutching her haul of foodstuffs in her skirt and sprinting for the ShuttleDisc.

"It's been fun, Surg, but, well…it's not anymore. Twa-don!" Aimz shut the hatch and set the coordinates for Rhea.

TWELVE

THE HORNIEST ONE

✳ ✳ ✳ ✳ ✳

"Ooooo'Zeno," Xan said, at last, when he could speak, quietly uttering the holy name as he exited the cabana over May's inert form. "O'Zeno. O—" he superstitiously stopped himself from repeating the name a third time. He highly doubted that repeating the deity's name three times would summon him, as the ancient scriptures claimed, but he had enough trouble on his hands, and so he wasn't keen to test it.

He scooped her up, nervously glancing around at the tentatively concerned onlookers. "Heh, she had one too many Electro-Blitzes," he said with a nervous smile. The arcade goers were far too invested in their own games to bother helping a Carmnian and a drunkard.

"Alright, okay, alright," he told himself, carrying May out of the arcade. "I'm going to take you to Listay, okay?" he told her rather pointlessly. "And then we're going to have a serious chat with Aimz and get this all worked out. I don't know what she did to you, but if she doesn't reverse, I'm going to..." He tried to think of something appropriately horrible to do to Aimz to gain vengeance for

May's unsettled consciousness, but nothing came. "Well, she's just going to have to reverse it. No other option."

"Had too much fun, eh?" said the security guard at the park's exit, hiking up his weapon-laden pants with one hand and wriggling the pinky of his other hand in his ear.

The exasperated sound Xan gave him was meant to pass for a casual chuckle, but it failed utterly under the weight of May's lifeless body. "Yeah," he huffed.

"Need a hand there?" the guard removed his pinky from his ear and, not bothering to dispose of the greenish gunk that now coated it, began to walk towards them, hands outstretched.

"No, no, I got her. Thanks. Just need to..." he tried to shift his hands beneath May so he could tell the *Audacity* to teleport him back in, to no avail.

"I gotcha there, just a blip," said the guard, bending down to see the screen on Xan's BEAPER and then tapping it with his ear wax-encrusted fingers.

Xan looked away miserably. "Thanks," he said.

"Just doing my job." He hit the teleport signal and blessedly disappeared, leaving Xan standing on the *Audacity*'s teledisc. He gratefully offloaded her onto the couch and melted on the shag carpet for a moment to recoup before crawling to his knees and calling Listay.

She answered quickly, her face floating above his BEAPER. "Xan, hey! Good to see you," Listay said because, although it was true, saying "Zuut, you look like trok" would have been poor manners.

"Is Aimz with you?" he said, then backtracked. "Sorry, hello! It's good to see you, too, mun! So is she there? I need to talk to her right now immediately. May and I are having some trouble with reality."

Listay sighed. "Aren't we all? She's not here. If she ever comes back, I'll let you know. Anything I can do to help?"

Empathy kicked in and began to help him override his panic. "Probably not, but seeing as we're both waiting for Aimz to get tired of flirting her way across the galaxy, maybe we ought to stick together."

"I'll start some coffee."

* * * * *

This year's harvest was a dud, blunted by an early frost on the island of Mwe'munsk.

Listay had spent most of the day inside keeping warm, but the compound was confusing for new arrivals, so in an effort to save Xan any further frustration, she'd come out into the open to watch for him. She dug in the garden while she waited, collecting a handful of fingernail-sized wrinkled bits of shermel root.

From the corner of her eye, Listay caught sight of a flash of orange; she knew better than to watch it directly; on a bright day like today, staring at the ship's neon hull could cause permanent eye damage. She turned her attention back to the rows of shriveled shermel and waited.

"Listay!" Xan shouted from quite a distance. She tried not to reward shouting, so she pretended not to have heard him.

"Listay!!" he called again, this time closer. She sat back on her ankles and nodded at him, still waiting for him to come within comfortable speaking range before she replied.

"Listay," he said when he was finally close enough. He leaned over his knees, panting from the run. "Good to see you," he said.

"You too. Where's May? Aren't you cold?" She wore an insulated coat and gardening gloves, but he only had on a simple racing suit.

"I feel nothing," he said. "May's resting. She got stabbed by someone who looked like me and then un-stabbed by someone who looked like Aimz, and then she thought we were working at an Earth fast food restaurant, then she just keeled over! I can't keep up!"

"I see," Listay said, though she wasn't positive that she did. "You suspect Aimz is the cause?"

His shoulders drooped helplessly. "I don't know, but if Aimz shows up and weird things are happening, I'd say it's pretty likely she's at fault."

"Isn't she great?" Listay said, and Xan wasn't quite sure if she was being ironic or not, so he didn't answer. "Let's collect May and bring her inside. Get you warmed up with some home-brew."

The cottage Listay had built, in a subtle attempt to keep Aimz interested, was a paragon of craftsmanship and invention. Recycled colored glass stacked like bricks to create a shimmering rainbow chimney, a solar-energy-collection dome sparkled over the main house, and a heavy carved door guarded the entranceway.

Notably, there were no weapons, no surveillance, no pressure sensors or forcefields. Just a door, on Listay's insistence. She'd had far more than her share of overprotective, deadly secrecy in the military. Mwe'munsk was nearly deserted, anyway. The only other inhabitants were part of a wealthy little commune on the other side of the island, and Listay had nothing they wanted except for the occasional jug of llerke ale or shermel, and they always paid handsomely for it.

Though Xan had tried to carry May into the cottage, Listay noticed him struggling and silently gestured to transfer that duty over. The oversized couch in Listay's lounge became a landing pad for May, whose consciousness was off having an adventure we will get to shortly.

With the physical weight of May off him, Xan's attention was quickly redirected to the mental weight of the day's perplexing events. He'd never worried much about whether the events of his life were "reality" or not. In his mind, what mattered was whatever you happened to be perceiving at the moment, and that was usually more than enough to keep him well-occupied.

"Llerke ale or shermel?" Listay asked. He was shaken out of his thoughts to find himself sitting at a hand-carved table in front of an enormous window overlooking the bay and the setting sun. The ocean sparkled in the clean, cool air, and a variety of wildflowers still grew against the warmth of the house.

"Whichever's stronger," he said miserably, setting his head down on the table. The gravity on Rhea seemed stronger than usual.

Listay poured two tall flutes of her homemade shermel and sat in the chair opposite him.

He hefted a hand onto the table and began to move the glass closer to his face. He didn't have the strength to drink it, though. "Has Aimz mentioned traveling to alternate realities?"

"Not recently. I'm fairly sure she would've told me if she had access to other realities." Listay sipped the shermel, staring out across the ocean. "Though you never know with Aimz. She could be the queen of the universe, and I wouldn't know."

Xan nodded. "She takes after our Aunt Chrismillian that way. Any indication of when she's coming back?" he finally rolled up to a proper seat and began to drink the shermel.

"Has she ever once in her life given indication of where she's going or how long she'll be there?" Listay asked.

Xan laughed gently. "Not in this reality, no. So I guess we wait. Should we take bets on how long until she gets tired of...what is she doing, anyway?"

Listay winced. "We went to a Millharmten party on the mainland, and she snuck off with some guy. He looked a lot like me, only taller and...hornier."

"Hornier?" Xan asked.

"He had horns, I mean. Maybe he was half Titian."

Xan sighed. "Andolonian, I'll bet."

"Andolon's a myth," Listay said. "Or else ancient history."

Xan shook his head. "You see a lot working with The Agency. There are still some Andolonians out there, but, uh, well, I've never met a sane one. They're all convinced they're ageless gods. Go around pillaging emergent species."

"They aren't an officially recognized human subspecies," Listay retorted. "They can't be actual Andolonians."

Xan only shrugged. "Whatever they are, they prefer to tip in 'benevolent gazes' than crystals."

Listay's brow furrowed. "I wasn't going to do this, but if you have reason to suspect that Aimz is in some kind of danger with this person...”

"Yes?" Xan straightened.

“And you really need her...”

“Go on.”

“This might sound, uh, immoral, but you've got to understand who Aimz is--"

"I understand completely. Go on."

"Well, I put a tracker chip in her without her knowing. I know it was wrong, but I've never used it. I only did it in case I really needed to find her and--"

Xan raised a hand. "Shh-shh. It's Aimz. I get it. Aunt Kalumbits used to talk about putting a tracker in her at least every other rotation. We have to find her." He began to stand, but a drop of green blood plopped into his glass of shermel followed by the plink of a tracker chip. Xan and Listay looked up. Aimz was scowling down at them from the thick wooden rafters.

"You put a tracker in me?!"

THIRTEEN

A PIRATICAL INTERLUDE

* * * * *

May found a sea shanty halfway out of her mouth before she realized that she didn't know any sea shanties and, furthermore, had no cause to be singing a sea shanty. She squawked unbecomingly as she choked off the song and peered wide-eyed at the crew surrounding her. Then, again, wide-eyed up at the stars, which were decidedly not twinkling around her.

She was in open space. On a wooden ship. Around a fire. Surrounded by her stalwart crew, which seemed to consist of a long-haired and bearded Xan, Aimz with a sorta bird-thing on her shoulder, Listay sporting several scars May didn't remember, and two other aliens, Rheans possibly, that she didn't know.

"Fuck. It happened again," she whispered.

"That's not how it goes!" Aimz shouted, her bird chirruping and fluttering its wings at the sudden outburst.

May smiled tightly. "Right. I uh...forgot the words."

"It's 'the gorpowag spliced a felly in 'er...'" Xan said, leaning in, hoping to jog her memory.

She shook her head and found it weighed down by heavy, jewelry-laden locs, the ends of which reached down past her waist. "I don't remember any of it," she whispered. The admission was met by a frown.

"Well, I do!" Aimz said. "Xanwell, start the tune, please!"

Xan stretched apart the thumb and pointer finger of his left hand, both of which were saddled with long, silver rings, then wriggled the fingers of his right hand in the gap, producing a sound like an accordion playing the flute. Aimz breathed deeply to belt out, "The gorpowag spliced a felly in 'er nethers, so they say!"

Aimz's quick rescue took the attention off May for long enough that she was able to stare, horrified at her hands. The tip of both her middle fingers was missing. Dark tattoos in a language she recognized as either A'Viltrian or Rhean (she could never quite tell the difference) ran from her fingers and up her arms. She counted seven large, gemy rings.

"Xan," she said quietly, trying to call him away from the conversation that had struck up. He ignored her. "Xan!" she repeated, quieter but more forcefully. That's not what Aimz had called him, though. "Xanwell?" she tried.

"Hmm?" he said, finally realizing he was being spoken to.

"What happened to my fingers?" she said, showing him her shaking hands.

Xanwell laughed boisterously and patted her shoulder. "How'd you forget a thing like that, lav? Middle-Aged Biderot, the shalg monger sliced 'em off after you performed an Earth gesture at him. I think you referred to it as a 'tipping the birds' or something. I guess he realized it was a nasty thing to do and..." Xanwell shrugged. "No more birds."

Sonic, May knew how to navigate. Pirates, she did not. Why was the ship made of wood? And in space? Why pirates? She began to shiver now despite the heat thrown off by the fire.

"Zuut, Captain, what's the matter?" Xanwell slipped the instrument off his hand and pocketed it, shifting on the crate he sat atop to get a better look at her.

"I don't remember any of this. I don't think I'm supposed to be here," she said.

"Hey, Xanwell! If you're not going to play it, toss the apopolator over this way, eh?" said one of the crew mates May did not know. Although, she thought their name was Bondoony. And they weren't Rhean; they were Titian. She didn't want to know that, but she did.

Xan tossed the heavy rings to Bondoony, and as soon as they started playing, May leaned in to whisper to Xan. "What's their name and where are they from?"

He pulled away slightly to give her a concerned once-over. "May, lav, that's Bondoony. Their Titian. Do you..." He looked down at the dark, splinter-ridden wood of the ship's deck. "Do you remember me?"

Briefly, May considered saying, emphatically, that she did remember him. Then she realized the him she remembered was not this him. She opened her mouth to explain this, but recognition seemed to be dawning in stages lately. She remembered trimming his hair with a laser knife just a few hours ago. She remembered him convincing her to join the rest of the crew and regale them with some of her famously naughty shanties. She remembered the shanties, and they were, indeed, naughty.

"Xanwell," she whispered. It felt right now. "Of course," she said. "You helped me escape from the Peacemaker. We built this crew together. I gave you that--" she trailed off, pointing to the massive gold plug in his ear lobe.

He smiled beneath the bushy orange beard. "That's right. The night we--"

May quickly put a silencing finger to his mouth. "No. No, I'm sorry. We never...we aren't. Fuck!" May said, trying to rub her fingers through her hair and failing when her fingers hit only the tightly wrapped silk cloth around her head. "Don't make me remember, please. I don't want to remember. This isn't my reality. You aren't real," she affirmed, standing.

"Where are you going?"

"To my cabin," May said. She shouldn't have known she had a cabin, much less how to get there, but she found herself stomping off to her quarters without hesitation.

The singing stopped, and everyone watched her disappear into the ship's lower deck. "She probably wants to be alone," Xanwell murmured to himself. He looked to Listay. "Do you think she wants to be alone?"

Aimz interjected. "'Course she doesn't! Give us one more song, then you can go and help her polish the floors of her cabin!" She laughed, elbowing Listay gently to see if she was in on the joke, too. Listay didn't laugh, but she didn't scold Aimz either.

The Adventuresomeness, prized EtherGalleon of Tuhnt, creaked around May, or rather the captain, as she made her way towards the cabin beneath the helm, her quarters.

It creaked, not because it was composed of settling wood beams biting back tireless ocean waves, but because all EtherGalleons came installed with a creak-feature to simulate all the majesty and glory of Tuhnt's ocean fairing heyday.

May knew all of this, though she wished she didn't.

A sprawling desk conquered the middle of the room, the top barely visible under a spread of charts and maps. She avoided it. She pulled down the tap handle on a keg of Crennaltian floating ale and held a mug upside down over the spout to collect the yellowish-green brew as it defied the ship's artificial gravity and floated upward.

Two disparate memories of recent events played perfectly in her head. She shut off the tap and opened the smaller, thumb-operated spigot on the bottom of the mug, sipping up a hearty mouthful.

Satisfied, she crashed into an oversized armchair beside a glass bay window and stared out at the field of stars. She had the vivid impression that just moments earlier, she had been at a theme park, exiting a cabana...and Xanwell didn't have a beard. And there was a shawl...she would never wear a shawl, though. That would be absurd.

"What a strange dream," she whispered out loud. Her brow furrowed, and she leaned over to the side table to grab a pen and scrap of paper. On it, she drew something fish-shaped, but it didn't have an eye. Or it did...maybe it had three eyes. Large, round things. And a jet of flame generated from its tail fins.

"Orange..." she mused just as Xanwell cautiously slid into her room.

"Uh, everything alright, Captain? You went a wee bit strange out there."

Frowning, May scrunched up the slip of paper and tossed it onto the floor. "Fine, sorry," she said as Xanwell picked up the scrap and deposited it in a trash can under the desk.

He perched on the arm of her chair. "You're worried about the Clymasir fortune, aren't you?"

She hadn't been. She hadn't remembered until he brought it up. The boxes of goods out there on the deck belonged to the Clymasir ruling family, a horribly inbred group of Rheans protected by one of the largest armed forces on Rhea I. If they got The Adventuresomeness in their sights, it was over. They'd be slotted for sure.

"Not that," she said, waving her hand dismissively. "I had a dream...just now. I must've fallen asleep at the fire."

"In the middle of a shanty?"

May nodded. "Aye," she said, feeling for just a moment like that wasn't something she was supposed to say.

"What was it about?"

She took another swig of the ale before answering. "I don't remember. But I feel like I really need to."

"Well, then," Xanwell stood and took the mug from his captain, setting it down before grabbing her hands and gently coaxing her to stand. "Perhaps we ought to make for the bed, eh?"

She took her hands back and flopped onto the chair again. "Not in the mood," she said.

"To sleep?"

"No, I need to think. I need to remember," she drank deeply of the ale.

"That brew'll make you forget, lav—that's what it's for!"

"Ugh," she slammed the mug down, realizing she had only been drinking out of habit; she didn't actually like floating ale. She tucked her legs under her and buried her face in her arms. "You ever feel like you're not who you thought you were? Like you're looking out from someone else's eyes all of a sudden? Like you're just..." May sighed, leaning back on the chair and staring at the rough wood ceiling she knew so well. "Just passing through?"

Xanwell took the mug from her and drank from it himself. "Only when I'm in my right mind, lav. Fortunately, I'm not in my right mind much. Would make the whole"—he swallowed loudly—"murdering people to steal their hard-earned goods a wee bit more difficult."

"You've never murdered anyone," May scoffed. She had, though, apparently.

"I've been party to it! You ever think maybe we've got enough now? Maybe we clean up, settle down on the outskirts of a nice, quiet fishing town? Take charge of a few larvae and never ever tell them why we're so obscenely wealthy?"

"I can honestly say I have never thought that..." or had she?

Xanwell tilted his head at the thoughtful wrinkle between her eyebrows and put a thumb to it, gently rubbing until the tension released, and May sighed.

"Bed?" he said, scooping her up out of the chair in a way that felt far too familiar to her. She locked her arms around his neck, fighting the feeling that he wasn't strong enough to carry her all the way to bed. Of course he was. She didn't know why she doubted that.

He set her up against the lumpy but copious pillows on a massive round bed, which nearly drowned her it was so soft. Then, he pulled his shirt off and began to peel out of his pants like it was just the most natural thing. May was about to say something, but the sound of cannon fire saved her. The ship rocked on its gyroscope, absorbing the force of the cannon to keep it from being thrown wildly off course, and Xanwell, perched on one leg with half his trousers off, toppled to the floor.

"What was that?" he said, popping up beside the bed like he was spring-loaded.

May's eyes narrowed. "Clymasir. Gotta be," she snarled and launched out of bed, snatching a mounted weapon from the wall. She slowly came to remember it was called a baulbeetor. Despite the dire circumstances, she snickered at the name as she cranked the cumbersome thing to charge its battery.

Another cannon sounded, and the ship rocked the other way, tossing her into a wall and giving her the inaugural injury of this battle, a rather large splinter in her arm. Xanwell, shimmying back into his pants but leaving the shirt, bounded after her, and she spun to stop him.

"You don't have a weapon!" she said. "Get back in my room and lock the door."

"I've got a weapon," he said defensively and pulled a small pocket knife from his belt, showing it to her with an uncomfortable grin. He blew a clump of wood dust off the hilt. "I was whittling earlier."

May shook her head at him, but the shouting of her crew on deck was getting louder; she didn't have time to argue. If he got himself killed, it would be his own damn fault.

She sprinted through the hall, wondering why she wore so much heavy jewelry and layers of thick cotton clothing that slowed her down. The first thing she was going to do after the interlopers were dealt with was comb her locs out in favor of a shorter, lighter style. Maybe bumper bangs.

The deck of the ship, lit only by the massive fire pit, danced with energy.

But it wasn't the agents of Clysmar attacking the ship. It seemed their own crew was attacking. Two Aimz's were locked in battle. The pirate Aimz had only a short dagger on hand at the time of the attack, but the other one wielded a hefty harpoon gun. Fortunately, at close range, the harpoon gun was rather useless, and the pirate Aimz was holding her own.

A shaven doppelgänger of Xanwell wielded a porcelain figure lamp and held off the rest of the crew back-to-back with a duplicate of herself whom she found spookily familiar. Bumper bangs. Her double had a stunning plasma gun, which was, fortunately for the ship's crew, totally out of plasma. May watched her throw the plasma gun overboard in frustration and pulled a tiny pocket knife from between her boobs instead.

May shot a single bullet from the baulbeetor into the forcefield surrounding them, electrifying the air with a momentary freezing buzz before the forcefield healed itself. The fighting ceased. "What's going on here? Who are you?" she shouted down to the doppelgängers.

"Oh, come on. This is too much effort," said Aimz's double, and all three disappeared together.

FOURTEEN

AIMZ'S SOLUTION

* * * * *

"Aimz! Get down here," Listay said, pointing seriously to the floor.

Aimz swung her legs at Listay but remained perched on the thick wooden beam. "Insecurity isn't an attractive quality, Listy," Aimz teased. "Haven't you ever heard that if you love something, don't track it?"

"Come down here," said Listay, slowly, reasonably, "and we can talk."

Xan knew talking wasn't going to tempt Aimz down, so he grabbed a broom from a corner of the kitchen and prodded her with it instead.

"Where have you been?" Listay asked. "Who was that person you ran off with?"

Aimz swatted and hissed at the broom Xan tried to coax her down with.

"Oh, just some--stop it! Just some minor deity. I thought it would be fun being a--hey! Blitheon, that was my eye, you tchaag." Aimz grabbed the bristles of the offending broom and tore it out of Xan's grasp, flinging it across the room. She dropped down to the floor, one eye squinted shut and the other glaring at him. Her fingers found the half glass of shermel he had left on the table, and she tipped her head back to pour it directly into her eye. "Zuut that stings!" She shook her head, showering Xan and Listay with droplets of shermel, and sat down on the table, trying to blink away the rest of the alcohol.

"You thought it would be fun being a what?! A cheat?" Listay said, punctuating by chugging the rest of her own shermel.

"A god, Listy. Turns out it's about the most boring, repetitive thing you can do with an eternity."

"An eternity?" Xan asked.

"Yeah.”

Xan squinted at her, trying to wrap his head around what she was saying. He couldn't, but he rarely could with her anyway, so he changed the subject. “What about May?"

"What about May?" Aimz asked, rubbing her eye with the back of her hand.

“You had something to do with this, didn't you? Someone who looks exactly like me showed up, stabbed her, then disappeared. Then someone who looks an awful lot like you un-stabbed her, and now she's all... questioning reality and going unconscious. That sounds very much like a you-problem.”

“You're the one who's worried about it. Sounds like a you-problem to me.”

“Where's your BEAPER?” Listay demanded.

Perplexed, Aimz looked at her naked wrist. “Huh. I don't know.”

“Isn't there anything you can do for May?” Xan interjected.

“You lost your BEAPER? I bought that for you!” Listay said.

Aimz shrugged dramatically. “It's not lost! I just don't know where it is right now.”

“I'd really like to talk about May now,” said Xan.

“That's the definition of lost!” said Listay.

“I'll buy a new one, zuut!” said Aimz.

“May.”

"With whose money?!"

"Okay, that's enough!" Xan said. "May needs help now. Aimz, I've seen you argue and work at the same time. I know you can do it."

Aimz scrubbed her fingers through her hair, making it even messier. "I've got my own problems right now, lav. I need to be unfindable for a while…"

"What did you do?" Xan asked.

"Nothing! I don't know! I just took one of Surg's saucers and came right here."

"Perhaps you're being pursued because you stole a saucer." Listay's voice was steady; she crossed her arms.

"No, no, it was before I stole the ShuttleDisc."

"Who's after you, then?" asked Listay.

"All I know is that whoever they still use real, actual paper." She shuddered and threw herself onto the couch next to an unconscious May, arms covering her face dramatically, legs sprawling in every imaginable direction. This, though terrifying, was not strictly true. The Administrative Assistants used digitally projected real, actual paper.

"So as long as they didn't follow me, I'm just going to crash here for a while until they forget about me, okay?"

"Not okay. It's been three seasons! You left without saying goodbye!" Listay said

"You put a tracker in me!"

"Alright!" Xan said. "Both of you were bad partners to each other, and we can sit down and talk through it and come to some agreements later, but right now, May is unconscious, and it really, certainly, absolutely seems like it's somehow your doing, Aimz. If you don't fix her, I'm not helping you fix your relationship!"

"Zuut, unpin it. It wasn't me who un-stabbed the Earthmun. I've been otherwise occupied. Either it was an alternate universe thing or a clone thing. It couldn't be time travel. Time's too fragile to go galavanting around in. I wouldn't try it."

"You wouldn't try it?" Xan asked.

Aimz got a real wide-eyed, serious look on her face. "No. I would never, ever try that. You sound surprised."

"It's...I mean, it's you. You'll try anything."

"Not this."

"Alright, so it's not time travel," Xan agreed. "So is it clones or alternate universes?!"

"Where did the doubles show up?"

"Another me on the *Audacity*, the other you was when I took her to the shaman vet on Morpas station."

"You took her to the shaman vet?" Aimz started to laugh but covered it with a polite cough. At least she was trying to be sensitive to his dire situation. "You know the only reason to go to the shaman vet is to get prescription-strength hallucinogenics, right? She probably took some really mind-blowing drugs. That would explain the questioning reality and going unconscious thing. How long has she been out?"

"It feels like eons."

"But it's actually been how long?"

"Maybe half a beoop."

Aimz's eyes crossed with exasperation. "I once tripped so hard I spent three rotations organizing tree seedlings by how threatening their auras were on the forest floor in Flortsanct. To this day if you want to see any nice trees there, you've got to walk past a whole lot of shady zuxers."

"But she didn't take anything at the vet!" Xan whined. "We just got our ominous warning and left."

Aimz stretched, punched a pillow into a more comfortable place under her back, closed her eyes, and produced a ZipOut Stick from her pocket, lazily poking it into May's wrist and turning it on.

"Arg!" May shouted, vibrating from the mild electric shock, her hair standing on end.

"There, she's back," Aimz yawned and stood, opening the heavy wooden front door. "I'm gonna make sure no one followed me." She slammed the door, shaking the entire living room.

FIFTEEN

LEGAL COFFEE

* * * * *

May held her aching wrist. She wasn't on her ship anymore; she was on a planet. She could feel the difference between real and artificial gravity in her bones. Furthermore, no one was attacking her. Only Xanwell and Listay faced her, watching her in quiet confusion as if waiting on her to do something.

It had happened again, one of those too-real dreams.

"No," she said, shaking her head. "I have to wake up. My crew needs me. How do I wake up?" she asked Xanwell, but he was not Xanwell. His face was shaven, and he wore a skin-tight racing suit.

"You are awake," Xan said. "Aimz zapped you."

"Where are we?" she looked around the living room space and found nothing familiar apart from Xan and Listay. Her hair was right again, though. Light and fluffy. "I don't remember this place."

"That's alright—we've never been here before!" Xan said. "This is Listay's house. I brought you here while you were unconscious; that's why you don't remember coming. Last thing we did was the Adventure Asteroid. You had just defeated the Murder Rail and won your victory shawl when--"

"Right, I told you about losing time on the Murder Rail, and then I lost it again. Shit, Xan! It felt so real. I even remembered things that never happened this time. Fingers!" She raised her hands, noting that while all her beautiful rings and tattoos were gone, the tips of her middle fingers were back. "Good. That wasn't real, then. But I remember so much from that life still. Listay, you were there, and Xan, you..." Dropping her head back, she gave a frustrated, guttural groan. "Listay, would you mind making me a coffee?" she asked. There were things she needed to discuss with him in private.

"Sure," Listay said, and as she left for the kitchen, May moved to the table by the window, where Xan joined her. Once he was seated, leaning forward, keenly interested in what she had remembered, May continued in a whisper.

"I remember everything. My parents sold me into servitude on the Peacemaker, and it was... I mean, it was a spaceship, but it was made of wood and iron and... That doesn't make any sense, does it? How could it possibly have been made of wood? It had a force field. But why?" she grabbed the sides of her head, combing her hair back. "And you, but not-you, Xanwell rescued me, and then we...our relationship was different." She concluded, looking at him searchingly, trying to separate which memories she'd made with him and which she'd made with Xanwell. The lack of a beard helped distinguish most of them but... "Xan, have we ever stolen a sacred artifact from ancient Pan that made us switch bodies?"

Slowly, Xan shook his head. "No...no, I would probably remember if that happened. We're not really into stealing. Or sacred artifacts."

May nodded. "Right," she closed her eyes, still trying to remember important events and sort them by fact or fiction. There was another thing she was finding difficult to sort out, and she didn't want to ask, but she needed to know for certain. "We've never," she lowered her head and her voice to a barely audible whisper. "Fucked, have we?"

A coffee cup appeared on the table in front of her with

Listay attached to it.

"That's the fastest anyone's ever brought me coffee in any reality," May said to Listay as she joined them at the third seat at the table, setting down a tray with two more coffee cups, one for Xan and one for herself.

"Sorry, that sounded like a private conversation."

"It's alright. Not much privacy on an old wooden EtherGalleon, either," May said, sipping her coffee. It was watery, reddish, and earthy. She swallowed hesitantly. "Is this coffee?"

"Yes," Listay said.

"It's not Earth-coffee," Xan explained. "I had some Earth-coffee back on the *Audacity*," he told Listay.

"Had?" May asked. "Is it gone?"

Xan crouched down sheepishly. "...no"

"Xan! That's illegal," Listay admonished. "Earth is a no-contact planet."

"If it's a no-contact planet, why did you invade it?" May said.

"Because I was under orders by a highly decorated Rhean captain...or so I thought. Sneaking exports off a no-contact planet is not only dangerous, it's unethical."

"You razed the planet to install a totalitarian regime!" May argued.

"Well, everybody makes mistakes," she said sheepishly.

Xan decided to rescue her from May's accusations by turning the conversation back to his highly illegal dried beans. "There were a lot of smugglers connected with The Agency, I got hooked," he said with a small shrug. "It's pretty easy to purchase in some corners of the galaxy. I didn't hand-smuggle it."

"That explains why we only get it from the sketchier spaceports," May said, drinking more of Listay's coffee. She could see why it translated as coffee; it was similar enough. She could also see why Xan always bought the Earth-coffee instead.

"Only the nicest sketchy spaceports," Xan corrected. "And, to answer your other question, no," Xan said, referring back to a question asked way before he had been accused of immoral caffeination.

Though Listay was surprised by this, she covered her shock neatly by taking an extra long gulp of perfectly legal coffee.

"Good," said May, absolutely unable to determine whether he felt that was good or not. "So what does Aimz have to do with this?"

"She didn't seem to know anything," Xan said. "Even what she did know, she couldn't explain."

"Wish I could've been more help," said Listay. And she did. She still felt awful about the whole invading Earth thing and had made it a sort of mission of hers to help Earthlings whenever possible, even though in this timeline, the invasion hadn't happened thanks to Chaos being kicked out of history.

"Coffee always helps," May said to her, just holding the mug now and letting the heat from it anchor her to reality. She closed her eyes and breathed deeply, but before she could exhale, her calm was shattered by a familiar sound. "That's the *Audacity*'s pre-launch splutter," she said, her eyes open wide now. Jumping up, she ran to the window and found that the *Audacity* was, indeed, prepping to launch. Without thinking, she teleported back into the ship, and Xan, only thinking that he shouldn't let her do that alone, teleported, too, leaving Listay alone with two half-empty mugs of coffee and no clue what was going on.

A polite knock came at the door. "We are the Administrative Assistants," Listay heard. "Open up." Listay had never had much trouble with paperwork. She actually rather liked it, and so she obliged.

SIXTEEN

DUST GHOST

* * * * *

"How'd you get in here?" May asked as soon as she was corporeal enough to do so. She hadn't known for sure that it would be Aimz at the controls, but she could've guessed.

"There's a loose panel in the nozzle," Aimz explained, continuing to steal the ship.

"Yeah, where the muns get in!" May said. "You're not the size of a mun; how'd you get in?!"

"I just squeezed in!" Aimz said, still playing with the controls. "How the trok does this thing start? I can't find a take-off checklist." May rushed up to the console and shooed her away.

"It's the red button marked 'GO,'" Xan said helpfully, appearing on the teledisc.

"You just told her how to steal our ship!" May said.

"It's not stealing if you're in it and not tied up," Aimz said, launching the ship and turning around. "I could tie you up if you want, though."

"Not right now," Xan said. "Aimz, what's going on? You said you were going to smash a tracker."

"I tried! They arrived before I could even find the zuxing thing, so I ran."

"Who?" May asked.

"The...the people! From the place with the paper."

"The place with the paper?" May said suspiciously. "You aren't making sense, Aimz." And with that, May's world began to morph and twist and then blinked out altogether.

Xan caught her and held her like a cumbersome sack of potatoes. Her mouth hung open in slumber, and her eyes were mostly, but not entirely, closed; a little crescent moon of white sclera peaked out from under her eyelashes.

"Fuck!" Xan said empathically.

Aimz tilted her head. "That's the Earth curse word, isn't it? I don't think you're saying it right. 'Fook'. It's 'Fook'"

"Aimz, I've been living with May for five orbits. It's 'fuck', I'm sure of it." He set May down in the pilot's seat, then realized that if anyone needed to be conscious, it was the pilot, so he shuffled her over to the co-pilot's seat instead, gingerly sitting in her chair and leaning over the console miserably.

"Want me to zap her again?" Aimz asked.

"No, it's alright. I can't just keep zapping her back to reality for the rest of her life. I'm taking her to the Andolonian Tree Museum. The trees will know what's wrong with her."

Aimz wormed over the back of the couch until she was staring at him upside down. It looked as if she were trying to physically meld with the couch. It looked like she was succeeding, actually. "Ugh, the trees are boring. So many rules," Aimz moaned. "Launch the ship, I don't know how long Listay will be able to resist them."

"You're just going to leave her to deal with your problems?" Xan asked.

"Yeah," Aimz said, closing her eyes.

"And...you don't feel at all bad about this? Or about cheating on her?"

Aimz's eyes rolled so far into the back of her head, her eyelids fluttered at him. "I feel bad, Xan, okay? I fooked up. I was only trying to keep it interesting. Thought she'd come after me. She was tracking me, after all."

"You knew?"

"Of course I knew there was a tracker in me! I wanted her to track me! But she didn't."

"Aimz, if you want someone to do something, you need to let them know," Xan said. "What do you think these people are going to do to her?"

Aimz shrugged. "Probably nothing she wouldn't do to herself sooner or later."

"What on Blitheon's great round buttcheek does that mean?"

"It means don't worry about her! She'll be fine," Aimz rolled along the couch until she was out of Xan's sight, smooshed against the crack between the cushions and the back of the couch. "Just launch the ship. Please?"

Xan shook his head at her but obeyed, setting coordinates for the Andolonian Tree Museum and taking his customary launch position in the fetal position underneath the console with his eyes jammed shut.

Once the ship escaped Rhea's gravity, the rattling calmed down, and he crawled back into his chair, double-checking that nothing important had been blown off the ship during launch. He didn't mind living in empty space, stopping at space stations here and there, but entering and exiting the atmosphere of a planet still blew and sucked.

He wobbled down the stairs and stood above the couch, trying to put on a tough, no-nonsense face to talk seriously to Aimz. He quickly changed tactics when he saw the state of her. Her usual self-confidant smirk was gone, her eyes glassily gazing at nothing. He hadn't seen her like this for centuries.

Honestly, he was relieved. Tough and no-nonsense serious talk didn't agree with him. He relaxed, sitting opposite her on the coffee table. Gently, he tucked a strand of pink hair behind her ear, which was filled with golden jewelry. Her outfit was truly spectacular.

"The guy you ran off with must've owned some stars. All this jewelry's worth more than both our inheritance plugs combined."

Aimz closed her eyes at him. "Money's crosh-wopple. He was boring." She began pawing at the jewelry on her ears until it released and tumbled to the carpet, becoming lost in the shag. She sighed, then stopped. It wasn't worth the energy to take it off.

"What do you want me to tell Listay?"

"Nothing." She spun around so she wouldn't accidentally give him the impression she wanted to talk to him.

He messaged Listay anyway, discretely, to thank her for the drinks, compliment her home, and let her know he would give Aimz a stern talking to. That last bit was wildly over-aspirational, but anyone who knew Xan would know that.

There was only one thing Xan could think of that might pull Aimz out of this dark spot. Another kind of dark spot. "Hey, Aimzy," he said, scooting over to the couch beside her to comb her hair back into a neat braid. "There's some kind of leak in the engine room, and it's making a really nasty, waxy stalagmite under the pipe." He tempted. "It's brownish yellow, and it smells like rotten fruit," a sing-song quality to his voice as he continued to braid her hair. "I think I saw some very small bones encased in it..."

She rolled over slightly, giving him the honor of her attention. "That's borbing fluid. Don't touch it. See a mechanic," she said. "Probably a mun got stuck in there," she sighed heavily and buried her face in her arm.

Xan frowned; that was all he had in his arsenal of weird, gross things Aimz might be invested in. "You want to watch some TV?" he said.

Again, Aimz sighed.

"Well, you let me know when you're ready to be a willing participant in life again, okay?" he finished off her braid, patted her shoulder, and went back up to the console, increasing the ship's speed slightly. He never thought he could be lonely with his best friend and his sister on board, but neither were interacting with him. He leaned lazily back in the pilot's chair, thinking perhaps he could just take a nap until they reached the Tree Museum, but his mind was utterly stuffed with thoughts. He needed to talk.

"May, if you can hear me, I'd really like it if you woke up," he said. "Where are you this time?" he wondered out loud.

"'m righ' here," she mumbled, her eyes still closed, her body otherwise unresponsive.

He sprung up. "May? You heard that?"

"M-hmm."

✳ ✢ ✳ ✶ ✳

Everything everywhere was orange all at once. May tried to blink, but there was no respite from the orange. She didn't appear to have eyelids at all. So how, exactly, was she seeing? And what? In one moment, she saw only orange all around; in another, she could make out the shapes inside the *Audacity* from the viewpoint of the console, then the coffee counter, the top of the TV...she was in the engine room and in her bedroom on the bed and in total darkness and in blinding light and—she was totally aware of it all.

That did not seem right. She wanted to be in one place desperately. She vibrated. She began to form a more cohesive picture. Slowly, one bit at a time, her awareness settled on the couch, where she focused all her attention on a single view of the TV. A black-and-white western shimmered on the screen. A man on a white horse. A man in a mask...The Lone Ranger? Sound became apparent to her now, and she heard the confirmation she needed: "Hi-yo silver!" shouted the man.

"...silver," echoed someone next to her on the couch. Xan! Had she ever seen him wear black before? That seemed unusual...Oh, she realized. Oh no. It happened again.

"Shit," she said.

Beside her, Xan startled, twisting to look behind himself, seemingly looking right through her. Not only was he wearing all black, but a black eye mask covered half his face, and his usual orange pompadour was smushed under a white cowboy hat. "Hello?" he hazarded. "Someone...there?"

"Yeah, it's me," May said, waving her hand in front of his face, confused as to why he couldn't see her. And then she wasn't confused. She looked at her hand. It was composed merely of a few hundred floating skin cells, barely visible in the low light, almost entirely see-through. She looked at her other hand; it was the same. She tried to touch her body, but there was no body to touch. "Whaa---" she said, her impulse to hyperventilate arrested by her distinct lack of lungs.

"May?!" Xan comically scrambled away from her over the arm of the couch, thudding on the carpet. He quickly regained a sense of direction and peeked over the couch arm at her, squinting to try to make out her vague dust-form scintillating in the dim orange light. "You're...a ghost?! You're a ghost! Zuut!"

She attempted to rub the back of her neck, but there was no neck to rub and no hand to rub it. The particles that approximated her face formed a wide-eyed cringe. "Yep..." she said. "I didn't make it off New-Tuhnt before it exploded, did I?"

Xan shook his head carefully. "You went back out to the planet to cut the tether anchoring the *Audacity*. You saved my life. I never got to thank you," he said shakily. "How are you here?!"

May played with her particles curiously. "Skin cells. You know the carpet's self-cleaning, right? Just push a button."

Xan shook his head, slowly crawling back to the couch cushion beside her, not blinking. "I did not know that, no."

May nodded, looking away uncomfortably. "I knew that...in another life," she said.

"Where are you this time?" Xan asked.

"I'm right here," she said, tilting her head in confusion.

"I can see that," said the Xan next to her.

"May? You heard that?" said Xan, but his lips didn't move. It wasn't THIS Xan asking. It was her Xan. She tried to think a reply really loudly without saying anything to the Xan next to her. Two conversations at once. One in a universe where she was nothing but dust.

"This is going to get confusing," she said on a sigh, which blew a puff of dust out of her particulate body.

SEVENTEEN

THE LONE RANGER

* * * * *

Xan sat on the edge of the pilot's seat, his attention raptly focused on May's inert form. She could hear him, somehow. She wasn't entirely gone.

It was at times like these Xan wished he had listened to what his Ness Instructor had said. He knew there was a way to access the great information store of the universe, that beings had spent lifetimes practicing the fine art of Ness travel. That wherever May's consciousness was currently trapped could be accessed...but he didn't have a clue as to how this was done.

He stared intently at May, hoping to will himself to wherever she was. This did not work. Not after a few blips, at least.

The subtle arts were not his specialty. So he tried this instead:

"May, come here. Follow the sound of my voice. May, May, May, May, can you hear me? May, come here, May, come on, you can do it, I'm real! I'm the real Xan! Come on back. If you can hear me, wake up. Wake up, May. May? May. May, wake up..." And he went on like this

89

while she mumbled incoherently.

* * * * *

Dust-May turned her attention back to the TV. She found that, oddly, she didn't need to actually turn to face it; she could just sorta sense the image over there if she decided to. "So you're...watching The Lone Ranger?" she said with a little laugh. "I always liked The Lone Ranger. Stoic," she said. "About the exact opposite of 'I Love Lucy,'" she said, but then she wasn't quite sure why she had said that. Had they ever watched 'I Love Lucy' together? Her memories were so old, so fuzzy. Being dead was really making it difficult to focus.

"What's 'I Love Lucy'?" asked the masked Xan beside her.

May just shrugged dustily. She didn't know why that question made her feel sad.

"May, come here," she heard distantly. Was she not supposed to be where she was? She ignored it.

"Just an old Earth TV show; you probably wouldn't get it." She transferred her particles a little closer to him on the couch in a familiar motion of snuggling in to watch TV with him. It would've felt more familiar if she had a body, but this was good enough.

The masked-Xan looked down at her, shifting back and forth until the light caught her just right, and she almost appeared solid. This must be some heretofore unknown stage of grief. Maybe no one talked about it because it was too weird. Seeing dust-specters. He'd never seen a dust-specter of Kalumbits, but he guessed that different kinds of grief manifested in different ways. While her presence was certainly comforting, her leaning on him had deposited a great deal of dust on his outfit, and he wasn't sure he'd ever have the heart to clean it off now.

"Pardon my asking, I know it may not be polite, but...are you real?" He turned off the TV, far more intent on understanding this most recent development than watching The Lone Ranger bring someone to justice for the thousandth time this orbit.

"I'm real!" May insisted, sitting up indignantly. "I wish people would stop saying that I wasn't."

"Right, of course, ma'am," he said, dipping his head in acquiescence. "Only, I can't help but wonder. Does a specter such as yourself have a consciousness of its own? Or are you an extension of my consciousness?"

"Follow the sound of my voice," May heard, but Xan didn't seem to hear it, so again, she ignored it. Maybe that was just part of being a ghost. She remembered the movie 'Poltergeist'...was she supposed to go into the light or not? It was unclear. She didn't want to go, though, so she stayed. Xan was questioning her reality again.

"I'm conscious! I don't know how to prove that to you. I know things you don't know," she said with a self-satisfied smirk.

"Such as?"

She paused. "May, May, May..." she heard. Damnit, that was getting obnoxious.

How to prove to this masked Xan that she was conscious? She did know things he didn't know, she was sure, but if he didn't know it, how could she prove it wasn't made up? Earth facts. She knew things about Earth the IFI would know, but he wouldn't. She thought.

She had lived on Earth for over twenty years; she must know some facts about it. Something simple would do. "The larch!" she said suddenly. "There's a tree on Earth called a larch. Look it up on the IFI. I bet you didn't know that."

Xan tapped on the device in his temple, and a holographic screen appeared before his eyes. "Search Earth Trees, Larch," he said, and almost immediately, an image of a tree appeared along with the words "No. 1 The Larch". So it was true. Or was it? He had heard of rare occasions of Ness spillage; in extreme states of being, anyone could tap into the Ness and know things they didn't know they knew. He shut off the device and thought for a moment, trying to rectify her existence in front of him with his knowing she was dead.

"Come here, May!" she heard, louder, more desperate.

"Why?" she shouted to the sky. "What do you want?!"

"I want you to wake up!"

The Xan before her watched her warily. "Sorry," she said to him. "I keep hearing things..."

"What are you hearing?"

"You, but it's not you. It's coming from everywhere. I can't pinpoint it. Maybe..." She looked again at her semi-corporeal hand. "Maybe I'm not as real as I think I am," she decided. "This is odd, come to think of it. I'm not usually made of dead skin cells. Usually, most of them are alive."

Xan nodded. "Yeah, usually. That's why I asked."

May nodded back.

"Maybe you should listen to him. The other me. Maybe that's your Xan."

She shook her head, "No. You're my Xan. We used to watch 'The Lone Ranger' together whenever there was Earth signal. We met in the crystal caves of Meeznalis after I hitched a ride from...no. No, I was abducted. And Ix helped me escape--"

"And I found you floating unprotected in space and tractor-beamed you into the *Audacity*!" she heard.

"It happened again," said dust-May. "Xan! You can hear me?" she shouted into the conical ceiling of the *Audacity*.

"I can hear you! Wake up!"

"Hold on!" She spoke again to masked-Xan, "This keeps happening. I don't belong to this reality, but I am real. In another one. I'm sorry for dying—that sucks. I'm sorry if my showing up here sucked, too. I don't know how long I'll stay here, but if I can, I'll visit you again, okay? I remember your May still. She's in here." May tried to tap her temple, but her finger went all the way through her head. "Damn, that's weird."

"Please visit," said masked-Xan, excitement opening up his face.

"Zuut!" she heard her Xan say from above. "May, I'm sorry, I need you back now!" Something bit into her shoulder with a sizzle of electricity, and she collapsed into dust again.

* * * * *

"Ahh!" May jolted awake, grabbing at her arm. "Ouch!" she told Xan. "I don't like that thing," she nodded at the little ZipOut Stick.

Xan was no longer near her. She was near herself, and she had a knife. "Who the fuck--?" she asked, pinned into her seat by a wild-eyed mirror image with a pocket knife to her throat. She'd been in this position before. Well, not her, and not with herself, but when she was a pirate, she'd had many a knife to her throat. She knew what to do. This other version of her was no expert with the thing. In a blip, May had the knife in her hand and was standing, hooking a leg behind her duplicate to drop her to the floor. OtherMay thudded.

"Aimz! What are you doing?" Xan shouted, busy wriggling away from a version of himself who was apologetically trying to ensnare him with the cord of a porcelain farmer lamp.

May sunk a knee into her duplicate's chest, holding her down at knife-point in a way that felt so oddly familiar. She turned to see Aimz's duplicate stabbing her repeatedly, gleefully, on the couch. Soaking it with pale blue/green blood. "Ouch," said the Aimz who was acting as a pin-cushion. She seemed bored. "Ouch," she said again. She blinked. "Xan, May? Either of you want to get her off m--" Mazelmez had stabbed her in the throat.

She sighed, annoyed, grabbed the knife, and lodged it in Mazelmez's shoulder. After a moment of perturbed gurgling, she said, "Not in the mood, half-brained dupe." She tossed her duplicate aside and brushed out her blood-stained, hole-covered tunic. "Oh, you thought you were smart for inventing a universe-hopping tongue ring? Now you're disintegrating. Not smart," Aimz affirmed. "Very, very not smart," she said, then sat back on the couch and turned on the TV while Mazelmez struggled to remove the knife. "You're in good company, at least. Seems like every version of me is a taagshlorph prunhip-brain."

"I want this ship!" other May shouted underneath May's knee. "This is the best one we've found. Use the harpoon!"

Mazelmez dutifully unhooked the massive harpoon from her back and pointed it at May. She had a perfectly clear shot until Xan bit down hard on his double's ear, shoved him off, and put himself between May and the harpoon.

EIGHTEEN

THE HARPOON

* * * * *

"Damn it!" Rage percolated inside May, brewing a strong blend of utter confusion and half-remembered piratical conquests that allowed her to stab the knife into her double's gut and twist. She flung her down the stairs, then rushed to check on Xan, who was still, for the moment, standing with a harpoon halfway through him. She hurled the knife at the duplicate of Aimz, but it only scratched her cheek and sailed past. "Xan, are you okay?" May didn't know whether or not taking the harpoon out would help, so she just slipped under his arm to gently lower him to the floor.

"Fine...I think," he said distantly.

May set him down and looked at her own hands, covered in his blood. "This can't be real." And then she was out again, slumping mouth open against Xan, who quickly joined her in unconsciousness.

Aimz laughed at the TV. She had happened across a stray episode of 'Everybody Loves Raymond.' She laughed not because she had found anything particularly funny but because the disembodied voices had laughed, and she figured it meant she ought to, too.

* * * * *

Music slammed into May's senses first, then the person beside her slammed into her. They muttered an apology and danced around her, squeezing her out of the circle of Tuhntians clad in colorful silks and moving clockwise around a fire raised on a central platform in a cheerful, choreographed four-step pattern that May definitely didn't remember how to do.

She backed away from the dancers, looking up into the smoky sky, too worried about Xan to really care where she had jumped to now. She needed a way back before their doppelgängers finished them both off.

"Xan?!" she called to the sky. "Zap me! Zap me!!" she shouted. She didn't like it, but it was the only way they'd found to get her back, and she needed to be back right now immediately.

"Shhh!" Xan had flung free from the crowd of dancers and clasped a hand over her mouth. He was dressed like them, decked out in glowing jewelry, tattoos of every imaginable color, and a scanty purple vest. "It's me. Your-me! I must've...what do you call it? Earthlings do it. Skipping out? I skipped out."

"Blacked out," May whispered, her hands exploring the two large puffs of hair on top of her head. "Why did you shush me?"

"Because if you're mumbling in real life, they might kill you, too," he said.

"You're not dead," May whispered back. "You said you were fine."

He bit his lip but said nothing as he rubbed his bare chest where the harpoon had speared him. It was perfectly fine here, in this reality. It seemed like they were having a good time here.

"What is this? Where are we?" May asked.

"I don't know. This is an old-fashioned Tuhntian Sun Begging, but...I mean, I've never participated in one before. They're just an excuse for people to dance and drink and get naked and... Well, that's probably why we're here, actually. I don't know where here is, though. Maybe in this reality, we live on Tuhnt?"

May nodded. "Maybe." Memories were not coming as quickly as usual. She was too concerned with the state of her actual body to be accessing information about this body. "How do we wake up?"

Xan's shoulders dropped, and he stared terrified into the flames. "I don't know. What if I can't wake up?"

"Hey," May put a hand on his shoulder. "You're going to be okay. It wasn't that bad, really, and you heal insanely fast. I've seen you take worse."

"Have you?" Xan sat down cross-legged in the soft Tuhntian grass. It was too soft, actually. Softer than he remembered it being. And the night was too pleasantly cool. The air too fragrant, the sound of music too comfortingly nostalgic. "Zuut, May, I don't like this. I think I'm dead."

"You're not!"

"Why am I here? You've been jumping realities, that's nothing new, but why am I with you now?"

May sat in the grass beside him. "You're always with me," she said, pulling up some of the soft, soft grass and rubbing it absently between her fingers. "Every time I've gone somewhere else, you were there, too." The music became louder, faster, changed key. The dancers switched directions and began ripping off their already meager clothing. "Different versions of you, but it's always you and me," she looked up to find that he was looking at her with such a strange mixture of alien emotions she couldn't comprehend.

"Well, that clinches it, I'm dead. You're probably not even the real May," he stared into the fire again, wrapping his arms around his knees, miserably watching the spectacle.

"You're not, and I am!" May tossed the bits of grass she'd desecrated at him, and they stuck in his hair. He looked at her, confused. "I mean, you aren't dead, and I am real."

His morose demeanor suddenly shifted as if he had just

woken up. "Oh! They're starting in on the good part! Join if you want!" He jumped up to rejoin the revelers, removing a few scraps of clothing to catch up with the rest of them and leaving May alone, perplexed.

"Starshine?" she heard a thin thread wafting on the smoke. "Please wake up."

May knew what she had to do. It was a terrible, horrible idea, but she had to do it. She rolled her eyes back into her head and clenched her teeth at how stupid she was about to be. "I'm coming, Xan," she said, stood up, and dashed through the circle of dancers, launching herself right into the flames.

The burst of light behind her eyes wasn't the fire, though. She was back in the *Audacity*, and there was Xan.

"Don't look at the carpet," said Xan the moment May's eyes fluttered open. "I appear to have been mortally wounded," he added, a great deal more calmly than May expected.

She sat up, rubbing her temple, feeling something hot and sticky when she did. She looked at her fingers, but rather than the expected red, they dripped with a viscous silvery-green fluid. When she set her hand back on the carpet to steady herself, it squished.

"Ahhh!" She scrambled back out of the puddle of Tuhntian blood, wiping her hands on her shirt.

"Yeah, looks like there's a bit of a dip in the floor there, doesn't it?" Xan said. "We should... should probably get that looked at. Get someone to level it or...or something." He sat against the orange wall of the living room, watching the pool continue to spread.

"Shit! Are you alright?"

"I seem to be," he said.

"But that's..." May pointed with a shaking hand. "That's a great deal of blood."

"You know, I noticed that, too, actually. Does seem like more than I should have, doesn't it?"

May looked at him as if he were a ghost. "Yeah!"

"Yeah. Weird."

"Weird!?" Rather than simply stare in horror, May

skirted the coastline to join him. "Was that you...with me and the fire and the dancing? Do you remember?"

He nodded. "Yep. That was me. Guess I'm not dead after all," he said with a nervous laugh. "How did you get back?"

"Jumped into the fire."

"Zuut, May! That's...I guess that's fine. It worked. Don't do it again, though, please."

"I don't plan to. Keep the ZipOut Stick handy, okay? Aimz! Help?!" May called over the noise of the TV, an old commercial playing now.

"Can't. I have to find out what it is," Aimz said, monotone.

"What what is?!"

"This"—Aimz gestured at the TV—"stuff. It looks like butter. It tastes like butter. It's not. I have to keep watching; they might tell me what it is."

"Your brother is dying, asshole!"

"No, he's not," Aimz assured.

Xan shrugged at May. All evidence pointed to her being right about that.

"What does asshole mean?" Aimz actually turned to look at May now, but May was too angry to answer.

She tapped on Xan's BEAPER, checking the ship's trajectory. Ten beoops left until we reach the Andolonian Tree Museum. "I'm going to search the IFI for something closer. Stay here," she told him and bounded up to the console. She paused. "Where did the others go?"

Xan shrugged. "They were gone when I woke up."

"Aimz! Where did they go?!" May shouted down to her.

"They left!" Aimz shouted back.

"They left," May repeated under her breath, annoyed.

The IFI had no good news. The Tree Museum was leagues closer than the closest planet. It would have to do. "Xan...are you okay?"

"Yep," he said behind her. She jumped, not expecting him to have come over.

"How are you standing?! Doesn't it hurt?" She eyed the massive harpoon. It wouldn't be easy to pull out; the sharp end had expanded into a three-pronged hook after exiting him. She looked away, trying to get her gag reflex under control.

"Oh yeah, I guess," he said. "I mean, it would feel better if I weren't harpooned, that's for sure! That would be ideal." He chuckled apprehensively. "I guess it didn't hit anything important."

"Important?! It went right through your spine! Your legs shouldn't work!" May said. "Come on, Aimz is being useless. Let's get you on the Diagn-O-scan. Aimz, don't bother cleaning up!" May said, wondering if reverse psychology worked on Tuhntians.

"I won't," Aimz confirmed.

It clearly didn't.

NINETEEN

A GOD OF LANGUAGE

* * * * *

The *Audacity*'s Diagn-O-Scan had never been so unsure of itself before. The machine was top of the line, installed with a religions processor, which gave it that extra edge over the faithless competition.

It was trying to save Xan's life—it really was. But Blitheon be praised, he just wasn't complying with medical precedent. He wasn't lying on the scanning plate properly, either, but under the circumstances, the Diagn-O-Scan didn't put up a fuss about that.

It feverishly swept its own systems, trying to work out why the vital signs and the diagnosis were not syncing up. Half of its circuits were alarming for immediate care, flashing out warnings in Danger Diaphatholene (a color slightly more urgent than red) and spitting out recommended courses of action. The other half were wondering where the fire was, metaphorically. The patient was fine, said the circuits. Heart rate normal, blood pressure steady, air sacs operational, blorpal blorpaling away.

There didn't seem to be anything wrong.

And so the machine conferred with itself. How could a patient who was losing a pint of blood with every heartbeat possibly be nothing to worry about? Finally, the religious subroutine kicked in, and a sudden clarity came to the machine. This patient was clearly favored by Blitheon himself. Perhaps, even, a prophet of O'Zeno whose mighty thumbs it would be an honor to kiss. This, here, was someone special they had on their scanning plate.

This was a god.

The Diagn-O-Scan stopped flashing the colors and sounding the alarms that May and Xan had been fearfully attending and, instead, displayed this simple message on its main screen in a fine script font: "Oh Holy One! Blessed be my circuitry, for thou hast siteth upon mine face."

"What?" May whispered.

Xan twisted around to read it. He read it once, haltingly. He read it again, just to be sure. He read it very, very slowly a third time. "'Siteth' isn't a word." He said, at last.

"My humblest apologies, oh Great One. Art thou a god of language?" the screen now read.

Clearly, he wasn't because he was having a difficult time finding the words to set this confused machine right. "I, uh...oh, zuut, I'll explain." As if he were the one being unclear. "A version of my sister from an alternate reality harpooned me."

"Confirmed," said the machine, the font still needlessly flowery. "There is a harpoon lodged between your third and fourth phenkaitak bones."

"And I need to know...uh, what to do about that?"

"Of course, your holiness. It would be my greatest honor to recommend a course of medical action."

"Also, could you not call me 'your holiness'? Please?"

"But it's my special feature!" read the screen.

"Right, yes, I gathered that. I gathered. It's only that I'm not a god."

"Humility suits you, oh Great One!" read the screen back at him.

There was no point in arguing with a machine that had already set its circuits on something—this he had learned first-hand from Sonan.

"Yeah, I guess it does. Can you please tell us what to do about the harpoon?" Mentally, he added. "Before May goes unconscious again," but she seemed present and alert.

"See a medical professional." The font had shifted back to its classic no-nonsense sans-serif white block letters. The religions subroutine had over-written both the machine's harm reduction and practicality programming.

"This was a waste of time," May grumbled. She opened a junk drawer in the counter opposite them and dug around its contents. Ten busted laser scalpels, a roll of gauze, a paperclip (which was odd because she'd never seen a sheet of paper on the ship), and, at last, what she was looking for: a sonic multi-slicer.

She tested the thumb-sized gadget on the paperclip, and it cut it in two nicely. The harpoon shaft was about as thick as 1,000 paperclips bundled together, but she had to try.

She strode confidently across the medibay, eyes forward, back straight, focused. Which was a shame because had she looked down, she might have avoided slipping catastrophically on the layer of blood coating the floor. She fumbled, searching for purchase but only succeeding in slathering herself with more and more of the blue/green fluid.

"Ugh!" said May, arms flailing.

"Sorry," Xan said.

"Arghhhh!" May said, losing purchase and crashing to the floor.

"You okay?" He leaned over the table, attempting to stand, but more blood gushed onto the floor.

"Stay." She held up a palm to him.

"Yeah... Again, so sorry."

"Mmph." May gave up and sprawled on the floor as if she were trying to make a snow angel.

"You know," Xan said to her. "I'll probably live long enough to get to the medic at the Tree Museum. You don't have to deal with this. You can go watch TV with Aimz until we get there. Explain all the Earth jokes to her so she gets why it's funny."

She grabbed onto the edge of the Diagn-O-Scan and pulled herself up. "No, I can do this. Besides, she was watching 'Everybody Loves Raymond.' Even I can't explain why that's funny," she said, eyes wide, shaking slightly, clutching the slicer in one hand, dripping in blood. "I can do this," she reminded herself.

"Blitheon, I hope I can," he said, giving the harpoon a gentle, testing tug and grunting at the sensation. "You know, it's alright, actually. We can leave it."

She shook her head. "You're still bleeding; we can't leave it. I need to cut off the barbs," May pushed him back down on the table and leaned over his side, rolling the edge of the slicer along the width of the harpoon shaft. Slowly but steadily, she sawed through the tip of the spear, and the barbed end dropped away. It clattered behind the Diagn-O-Scan and into a dark crevice neither of them would ever think about again.

"Okay." May used the edge of the table to steady herself as she stood up. She turned her face away and squeezed her eyes shut. "You can take it out now," she said, bracing for something as if she were the one who'd been impaled.

"Right, that is definitely, completely something I can do now," he confirmed weakly. He wasn't sure why, but he really wanted her to be watching him. Just in case.

"Did you do it?" she asked after a moment.

He stared down at the shaft sticking out of him, trying to will his arms to move. "It would seem I haven't," he said.

May breathed deeply in, followed by a nervous staccato exhale. She opened her eyes, slowly wrapped her hands around the shaft, shut her eyes again, and pulled straight out.

"Zuut! Blitheon's beans," Xan shouted, clutching the hole in his gut. "It hurt less going in."

May let the spear clatter to the ground and grabbed the roll of gauze from the junk drawer, wadding it up and pressing it into the hole in his back. "What now? Will it close up?" she asked as the gauze became soaked.

"Ngheh," he grunted. "Eventually." He hazarded a look at the damage, spreading open the hole in his Layflex suit to see it better. He couldn't see anything under the blood. He wiped it away with his hand. He still couldn't see anything. He ripped the hole wider. Nothing. He slipped a finger under the suit's magnetic seam and opened the top half, exposing the entire front of his torso.

"What?"

He shrugged his arms out of the suit and pulled it down his back. "No hole...Can you see anything back there?" he asked her.

She used the gauze to scrub off some quickly coagulating blood. "Nothing..." she said, confused. "Just like the fleam..." May tossed the gauze on the floor and sat on the table next to him. "You feeling okay?"

Xan stretched and twisted, testing the range of the muscles that should've been torn but weren't. "Yeah."

"Maybe weapons from other universes don't work. Like...they aren't entirely real," May mused, brow furrowed. "Does that make any sense?"

"Aimz zuxing knew," he sighed. "A lot of things make sense now, actually."

It did not make sense, and it didn't make sense because it wasn't correct. What was really going on here is a great deal more nonsensical, though, so we shan't shame them for thinking this way.

"You know what doesn't make sense, though?" May said. "Where did all that blood come from? If the weapons aren't real?"

"Yeah," Xan confirmed. "But hey, we can't know everything! All I know is we both need a sani-steam before we reach the Tree Museum.

"You're really stuck on that Tree Museum," she said.

"They know things! Some of them know the future, some know the past, some know the present. They can help." He smiled hopefully.

"Maybe. Promise you'll never bleed that much again, though, okay?" May said. "It might not have been real, but it was terrifying."

"I absolutely promise. I hated that, May, I hated that so,

so much. I was trying to stay calm for your sake!"

"And I was trying to stay calm for you!" May said.

"Alright, we certainly did a fantastic job of keeping each other calm, then. Well done us." He patted her on the shoulder. "Excellent work, team. Outstanding performance."

"We deserve a medal," May said.

"Oh, zuut, no, we deserve a trophy. Something big, too."

"Bigger than the one we bought ourselves after filing our Space Taxes?"

"Well, yeah, right? 'Didn't die at the hands of doppelgängers' is a massive accomplishment, don't you think?" Xan asked.

May carefully dropped to the floor. "You're right. We should order ourselves a trophy on the IFI. But first, shower." She slowly stepped around the puddle of blood and demagnetized her suit, crawling out of it and leaving it in a pile on the floor. Then she shed her bra and underwear and stepped into the medibay's clear-walled Sani-Steam pod and started the program.

Distracted by the blood, Xan hadn't noticed May get completely naked just a few steps away from him. He hadn't noticed anything, really. His eyes were open, but his attention was swept up in a torrent of thoughts.

"Are you coming?" May asked.

He shook himself back to the present and blinked, noting her clothing on the ground. "Uh...am I coming?" he asked, pointedly not looking in her direction. "I am not. Should I be?"

"We usually shower together. Saves water. Right?" May said.

Hesitantly, Xan got up and peeled off the rest of his soaking Layflex™. He was starting to wonder if he had changed realities somehow. They had not, to his recollection, ever showered together. But he did need one, and she was offering so...he stepped into the steam.

Though the SaniSteam used sonic pulses to shake the grime off, May still habitually 'washed' herself in the streams of steam. Because he didn't want to make her feel left out, Xan copied her movements.

"Am I good?" she asked, lifting an arm and gesturing at her unshaven armpit.

Tilting his head, Xan bent down and sniffed. "You're good," he said.

"Can you believe that in another reality, you and I were fucking?" May said. "That's so weird."

"Yeah...really weird," he agreed. "And you...remember it all? As if it happened to you?"

May scrubbed her fingers through her scalp. Somehow, the SaniSteam always left her hair soft and moisturized and completely dry. She never wanted to go back to Earth showers again. "Yep."

"Oh," said Xan. "Then that explains this."

"What?" May asked.

"Don't...worry about it," he said. He would worry about it for both of them.

TWENTY

WEEKEND AT BERNIE'S

* * * * *

May stirred her coffee with a plastic knife in the windowless breakroom. Her mind swirled along with the acidic brew. The whispers around the office were that a living extraterrestrial had been captured. It had been found orbiting Earth. They were storing it in the basement of this very building.

Sounded like an intern's idea of a fun practical joke, May thought. But there hadn't been an intern in three years. She continued to stir her coffee. She couldn't get the alien out of her brain. Just a few more minutes of stirring, she thought. Then she'd drink it down and get back to work on...paperwork. She'd finished the day's tests. Working with the machines might have distracted her, but filling out reports certainly couldn't.

She took out her phone and called Aulani July. If there was an alien somewhere in this facility, he would know.

She got the voicemail, hung up, and sent him a text instead. "There's a rumor about that space junk your team brought in last week. Wanted some clarity. Love you."

Pocketing her phone, she resolved to drop it until he got back to her. She felt a jolt of electricity in her side, checked the phone for notifications...nothing. A strong whiff of coffee reminded her of orange shag carpeting. Of space. Of...an alien. She couldn't wait. Without taking even a sip, she abandoned the coffee.

She walked the halls of the facility as fast as she could without raising suspicion. The alien was likely being held somewhere she didn't have clearance to access. She didn't care. She had to see it, and she had to see it immediately. If she walked with confidence, she could get anywhere in the facility.

In the elevator, the strange liminal weightlessness made her even more determined to find him, as if her soul was hovering a few feet above her body and it knew something she didn't. In a fugue, she reached the lowest level her badge would take her. The lower two basements she couldn't access, but if she set off the fire alarm, the normally locked stairwell accesses would unlock.

Her hand, almost without the consent of her brain, reached for the fire alarm. She would lose her job for doing this if they caught her. Years of study wasted. Her dad would be pissed. But somehow, those fears didn't overcome her need to see him--it. She pulled the alarm and began to run.

She squeezed by confused co-workers on the stairwell, muttering excuses like "Sorry, forgot something," or "Just looking for someone," which wasn't untrue. Finally, she hit the lowest level. Everyone else had exited, and she was alone in the underground lab. Much different from her own messy lab upstairs stacked round with boxes of various parts and wires, this lab was clean and clinical. She wondered if she'd been accidentally working in a storage room instead of a real lab.

"Hello? Uhhh...help?"

The accent was strange, but the voice she knew. As if she'd heard it in a dream. It came from within a cubicle near the back, and she jogged over to it.

"Xan," she said upon seeing him. He was cuffed to a chair, wearing a grey jumpsuit which, though she had never actually seen him before, she knew was not what he was supposed to be wearing.

"^AJN%dfkjn! Fgnsjadf^ knaif %d?"

May shook her head. "I can't understand you. Don't you speak any English?"

"Lucy, I'm home!" he said in confirmation.

May wiped her cheek; she had no idea why she was crying. "I'm going to break you out of here. Nod if you understand."

He did—his translation chip was working fine, but she didn't have one. That had been the main source of his frustrations on Earth so far. The little English he did know wasn't enough to convince the people who had detained him that he wasn't dangerous. It had barely been enough to convince them not to kill him on sight.

"Why do I feel like I know you?" May asked as she searched the room for a way to unlatch his wrists and ankles from the chair. "Do you recognize me?"

Xan shook his head no and then shrugged. "Just got one of those faces?" he suggested because he'd heard that once and the melodic timber of the phrase had stuck with him. He wasn't quite sure what it meant.

"You're blue!"

"Yes," he confirmed, not quite seeing what that had to do with anything.

May found the key and unlatched the cuffs, but he couldn't remember how Earthlings expressed gratitude, he was sure there were several variants depending on the context. He tried one. "Aw, you shouldn't have."

May smiled, then winced. Something had shocked her again, right on the wrist under her watch. She took the watch off and stuffed it in her pocket. "Sorry, this thing must've had a short circuit. Let's get you out of here."

* * * * *

"I'm going to have to buy genetic muscle enhancements if we can't fix this," Xan whined, dragging an unconscious May out of the Sani-Steam and carefully laying her on the floor away from the blood, which he was not yet emotionally prepared to clean up.

"May, can you hear me again?" He crouched down beside her inert, naked form. "Can you please come back? I don't want to zap you." Nothing. Not even a mumble. She was truly out. He sighed and went to the closet, taking out a crisply folded sheet that was meant to cover the Diagn-O-Scan scanner bed, but he'd never bothered to put it on. He draped the sheet over May so she wouldn't get cold, she was always so much colder than him, and sat with her for a few blips, gently tapping her arm and staring at the blood on the floor as if he could clean it up with an intent enough gaze.

The ship jostled, and the engine sound shifted from the regular burring of space travel to the effortful chug of the auto-park. They were close to the Tree Museum now, entering the station's faux atmosphere.

"Zuut," Xan said. "Alright, May, I'm going to get dressed. If you're not awake by the time I get back, I'm going to set Aimz on you."

Xan rose into the living room via the intershoot and called out to Aimz. "Hey, I need your help with May; she's out again."

The TV was still chattering away, Aimz still slumped on the couch, and copious amounts of blood, both his and hers, splotched the orange carpet and walls with darkening blue.

Aimz did not answer.

"You okay?" he asked, setting May down in a chair at the table. The porthole showed the view outside, massive ancient tree tops quickly approaching. He jogged over to Aimz. "Aimz? You okay?"

"Mmm," she said.

"May's naked," he said. "And I need you to wake her up so I can take her to the trees."

The word naked had piqued her interest slightly, and her eyes flicked to him. "Zap her," she said.

"I tried! She's really out. Can't you do anything else?"

Aimz shrugged. "Bernie her."

"Huh?"

Aimz nodded towards the television, where a

mustachioed, sunglass-wearing man lounged on a couch almost as bright pink as Aimz's hair. "You got some sunglasses?"

"Yeah, but..."

"This guy's dead, but they need to pretend he's alive to use his fancy house. Put some sunglasses on her."

"People are going to know she's not awake, Aimz! I'll have to carry her!"

Aimz shrugged. "That's my idea. You want me to get her dressed?" Aimz asked.

While he appreciated the offer of assistance, he didn't quite trust her eagerness somehow. "No, I'll do it. I'm not Bernie-ing her, though. That's silly."

Aimz reached into her Largish Bronda's Flexidimensional Utility Belt and pulled out a pair of cheap plastic sunglasses. "Here. Do it," she said, tossing them on the couch next to herself.

He sighed and took the glasses.

Now please imagine a lushly sprawling, pages-long description of the beauty and majesty of that most singularly beautiful and majestic place: The Andolonian Tree Museum. Not so much a museum as it is a forest. Not so much on Andolon as it is on a manufactured spacestation near where the planet Andolon used to be before that unfortunate hubris incident. Not so much trees as they are ancient beings with multifaceted wisdom regarding what was, is, and is to come.

These more-than-trees soared into the lovely artificial sky, glistening geodesic domes made of something far more expensive than glass glistened glisteningly. Secluded paths snaked snake-like through snake-free forests. Or, at least, in the easily accessible areas they did. Beyond the museum's boundaries, the ancient forests grew wild and evil. But more on them later.

The trick to safely visiting the Andolonian Tree Museum is to have 2-3 extraordinarily clear questions and to be totally detached from whether or not you get a comprehensible answer. It's not that the trees aren't good at what they do; they are very good. It's that the trees, well accustomed to communicating information between each other, are extremely bad at communicating information to other sentient species. The process alone requires an act of pseudoscience so heinous, I daren't disgust you with the details. The outcome is often garbled, meandering, and/or terribly rude.

The museum lobby was entirely made of glass so that the majesty of the enormous millennia-old trees would never be too far from the minds of museum-goers. It was busy, but in a quiet, respectful sort of way, when Xan teleported in carrying May, who was now clothed properly in her favorite striped t-shirt and green overcoat, besunglassed, and still asleep. A prignette sister rushed gracefully over to him, bowing her head slightly so she could speak to him at eye level.

"We are no longer offering burial services on account of the IFI ghost situation. I am sorry, but you will have to leave."

"Oh! No, she's..." He chuckled nervously. "She's not dead. Just asleep."

The prignette's long-lashed lemon-sized eyes blinked very, very slowly.

"I promise."

"If she is not dead, why are you attempting to 'Weekend at Bernie's' with her?"

"H-how do you know about that?"

"I am a tenant of the ocular forests. I know many things. Several of those things happen to be films. It is not strange at all."

Xan nodded, though he still thought it was strange. He shifted May in his arms. "Look, she's getting really heavy. If I can just set her down, I'll prove to you she's alive. She's got a pulse and everything!"

The prignette stood back up to her full height. "I believe you. You may enter, but you must purchase two tickets, not one. Do not perform a 'two kids in a trench coat.' I will know."

"I won't. I don't even know what that means," Xan assured her and bending his knees a little more so he could try to shift May's weight higher, he brought her to the ticket line, paid for both of them with a quick facescan, accepted two paper maps, which he clutched in his teeth, and entered the main hall.

An overwhelming display of informative signs called for his attention, but one stood out: 'Museum Historical Film - Thirty Bloops.'

"Thank Blitheon," said Xan. He quickly entered the theater and deposited May in a seat near the back. He spent a few minutes trying to prop her up in such a way that she looked awake and alert but eventually gave up and let her slump against him as the film began.

TWENTY-ONE

TREE MUSEUM!

✳ ✳ ✳ ✳ ✳

"Here are the things you must know before interacting with the ocular trees," explained the narrator, whose rich, comforting voice defied interpretation of gender and species. This was called the TransGalactic Accent, and this accent had been developed specifically so that intergalactic businesspeople could easily judge whether or not someone sounded professional.

"The ocular trees, so called due to their many literal and metaphorical eyes, are the offspring of one single sentient tree cultivated millennia ago on the now-extinct planet of Andolon. It, and its offspring, on account of having knowledge of the future, were moved by their own request to a self-sustaining space station just a few orbits before Andolon's infamous reality failure." The screen displayed scraggly, degraded footage of the original ocular tree, and it was, indeed, covered in slowly blinking wooden eyes.

"Communication with the trees is more of an art than a science, and so the scientists who have dedicated their lives to the practice are rigorously trained to endure ridicule and slander prior to their onboarding.

"Due to its proximity to Primox and the prignette's cultural inclination towards deep-listening, the Prignette Order of Ultraphysicists are the main proprietors of the Tree Museum. If you see a Prignette sister at work, please avoid asking foolish questions, attempting to feed them, or offering pleasurable sexual engagement."

"That's going to be a challenge for you, then," May whispered in Xan's ear.

"May! You're awake! And you're being mean."

"It was a loving jab," May corrected.

"How did you get back?"

May shrugged. "I don't know."

"Zuut, I'm glad you are. My arms are aching."

The film paused. "Silence is requested in the theater," said the narrator.

Xan nodded sheepish acquiesce, and the film began again, displaying an image of an assortment of bones and skulls swimming in soupy, bubbling mud. "Failure to comply with the aforementioned guidelines will result in an agonizing and lengthy death.

"Section two," said the narrator, cutting to a cheery view of families gathered around a single, enormous ocular tree trunk. "Preparing your questions. Guests are asked to limit their questions to one per tree and to refrain from asking the same question twice. The trees talk. They will know, and they don't take kindly to being second-guessed. Politeness confuses the trees. Be sure to avoid addressing the trees respectfully, inserting flippant gratitude markers, or saying 'please.'"

"That's really going to be a challenge for you," May whispered at Xan with a snicker, but he had already been asked not to talk once, so he only replied with a pained look of confirmation.

"Each tree in the museum specializes in quick-recall of certain areas of expertise. Do not, for example, ask a history of Andalon tree what you'll have for supper next week. It will answer, but the massive amount of energy it takes to recall information outside of a tree's scope may result in museum-wide power outages.

"For an extra fee, a Prignette sister interpreter guide

may assist you personally in forming your question and choosing your tree. New guests are encouraged to interact only with the Certified Friendly trees growing nearest the museum lobby to avoid contracting chronic existential turmoil. In the event of existential turmoil, please report directly to the mind-draining clinic to be decanted.

"The museum runs on a half-rotational sleep/wake cycle. Every sixth half-rotation, the museum will be closed for one full rotation to perform maintenance. Guests wishing to remain longer than a single half-rotation may camp on the forest floor beneath the canopy-hub for up to twelve rotations."

May crinkled beside him. She was opening the large, folded paper map they had been given. "Alright, which tree should we go to?" she whispered.

The film paused. "Silence is requested in the theater."

"Come on, we don't need this," May said, side-stepping past Xan to exit the theater.

"I think we do!" Xan whispered, standing to follow her.

"All the rules are on the map. I know how to read," she said. And he couldn't argue with that, so he followed her back into the lobby, grateful she was ambulating under her own power again.

May took the map to a low table and spread it out. Illustrated tree tops dotted the paper, each labeled with a name, title, and a comprehensibility rating. They both searched it for a tree that understood reality and could help them to understand it, too.

"What, exactly, are we asking the trees?" Xan said. "Because a lot has been out of sorts lately, and I honestly have quite a few questions, and I'm not really sure where to start."

"I want to know why I keep losing touch with reality," May said.

"Why not ask how to stop losing touch with reality?" Xan suggested. "Or why duplicates of us tried to kill us? Or who's after Aimz, because it wasn't the doppelgängers. Or maybe where all that blood came from? I mean, if the weapons didn't work, why was there blood?"

"If I know why I'm losing touch with reality, I'll know

how to fix it. If the tree tells me how to fix it, it might not tell me why it happened."

"Does it matter?"

"I want to know!"

Xan tapped the map absently, considering. "I think we need a guide."

"We don't need to pay for a guide," May said. "Look," she pointed at a tree on the outskirts of the museum's border. "EkoDoDo, Tree of Singular Multiplicities. That sounds promising. I've been feeling a little multiplied lately."

Xan cringed. "That's way at the edge of the map. It's got a comprehensibility rating of negative two. Benny G's close by and knows things about the recent past as well as every song in the known universe. That sounds good, right? And it's rated a five out of five for comprehensibility!"

"That one's on the way to EkoDoDo, so we can hit that first. You ask one of your questions, and I'll ask what happened to me," May said.

"You really want to go to a tree of singular multiplicities? With a negative two rating? What about existential turmoil? That sounds like the kinda tree that would cause existential turmoil."

"I'm already in existential turmoil; it can't get any worse," May said. "Xan..." She folded up the map and stuck it in her pocket. "In the last jump, I was working with my dad."

"Oh," Xan said. He hopped up onto the table and sat on the edge of it, patting beside himself so she would sit next to him. "Do you want to talk about it?" He meant HE wanted her to talk about it. She'd mentioned her mother, and he had figured that meant she only had one guardian, which wasn't really unusual on Tuhnt, but on Earth, where they were raised by their own progenitors, he'd learned that was the exception, not the rule. He desperately wanted to know why she never talked about her father, but he also desperately didn't want to upset her.

So he'd never asked.

"No," May said.

"Why did you bring it up?"

"Because!" May dropped her head back on her shoulders, groaning her frustration. "I've got four different versions of my past cataloged in my brain somewhere, and some parts, I remember so well I know they must've happened, but other things I can barely make sense of, like a dream. I called him! I haven't seen him since I was twelve! He supposedly went MIA, but apparently, he was somewhere! I think...I stayed on Earth in that lifetime. But then you showed up in the subbasement strapped to an interrogation booth."

"Yikes," said Xan. "That sounds unpleasant. Good thing that's not real!"

May sat on the table next to him. "I can't shake the feeling that this version of reality isn't real, either. Why else would I keep showing up to myself? Where did the doubles come from? Oh...shit. It's happening again," she said.

"Look at me," Xan said, holding onto her as her gaze became distant. "This is real. I'm real, and you're real. We're at the Tree Museum, and we're going to figure this out, okay? Stay with me." He hoped maybe direct, forceful instruction would help, but May was so unused to him being direct and forceful that it only enhanced her sense of unreality, and she dropped off into another life.

* * * * *

"Right, all sealed up and ready to finish yourself off," Mazelmez told May with a grin, smoothing down the edge of a plasma-plaster against her midsection and shoving a cheap-looking steel ray-gun and a rope in her hands.

May looked down at the plasma-plaster Mazelmez had taped to her, recognizing the location of the wound. She was the one she'd attacked, or...she was the one who had attacked her. This was good. This was a way to get information, as long as she kept remembering that she was really at--she was at the EZ Lab, Mazelmez's dusty hovel of a lair.

And the walls were clipping out.

"What's going on with the walls?" she asked.

Mazelmez beamed, gazing proudly around her at the disintegrating room. "Clever, isn't it? This is the very last bit of this universe that's left. The locus of destruction! I wanted to see it one more time before it unexisted itself. Proves my theory, too. All my fault! I destroyed this entire universe, May! Isn't that awesome?"

May gave a tight-lipped smile. "I think that's a translation error. You mean 'awful,' right? Awful."

She shook her head, still grinning. "Not at all, right, Xan? Confirm to May that this is awesome."

"I don't know...I think I agree with May. This is kinda awf--f--f---f" He seemed to get stuck on the word, repeating it over and over, parts of his body beginning to fizzle out until Mazelmez reached up for his hand and pulled him a little closer to her, where he stabilized. "Mazelmez! Zuut! You're going to kill us!"

"Relax, ya zingnat, I'm not going to let you die. I needed to re-up my weapons game." She held up a very old model classic laser-pistol, so old it didn't even have a brandname, and shot it into the ceiling. It gave a geriatric sizzle. "Back into the fray!" She grabbed both of them by the arm and clicked her tongue, and then...

✳ ✳ ✳ ✳ ✳

"Tree museum!" May said, sitting up suddenly. "I'm at the Tree Museum." A small group of tourists looked to see what the commotion was about. Just someone overly excited to talk to some trees, they guessed, and continued onward.

"Yes!" Xan said next to her. "You did it! Good!"

She shook her head. "Not good. The reason they attacked us—er, we attacked us—is because their universe is disintegrating. What if ours does that? Where will we go? There wasn't anywhere to go!" May said.

"Hey, it's okay. It's not disintegrating. Aimz would've told us if it were. Probably. Most likely, she would've known about that and said something. Seems like the kind of thing she's likely to know about, right?"

May nodded, wide-eyed. "Yeah. She caused it in their universe."

"Also seems like the kind of thing she's likely to do. But she's just lying on the couch in the *Audacity* right now, watching a comedy about a sunglass-wearing corpse. She's not disintegrating anything, I promise."

"She better not be," May said. "Okay, I need to pay attention to my surroundings." She opened her eyes a little wider, purposefully taking in every visual stimulus she could get her sights on. "This is real."

"Right, and stop questioning it. Every time you question it, you get...unreal."

May nodded. "Let's go. Benny G first, then EkoDoDo."

"I'm starting to think you just like saying its name," Xan said.

"What, EkoDoDo? You think I like to say EkoDoDo?"

Xan shrugged.

"Yeah, I guess I do like to say EkoDoDo. Is it not as fun in Tuhntian?"

"It's a name, so it's exactly the same in Tuhntian. But you're not pronouncing the % right. It would be E%oDoDo. E%oDoDo."

May frowned. "I literally cannot do that with my mouth."

"Well, no. It's not done with the mouth; it's done with the gloxalatal."

She blinked at him, waiting for him to remember who he was talking to.

"Which...you don't have, right," he said. "The way you say it's fine, I'm sure. It's a tree. It probably can't get offended."

"Come on. The museum closes in three beoops, and it'll be a long walk out to EkoDoDo," May said, emphasizing the 'k.'

BENNY G

* * * * *

Benny G was a gnarled, burly tree with bark so dark blue it nearly looked charred black, apart from the light-filled eyes that dotted its exterior. On a stand, a silver tray, up-lit by the landscape lights, presented to May what appeared to be a pair of metal sporks labeled 'Spork Provided For the Convenience of The Tele-Challenged. Please wipe residual brain matter off after use.'

May grimaced at the image of residual brain matter. "Hello?" she asked the tree quietly. "Can you hear me?"

The tree, like most trees, did not respond.

"Don't tell me I have to use that thing," May spoke again to the tree, which seemed to be ignoring her.

"Alright," Xan said. "So last time I was here, these were a lot longer! Good to see they've innovated a bit." He inspected the tines carefully, thoughtfully, a note of concern dipping his brows. "Still doesn't look comfortable, but that's what we get for not taking the time to learn the skill of speaking to trees telepathically, right?"

Xan gently placed the tines to his temple, squinted one eye in readiness, and thrust them in. Though he was still standing perfectly upright, his eyes rolled into the back of his head in a way that was highly unsettling.

"Why does advanced technology always interface with your brain? What's wrong with a screen?!" May said, squeezing her eyes tight before carefully pricking the tines into her temple.

In a moment, she was in a different location altogether. A grey-skinned old man sat on a porch beside her, lit with a yellow, bug-infested light. Beyond the porch, May could see nothing, but she heard the sounds of frogs and cicadas. The old man removed a moth-eaten felt hat from his head and leaned over one knee, uncannily bright, young blue eyes observing her from beneath heavy, wrinkled lids.

"Screens only display information. Brains can process it," said Benny G's dry, rustly voice. His mouth didn't move.

"Oh, I see," May said out loud.

"You don't need to do that; I can hear your thoughts just fine."

"You can?" May said, louder this time.

"Yes, yes, sapling! No need to vibrate your vocal cords at me. Just think, I can hear you."

"Oh, right," thought May quietly. "HELLO!" thought May loudly. "MY NAME IS MAY JUNE JULY AND--"

"Whoa there, no need to shout! Benny G hears just fine if you think at a comfortable register. Now, what brings you to Benny G?"

"Sorry. My name is May June July, and I would like to know..." May tried to focus on her intended question, but her thoughts became muddled suddenly. She knew she wanted to learn how she'd been jumping into different realities, if they were real at all. And what had Aimz allegedly done to disintegrate their universe? Would it happen to hers? Where was her father in this reality? Could she have found him if only she had—

"That's enough, fleshling! One question."

May hadn't realized that the thoughts she was trying not to think had, in fact, been thought.

"Don't be surprised. This is your first encounter with

the IFI, you have many questions."

"I've used the IFI before," May thought. "It's like the internet. I use it all the time on my ship's computer," May said.

"The audacity!" said Benny G, his body leaning back in the rocking chair.

"Yeah, that's the ship."

"No, I mean the audacity to think you've touched even a speck of what the IFI has to offer. You've played around in the contextualized, monetized IFI. A single dimension of data. This is your first encounter with the unfiltered thing. It is overwhelming."

May didn't feel overwhelmed and tried to keep herself from thinking that she didn't feel overwhelmed but thought it anyway.

"My, but you are a stubborn sapling," said Benny G in her head, his fingers coming to his stubbly grey chin and scratching.

May was overwhelmed.

"Calm down now. You wanted to know how you became unstuck in space/time, is that right?"

"Please," May thought, working diligently to think nothing else. To Benny G, this sounded like "Please, please, please, please..." And had Benny G not had centuries of experience with poorly controlled minds, it would've found this obnoxious. This one clearly had not watched the introductory film.

"Hush! You best be more careful what you think, sapling. You're lucky I put up with you. I think you're cute, though. You're quite short, you know? That is cute."

May was so afraid of thinking that she'd been offended by that, that her brain went totally offline.

"Good. Quiet. You've been infected with traces of the element Tuhntians call invilitex. This happened when a person from an alternate timeline entered yours and stabbed you with an unclean fleam. Do you recall this incident?"

"Yes," she thought calmly.

"That fleam had been used to shave a block of invilitex for the purposes of building a miniaturized universe-shifting device in the shape of a tongue ring. Nasty things, tongues. I do wish humanoids would finally outgrow the need for them." He smacked his mouth, and May could see that it was devoid of teeth and, presumably, tongue. Just a dark cavern in his uncannily human face.

"So my blood is infected? How do I fix that?" May thought carefully, one word at a time.

"One question only! Now I suggest you go watch the introductory film and learn to have some control of that lukewarm, festering wading pool you call your mind."

"Yes," May thought. Then, quietly, to herself, she thought, "For a certified friendly tree, this guy can really throw shade."

Apparently, she had not thought that part quietly enough and, repulsed, Benny G tore the spork out of her temple, the imagined scenery whipping away around her.

TWENTY-THREE

THE DUDE

* ✝ * ✝ *

May rubbed her temple, readjusting to being back on the Tree Museum platform. It didn't take long, though; she had become accustomed to suddenly being somewhere she wasn't a moment before. Beside her, Xan was pulling the spork from his own brain, winking his eyes in turn to readjust his vision.

May decided to ask the important question first. "So did Benny G look like an old white guy sitting on a porch for you, too?"

Xan nodded. "He was more greyish blue than white, but yes, I guess so. What did you find out?"

"The fleam I got stabbed with had a universe-melting element on it, and now it's in my bloodstream."

"Ah," Xan said, looking pensive. "That's why we can't fix it, then."

"What?"

"I asked Benny G how to fix whatever was wrong with you, and it said we can't."

"Great." May picked up the spork that the tree had pulled away from her and hung it back on the edge of the pedestal.

"It said EkoDoDo might be willing to show you how to cope, though. Not sure why it said 'might.' Thought the trees knew everything. I guess that's a future question, and Benny G's a past tree."

A soft, three-note trill echoed in the glass hall. "Museum closing in one beoop. Please collect your younglings, personal items, and sanity before returning to the lobby, where you may disembark or stay in our campsite accommodations."

"I guess we're camping," May said.

"Can't we sleep in the *Audacity*?"

"It's soaked in blood, and Aimz is there."

"Camping sounds fun!"

Camping would not be fun.

The campsite was a hard-packed dirt clearing many stories beneath the glass dome of the museum lobby. Its only amenities were crackling faux-fires (real fire was absolutely forbidden), amorphous nano-bot chairs that doubled as sleeping pods, and a row of outdoor showers because beings of all species started to get a little rank after their third or fourth day straight of plugging themselves into trees.

Campers gathered around the illusory fires, singing songs they'd written about the trees, talking about the grand universal insights they'd learned from the trees, and repeating stories the trees had told them. Although the intention of the rest periods was to keep guests from becoming entirely absorbed by thoughts of the ocular forest, anyone who'd spent much time with the trees had a difficult time talking about anything else.

Around a quiet fire near the intershoot, which transported people to and from the lobby above, Xan and May had settled into a single extra large nano-pod, which took the shape of an oversized bean bag chair as they sat around the fire, both distractedly listening to the various extraordinary tales of universal insight their fellow campers were sharing with each other.

"Rikokory?" A prignette robed in white offered May a metal mug full of hot, dark liquid.

"What's it cost?"

A prignette's muzzle lacks the necessary muscles needed to smile, and so the prignette blinked slowly to reassure her. "No charge. We find offering a free mood stabilizer to guests is mutually beneficial." May took it, and the prignette produced another cup from a small teledisc in her palm and offered it to Xan, who drank it happily.

May took a sip of the hot drink and then immediately spit it back out. "Looked like coffee," she said, considering whether to try again or to dump it out on the ground beside the fire.

"You should probably finish that," Xan said between sips. "Benny G was rated a five out of five on comprehensibility and was certified friendly. EkoDoDo has a negative two. That could really mess with our wiring."

"My wiring's already messed up," May said, swirling the liquid in the mug, watching the eddies she created in its oily surface. "I don't want to think about that right now." She sat back in the nano-pod, leaning into Xan and curling her legs underneath her as she looked up at the stars, surrounded on all sides by the tops of the dark ocular trees.

May was so used to seeing different sets of stars from different angles while traveling in the *Audacity* that she almost forgot that from the surface of a planet, one could see the stars from the same perspective night after night and pick out meaningful patterns in them. She hadn't thought about constellations in ages. It was high time for some new ones.

"That, there." May pointed up into the sky. "That's the jackalope constellation. American mythology tells of the great sky jackalope who visited lost travelers in the Midwest and led them to the nearest town. The legend goes that you had to give the jackalope a small felted hat in return, which is why, as I'm sure you can see, there are several styles of hat on the tips of the jackalope's antlers."

"What happens if you don't give the jackalope a hat?" Xan asked, rightly concerned about the available supply of small felted hats.

"That's what the teeth are for." She then gestured to the jackalope's face, where four stars appeared to form a rectangle of sharp rodent teeth in its maw. "You see it?"

Xan squinted, but he didn't see it. "Yeah, I see it," he said. Ancient Tuhntians used constellations to navigate Tuhnt's surface, but once space travel became commonplace, it was difficult for anyone to think of the stars from a two-dimensional perspective again, and the tradition was lost.

May sipped the rikokory ponderously. The only way she could stomach the drink was by distracting herself with deep thoughts while she drank it. Fortunately, a perfect external distraction grew increasingly louder at the bonfire nearest them.

"This isn't right!" shouted a thin, haggard red-skinned man with a crest of horns reaching from his brow to the nape of his neck. "This gorphlorting place isn't what it used to be, man." Two prignettes in robes appeared beside him, gently grabbing his arms. "You can't shut out EkoDoDo! That's censorship! It's the only tree around here that gets it, man!"

May wondered what he was saying that kept translating to 'man' since she'd never heard another being outside of Earth use the word. The word he was saying was, actually, man. This guy spoke Panseen, and the Panseen are Earth's closest biological and cultural ancestors. Most Panseen are men, women, dudes, chicks, guys, gals, ladies, bros, etc. Some have evolved beyond this, though.

"Please follow us," said one of the prignettes to the dude.

"You don't get it, man!" he shouted, pulling his arms away. "You're all caught up in the game!"

May set her mug on the ground and, with some effort, pulled herself out of the cozy nano-pod and headed towards the conflict.

"May, what're you doing?" Xan asked. He generally walked away from conflicts.

"He's talking about EkoDoDo."

"He's raving about EkoDoDo," Xan corrected, but May

was already out of earshot.

The prignette to the fellow's left pressed a thin, buzzing wand to his temple, and he dropped into their arms to be carried off. May took his place at the fire, whispering to the person nearest the events, a pale green Udonian whose customary mustache curled out in all directions, trapping small twigs and bits of leaves. "What did he say about EkoDoDo? They're shutting it down?"

"That's the rumor. Seems ol' EkoDoDo has outlived its usefulness to the museum. They're shutting down the access path to it from the canopy-hub. Marked it senile," they said.

"Damn, I need to see that tree tomorrow. Do you know how to get to it from here?"

"You can't; it's not safe to travel on the forest floor without a guide. Barely safe with a guide. Especially in the dark. Besides, you don't want to end up like that man-bloke, do you?"

"I'm afraid I will if I don't talk to EkoDoDo soon," May said seriously.

The Udonian dug in the well-worn backpack next to them, producing a flashlight and a folded map that smelled of mildew and was so worn at the edges it had turned white. "Here, you can take these. Old map of the place before the canopy-hub was built. That'll get you to EkoDoDo the traditional way, on the ground. You can telepathize, I'm assuming?"

"No," May said, taking the map.

"Well, good luck," the Udonian shrugged.

"Thanks," May said. She brought the map and flashlight back to Xan, who was trying to sit forward alertly in the nano-pod, which had not been designed for alert sitting.

"What was Mr. Dude's man-problem?" Xan asked.

She gave him a crooked smile that he both loved and dreaded. This smile meant she was about to suggest something crazy. His love of that smile meant he was about to go along with it.

"They're shutting down EkoDoDo from the main walkway, but I got an old map that will take us there on the ground," she said, holding up the moldering bit of paper triumphantly.

"Sounds fun," said Xan.

"Really?" May asked.

"Not at all. Can we at least wait until the sun turns on?"

"No, they'll see us," May said, already looking around suspiciously, trying to locate all the prignette sisters in the area to avoid them.

Xan finished his mug of rikokory and then picked hers up. "Are you going to finish this?"

"No," May said distractedly, studying the map.

"Alright." Xan finished off her drink, too, and she paused to look up at him with a questioning eyebrow.

"You know I spit in that, right?"

"If I catch some kind of Earthling virus from you, it wouldn't be the worst thing to have happened this rotation," Xan said with a shrug.

"Fair point. Let's go."

TWENTY-FOUR

WE FELL INTO THE PIT

* * * * *

For a while, the path on the forest floor was lit by a trail of old solar lamps from the museum's first iteration that no one had bothered to tear down. The path was once well-trodden, now covered in a fine layer of dead leaves and weeds.

The woods beyond were dark and silent. May used the flashlight to study the map. "Alright, at the first fork, we're going left," she told Xan, then she shut off the light and tucked the map into her coat pocket.

"It's kinda nice out here," Xan said, his boots crunching steadily along the path. "There aren't any forests like this in Trilly. Not for thousands of orbits, anyway. Aimz and I went on a trip once to see a forest, but the filporthean weet warning was too high the day we were planning to go out. We went out anyway. Didn't go well. Kinda ruined my view of forests, honestly. But there are no weets here. Hopefully. They would've told us if there were, right? Zuut..."

"Don't worry. This is a manufactured museum floating out in space. I doubt there's anything alive around here besides—"

Something scuttled across the path, interrupting May. It was the size of a small raccoon, but its skin reflected the solar light like a salamander. "Probably nothing dangerous," she assured herself. Xan would not be assured.

"What if there's another tree that could help? If EkoDoDo is really as dangerous as they say, maybe it won't be able to help us anyway. There was a tree that specialized in folk remedies! Or the psychology tree?"

"I doubt there's a folk remedy for reality shifting," May said. She did pause, though. "Any quantum physics trees?" Xan pulled out the new map, and May held the light to it. They studied it.

"Nope. This one knows every recipe for ice cream in both the known and unknown universe, though. That's pretty neat."

"Come on, I want to get there before sunrise."

"You mean sun-on?"

"Can't we call it sunrise?"

"We sure can," Xan said. And they wandered on, taking the left fork, trying to enjoy the peaceful quiet of the dark forest surrounding them. The only sound beyond the crunch of leaves under their feet was melodious birdsong, which comforted them into thinking there was nothing predatory nearby.

Some things don't prey on birds, though.

Some things don't announce their presence before it's too late.

A crackling in the air, the scent of cherries jubilee, and in an instant, May and Xan's arms were pinned to their sides. May with a scratchy hemp rope and Xan with a long lamp cord.

"Don't struggle, please," Xan said to Xan. His doppelgänger pulled him to the ground, which wasn't difficult because he had a particularly high center of gravity. May's double was having more trouble as May wiggled and twisted, instinctively crouching down to avoid being overtaken.

"Xan, fight him!" May shouted, noticing that Xan was

already on the ground and his double was currently wrapping up his legs. She attempted to bonk her forehead into her double's, but otherMay was prepared for this. She secured the rope around May's arms and dropped to the ground, grabbing onto one leg, tying the rope around it, then glomming May's other leg and, with a grunt of effort, she pulled, throwing May face-first into the dirt.

"Fuck," May cursed, spitting to get the dirt and hair out of her mouth. She continued to kick her legs like a beached, ferocious mermaid, but she was well tied. OtherMay stole her anchor button and BEAPER, then sat back in a pile of leaves, catching her breath as she watched herself struggle.

"These are nice knots," Xan complimented his double. "You must have also spent some time with Zilla," he remarked. "A little tight, though. And attached to a truly hideous lamp, ugh. But we didn't agree on a safeword so, as Zilla might say, you failed, and you should feel ashamed of yourself."

May rolled onto her side to give Xan a questioning look.

"She was joking," Xan clarified. "Mostly, I think."

"You knew Zilla, too? Is she...still around in this universe?" otherXan asked.

"She sure is!" He wormed around onto his back and, with some cajoling of his under-used stomach muscles, sat up, his arms still tied behind him. "Moved to Peeperhoip after the war. I hear she's running the cleanest brothel on Tuhnt now. You want to untie me and we can go see her? After...we do the thing we were doing. We gotta finish that thing," Xan said, mostly to May.

"May, Zilla! In our universe, she was on Tuhnt when it... Hold on, she's on Tuhnt? And alive? Tuhnt's not a scorched, barren smattering of rocks?!"

"Not anymore! It was. But we fixed it. Kinda of. Chaos fixed it, actually. No, actually, she caused it. But Chaos's meddling caused the Seam to fix it. Does that make sense?"

OtherXan shook his head, but he was smiling. "None at all, but I don't really care. It sounds wonderful. This universe is wonderful!" he told otherMay gleefully.

"Their rocket is orange," she said with a scowl. "That's going to be expensive to re-paint."

"I've gotten used to it," May informed her.

"So what's the thing you two need to finish?" otherXan asked his captives cheerfully, but otherMay motioned him aside.

"Don't befriend them; we can't keep them. There can't be two of each of us in this universe."

"Why not?" he asked.

"I am not sharing command of the *Ostentatious*," she snarled.

"And you're not going anywhere near the *Audacity*!" May shouted from the ground. "You crashed it in your universe!"

"How did you know that?" asked otherMay.

"I'm smarter than you," she said, although she was in no position to say this, tied up on the ground.

"Can't you two just get along?" both Xans said in tandem. "Oh! That's neat," they said. "We really are the same. Isn't that neat, May?" they asked their respective Mays, who shot them matching glares.

"Stick to the plan and stop talking to each other," otherMay said. She put the ring on Xan's finger and showed otherXan that it was solid black. "See? Not conscious. They're ghosts of our own personalities; that's why they're exactly like us."

"Not exactly," May said again, though she went ignored.

"Mazelmez is probably waiting for us on the ship already. I don't know how long I trust her to wait."

"She is a wildcard," both Xans agreed.

"How will we know it's our Mazelmez and not the other one?" said otherXan.

"Ring," said otherMay, twisting it off Xan, along with his BEAPER. She found the anchor button on his lapel and took that, too.

"Right, the ring. Do we just leave them here, though? Maybe we should contact the museum and let them know there are two people tied up somewhere in the forest."

"So they can come after us? No," said otherMay. "We need to drag them off the main path and shoot them."

"Oh, sorry, your weapons don't—" Xan began.

"Scare us!" May finished. "Your weapons don't scare us," she insisted, giving her Xan a serious, wide-eyed look, hoping he would get the idea.

He got it. They were going to act tough to intimidate their duplicates. He winked his understanding.

May shook her head no.

No... Oh! No, now he got it. They were going to pretend to be dead even though the otherworldly weapons wouldn't work. That made sense. He winked the other eye to show that he really did get it this time, and May nodded in return.

"See? They aren't scared to die, so it's fine to kill them," otherMay reasoned. Usually, she wasn't the one handling the ethical quandaries, and there was good reason for this.

"I don't think that tracks," otherXan started to say, but his May had already pulled the ray gun on them. With two quick zaps and a tastefully brief death scene, May and Xan slumped against each other in alleged slack-jawed lifelessness.

"Zuut! You just did it," otherXan said. "How did you just do that?"

OtherMay shrugged. "Losing your entire universe changes you."

"I mean, I also lost my entire universe and—"

"Also, she stabbed me with my own pocket knife. Come on, we need to drag them somewhere they won't be found." OtherMay tried to drag herself along the forest floor with the free end of the rope, but having recently been stabbed, she didn't get very far before doubling over in defeat.

"I'll take them," said otherXan. "Wait here."

Catching her breath, otherMay nodded. She pointed towards a sign leading down a thin trail off the main path which read: Danger. Sentient Ravine Ahead. Hungry. Do Not Interact. "Put them in the ravine; no one will find them."

"Alright, you sit and rest." He helped her sit up against a tree. "I'm going to have to do this one at a time," he said, more to himself, as he struggled to pick himself up.

A ways down the road, a kind of warbling bird noise spooked otherXan and, as was his custom, he started talking to himself. "Zuut," he whispered. "I really, really wish she hadn't killed you."

"She didn't," whispered Xan. "Your weapons don't work in this reality."

Startled, otherXan dropped Xan and helped him to his feet, only untying the bounds around his ankles, holding onto the porcelain farmer lamp that was still wrapped around Xan's arms.

"Thanks."

"No problem! I'm sorry about her. She's been under a lot of stress lately." They continued walking toward the ravine.

"We all have," said Xan.

"Once she heals down and cools up—"

"You mean heals up and cools down?" Xan asked.

"Zuut, this universe is more different than I thought!" said otherXan. "Once she's better, I'll try to convince her to come back for you two, okay?"

"Well, ideally, you might untie me now, and we could both try to convince her again."

"Ideally, yes, but I don't think she's ready for that. I'll just drop you two off into the woods here and be back within a rotation."

"Promise?" asked Xan. Usually, typically, he would promise. If he had any scrap of hope that he could do what he said he would do, he would promise.

OtherXan only made a noncommittal sort of groan, and Xan knew exactly what this meant. That hadn't been a promise.

TWENTY-FIVE

REGRETS AND CONFESSIONS

* * * * *

"Welcome to the ravine," said Xan as otherXan carefully lowered a tied-up May down next to him. May peeked a worried eye up at him. "It's alright; he knows we aren't dead. Might try to help us?" Xan asked hopefully up at otherXan, who stood a few feet above them at the edge of the ravine.

"I'm sorry," he said down to them. "Blitheon, I'm going to pay for this," he whispered to himself and walked away.

"Yeah, yeah, he's going to send help. I'm sure of it," Xan told May.

"I'm not," May growled. "Coward," she shouted up at him, right in Xan's ear.

Xan winced. "Okay, but consider he did this for your benefit. The other-you."

"I will not consider that. Can you get out of these ropes?"

Xan struggled audibly with them for a moment, twisting and turning in the mud, sliding a little further down into the ravine. "Nope."

"Then we're fucked," May said.

"Until Aimz comes looking for us."

"We're fucked," May repeated, resting her head on the muddy slope behind her.

"You know the worst part of this?" Xan said, kicking at the porcelain farmer lamp beside him. "In 10,000 orbits, when archeologists dig up our bones, they're going to think we loved this lamp so much we were buried with it. I don't want my anthropological legacy attached to this ugly, ugly lamp."

"I can see the headline," May said. "Earthling and Tuhntian Remains Found in Sacred Burial Site."

"Shepherded into the afterlife by a porcelain representation of a pastoral farmer," Xan added.

"Their relationship to each other is still unclear," May said.

"But they were found together?"

"They were found together," she confirmed, wriggling nearer to him so she could use his stomach as a pillow.

Xan laid his head back against a rock that jutted tooth-like from the ravine wall and gazed up at the stars. "Oh. The jackalope...with the little felt hats. I see it now."

Spinning around to face him, May chuckled. "You lied about seeing it earlier?"

"Heh, yeah, guess it's a hard habit to break."

"Anything else you need to confess to me before we die?"

He took his time to answer since they weren't dying anytime soon at this rate. "I wish I'd taken you to Tuhnt to meet Kalumbits, now that that's an option."

"That isn't a confession; that's a regret," May pointed out.

"Eh, there's a lot of overlap."

May sighed. "I regret not asking one of the trees what happened to my dad," she said.

"You know, you don't talk much about your life back on Earth," Xan said hesitantly, fearing that there was a good reason why she didn't.

"Earth's boring, and it sucks," she said, which was a pretty good reason, but not great.

"Yeah, but I mean...I didn't even know you had a dad, and now you've mentioned them twice in one rotation. It sounds like you want to talk about it."

May shrugged. "There isn't much to talk about."

"But there is a little to talk about?" he prodded.

She relented.

"Ugh, fine. He did something important in the military, I don't know what his rank was or anything, but he was away a lot and we moved around because of it. He went missing when I was twelve. Mom threw out any photos we had of him. I sorta stopped talking to her after that. Got a job as soon as I turned 16, and I lived in his old car for a while until I could afford an apartment."

"You never found out what happened to him?"

"I tried to get into the Air Force after that. I thought I would be able to get my hands on some records, find out more. But they turned me down. Bad eyesight." She smiled at the irony of her racing a rocket ship with eyesight that wasn't good enough for her to fly a plane.

"You've been hurling us through obstacle courses at nearly light-speed with bad eyesight?" Xan asked. "That's your final confession?"

May laughed and closed her eyes. "No, my final confession is that getting shot, tied up, and thrown into a ravine isn't so bad with good company."

"Zuut, you two have some weird kinks," Aimz said from somewhere above them.

"Aimz!" Xan shouted up at Aimz, who peered down at them over the edge of the ravine on her hands and knees. She popped a golf-ball-sized wad of groonhaas in her mouth and chewed. "Got anymore groonhaas down there? This was my last one."

"Where'd you get groonhaas?! And aren't you high enough? One of those things used to feed a party of twelve." Xan shouted at her.

"Not enough. Never enough. Not for this trok." She swung her legs around to dangle over the ravine. "My zuxing double showed up again. Said she just wanted to swap notes and groonhaas. I said I'd take the groonhaas; she could have the notes. Then she got me splattered, shot me with a stupid little ray gun, and tossed me out the ship!"

"Go back to the museum and tell them we're here," May shouted up at her.

"Hold on," Aimz said, then hauled herself over the edge of the ravine and slid gracefully down the muddy slope until she was close enough that May could smell the groonhaas on her breath. "What?"

"Never mind," May said. "Just untie us."

Aimz crawled on top of May, observing the knot binding her arms and legs. "How'd you manage this? Tying each other up? I know you're good with knots, Xan, but not this good. Forgot the safeword, huh?"

"Just untie us!" May snapped, angrily shimmying at her.

"Alright! Hold still. It's lucky for you I used to be the Tinsel Merkin Fiasco's lead knot-master. Would've been Xan, he's better at knots technically, but someone needed to be on after-care, and Zilla said I don't have a nurturing personality. Can you believe that?"

"Yes," May said as Aimz freed her from the rough ropes. Her arms and legs had fallen asleep, and she winced as she shook them out, trying to regain feeling. She surveyed the steep, muddy walls around them as Aimz untied Xan. "I don't think we can climb this. We'll have to walk along the creek until we find a way out."

Aimz played with the rope, wrapping it around herself decoratively while Xan rubbed his wrists.

"No need to walk."

"Who said that?" May asked. It hadn't been any of the three of them, but no one else was nearby. The sound had seemingly come from inside her own head, exactly as it had when Benny G spoke to her.

"One of the trees?" Xan suggested.

"Sentient ravine," Aimz said, tapping her temple. "Telepathic sentient ravine! Hello, ravine! Do you want to eat us? Hungry buddy? Who's a hungry buddy?" she teased the muddy ground.

"I am," said the ravine, and the ground beneath them began to tremble, rough-edged rocks churning around their feet, chewing them into the ground.

TWENTY-SIX

AIMZ IS THE ASSHOLE

* † * * *

If you've never been eaten by a sentient ravine before, here is what you must know: It is nearly, but not quite, as horrific as being killed by a garbage disposal. It is like being put into a blender full of mud and rocks. It is a bit like quicksand, but unlike quicksand, which doesn't care whether you live or die, it thoroughly enjoys the thrashing and wailing of live prey, and so it tries to keep its prey alive as long as possible.

May became caught in the churning rocks first, flailing her arms to try to keep herself balanced physically and emitting a number of curses to try to keep herself balanced emotionally.

"May! Grab my hand!" Xan said, hopping on the shifting rocks, dancing from one foot to the next as he tried to keep from being pulled under. He at last caught one of May's hands and then slipped, landing sideways in the mud, two rocks taking the opportunity to crush his leg in place and drag it deeper into the ravine.

Aimz sighed, her arms crossed as she let the mud consume her. "I knew this was going to happen someday," she said.

"You knew this would happen?!" Xan asked, tugging his leg to try to free it.

"Well, sure. That's statistics. If you live forever, you eventually experience every possible death scenario. Just didn't have this one pegged as happening quite so soon..." Aimz said, already sunk to her knees.

"What are you talking about?!" Xan wheezed, up to his chest in crushing rocks now; he tried to wiggle backwards toward the ravine wall and May but couldn't move.

"Hold on, do you..." Aimz snorted with laughter. "Do you not know yet?" Aimz looked suddenly like she had just won an interstellar lottery. She clapped with delight. May and Xan, momentarily distracted from their horror, looked at her, confused. "Zuut! You don't know! Ahaha! Okay, watch this." She pulled a palm-sized laser zapper from her belt, held it to her temple, and pulled the trigger. A bolt of energy sizzled through her body, the pink baby hairs around her face standing on end to create a crazed halo.

"Aimz!" Xan tried to pull away from the rocks that held him to rescue his sister from the zapper, but there was no saving to be done. Aimz was fine.

"We're immortal, you zingnats! The Seam forgot to hook us back up into the system when it reset the timeline! We're in cosmic free-float. Our consciousness and, to some degree, our physical forms are now a constant. We're timeless classics!" Aimz's left eyelid was twitching madly, and she clasped a hand over it to calm the nerves. "There are some side-effects, of course."

"What the fuck, Aimz?! You couldn't have told us that earlier?" May said. "Maybe when Xan got harpooned?"

"I figured you knew!"

"How would we have?!" Xan took his turn to shout at her. "How long have you known about this?"

"Only three seasons," Aimz whined. "Surg said he sensed it on me. What a pick-up line, right?" Lowering her eyelids, Aimz wiggled her shoulders sensually at Xan. "You smell like forever," she said in a husky voice, then laughed. "He showed me his ShuttleDisc and, zuut, that thing is zing up to caliber! Andolonian technology is eons beyond A'Viltrian junk. You know they invented the ocular forests, right? Surg wouldn't shut up about them," Aimz muttered. "One of the reasons I left him. Now his dumb smart trees are eating us. Is that ironic? I think that's irony," she said, musing at the trees around her, which shuddered slightly. They hated watching the ravine consume living prey. Their food was long dead by the time they ate it. Live meat was so uncivilized.

"So what's going to happen to us? If the ravine eats us?" May said, terrified, still trying to swim towards Xan.

Aimz shrugged. "There are legends about immortals who became separated from their physical forms. Trapped in objects, possessing other forms at will."

"Chaos," May and Xan said together.

"Yeah! Chaos did that. Surg said he knew her before she got de-boned. Bretsy. What a name, right? Tracks that she changed it. Chaos is much scarier sounding."

"So we're going to become like Chaos?" May asked, her mind so occupied that, for the moment, she wasn't fighting the ravine.

"Oh no, no...no, that takes eons to master. No. We'll be trapped under the forest for however long it takes us to be discovered again. Or to dig ourselves out. You know, I was miffed at the idea I'd never be able to be a zombie, but now I think about it, this is better."

"Better!?" Xan shouted. "In what possible way is this-- No. Alright, you know what? This is fine. This is alright. I've accepted it. May, we're going to be buried alive for the next foreseeable forever. Nothing we can do. I'm going to use this time to think about writing a holobook. Zuut, I could write a twenty-holobook series. Hopefully, by the time someone digs us up, people still read books! If not, I'll just have to adapt it, I guess. You want to know the theme?" he said to Aimz, his neck half-buried in silt now. "You want to know? The theme is going to be horrible, horrible sisters who are horrible." And then he disappeared beneath the mud.

"Fuck! Fuck! Xan!" May began crawling toward where he disappeared, but her movement only made the shifting mud eat her faster.

Aimz twisted her lips to the side, her brow furrowed, still slowly sinking, up to her waist now. She sighed. "You think I'm horrible?" she asked May, soberly.

May had found Xan's arm under the mud and was doing her best to pull him up, but now her shoulders were covered. She couldn't even turn to look Aimz in the eye when she said, "Figure it out for yourself. You're going to have plenty of time." May said before she, too, disappeared into the muck. Aimz went a few moments later.

I should've told Aimz to fuck all the way off, May thought in the cool dark wetness of the mud once the churning had stopped and the panic had settled down a little. Or I could've been really cool about it and just said 'yes.' "Yes, I do think you're horrible." She's honest, at least. Brutally honest. Xan's not. Xan's been known to lie to keep the peace, actually. I'm honest, thought May. But not like Aimz, right? The other me was pretty intense. I've got some empathy, though. Maybe not for myself, but for other people. Aimz doesn't have a scrap of that. Is she a narcissist? Is that what a narcissist is? Can't look it up, I guess. I'm going to say yes. Doesn't matter now. How long has it been? It feels like it's been hours.

It had been six minutes.

TWENTY-SEVEN

EKODODO

* * * * *

Time passed. Several times, actually, and May did not shift realities. This wasn't for lack of trying. Desperately, she wanted to be anywhere but where she was, the warm, wet dirt so heavy on her body she couldn't even wiggle her toes. Sleep was her only reprieve, and there was only so much of that she could usefully do.

The darkness behind her eyes was absolute, but out of boredom, she decided to see if she could actually look at it. Intently, she stared at the darkness behind her eyelids. She was waiting for visual information, but none was forthcoming, so her brain had the clever idea to send in the reserves and create a faux light show to project on the inside of her eyelids. Lights, colors, and shapes started to dance madly in front of her, coming together and then coming apart in a kaleidoscope of nearly but not quite recognizable images.

And then, the patterns became more complex, showing her hands with too many fingers, eyes with too many pupils, platypuses with neither plat nor pus to speak of. Light pervaded the darkness as if she were looking up at the sun with her eyes closed.

The weight above her shifted, and her body felt light again. Her lungs filled with air. She tried to move her hand and found it was free to touch her face. A fuzzy background noise resolved into the sound of the ocean.

Finally, she got brave enough to open her eyes.

Upside-down above her, framed with blue sky, she saw the face of a wrinkled old woman, her long, natural grey locs tied back and an open welder's mask shading her face from the bright sun.

"That's better, huh?" she heard in her mind. And then she heard, "Oh, you humans like it when the mouth moves, I almost forgot," said the old woman above her, moving her black-stained lips in a way that only vaguely matched the words, like she was being dubbed from another language. The translation chip usually took care of that, altering the visual cortex's perception to perfectly sync a mouth with the words it was supposed to be making. The translation chip didn't work on visual hallucinations, though. So the mouth was a bit off.

"Thanks," said May, rolling over so she could sit up. Though it wasn't her actual body that was rolling over, just a strong impression in her mind. She thought herself to be on a driftwood beach, dark rotting wood and behemoth abstract metal sculptures contrasting sharply against powdery white sand. She even felt the hot sun and humid breeze, though it wasn't really there.

"Who are you?"

"Guess," said the old woman with a grin.

May squinted out the excess light and studied the woman's warm brown complexion, her nose, her chin... it all did seem familiar. But the eyes, in particular, she knew.

"You're...me?" May said cautiously, worried she sounded utterly bonkers.

The old woman winked. "Everyone loves that trick. The inner wise-one, eh?"

"If it's a trick, then who are you, really?"

"Don't you know? You're the one who came to me."

"I haven't moved," May said. "I've been buried alive!"

"Mmm, yet here you are," the old woman said, sitting down on the sand and staring out across the ocean. May realized, now, it wasn't an Earthly ocean. It was the cream sea of Taeloo VII, foaming white against the pink sands.

"This is a dream," she said. "Or a hallucination. I'm not really here." She pinched the sand, rubbing it between her fingers. It felt real enough.

"You are too concerned with what's real. Too concerned with what's actual to envision what's possible. You'll never be able to sculpt anything with a mind like that," she waved a hand at the many tall, dark metal sculptures surrounding them. "You intended to make contact with EkoDoDo, and it is here. Ask now your question."

The original question, about how to stay rooted to her own reality, seemed unimportant now because all she wanted to do was be in a reality where she wasn't trapped underground. She needed to know how to escape her muddy prison.

She didn't even have to form the question, EkoDoDo answered.

"You're so convinced that you know which reality you wish to live in! Just live in it." EkoDoDo squinted at her.

"I am living in it; I don't know how to get out of it!" May said.

"Well, do you want in or out? You're acting like the universe's feral cat. Make thine eye single!"

"I don't know what that means," May said.

"It means you eye should be single," EkoDoDo clarified.

May squeezed one eye shut, effecting a dramatic raised eyebrow. "How is this going to help?"

EkoDoDo sighed deeply. Sighing was not something it had picked up from its interaction with humans. All trees sigh. Humans picked up this habit from trees, actually. "You aren't doing it right."

"Then teach me! I don't know what you're talking about!"

"It is simple, sapling. It's no harder than absorbing photons with your leaves or sucking up water at your roots. Though, I suppose to you, that sounds impossible since you are not a tree," said EkoDoDo, displaying a brief flash of empathy. "You cannot end your confusion, then. That is all." The flash was very brief, after all. EkoDoDo turned away from her and began walking up the beach toward the verdant dunes.

"Please!" May begged. "When I want to shift, I can't, and when I don't want to, I do. Teach me how to control it."

"Pff," EkoDoDo muttered. "Humans and their precious 'control.'" It turned around and fixed May again with a mirror-like gaze. "I don't teach. I'm not that kind of tree... but since you are my final customer, and my roots have been feeding off your body, I will make an exception."

"You've what?!"

"Oh, that body you cling to is perfectly safe. It's been uprooted from natural law, which is disturbing but not altogether unusual," said EkoDoDo, waving away the thought of immortality with its wrinkled hand. "Besides, this will be good for your untethered consciousness. Connected to my roots, you are connected with infinite possibility. From a reality where the only difference is that you're lying one inch to the left, to a reality where you are a wad of chewing gum on the underside of the universe's shoe, to—"

"I get it," May interrupted.

"You don't, but that's okay. These infinite realities don't become real until they are perceived, anyway. Consciousness is the catalyst that turns possible into real. And your human consciousness is generally so caught up in the idea of knowing its reality that it simply accepts whatever is nearby as 'real.' Except now, thanks to the toxic metal in your bloodstream, yours is partially unstuck. It's finding other realities to latch onto and thinking they're real. What a mess, sapling!

"At the base of the multiverse, your consciousness is whole. It's neither yours nor mine, but ours. Here, as in any other universe, our consciousness is divided. It must be, in order for you to think you are you and for me to think I am me. Do you see?

"No," May said, but fearing that EkoDoDo might try to make like a tree and leave again, she amended, "Maybe..."

It motioned for May to sit, and then it plopped down in

the sand, legs crossed. "How many of you are there?" EkoDoDo asked.

May counted on her fingers. "Including me, at least five. Maybe more. Infinite, even."

EkoDoDo nodded. "Maybe infinite. But how many consciousnesses do you have?"

"One?"

"There is only one. One eye looking through infinite peep-holes. One light refracted into infinite colors. Do you see?"

"I see."

"Yes. And that's all you do. In one way or another, you are a Seeing Thing, just like me. We are the same. If I can live comfortably in all realities, you can, too."

"But I can't control the other versions of myself. If I could, I wouldn't have shot myself!"

"Oh, and there you go, obsessing over control again. Consciousness attacks itself all the time. Put yourself in the shoes of your alter. She lost her ship and her universe. She found an alternate reality in which she hadn't lost those things, and believing you to be a soulless body-double, she took your place. In that situation, what would you have done?"

May nodded. "Same."

"And so, you are the same."

"What do I need to do, then?"

EkoDoDo shrugged, shaking its head. "What makes you think you need to do anything?"

"Because...I'm trapped underground."

Tilting their head, EkoDoDo looked around. "You're on a beach."

"This is annoying," May muttered. "My body is trapped underground! I want to get it out."

"Then get it out."

"How?"

"This is annoying," EkoDoDo muttered, exactly as May had done. "I see what's going on here. You want to fiddle." EkoDoDo crossed their arms judgmentally at May.

"I'm not good with instruments," she objected.

"No, you need to tinker! To putter. You want to affect

change in your physical environment, isn't that right?"

"Isn't that the definition of doing something?" May asked.

EkoDoDo shook her head with exasperation but didn't refute her. "Alright, then. Take your awareness to the Ranger. Tell him to come here to dig you out."

"But he's in another reality."

"That's what the PLOT hole is for," EkoDoDo said, its fingers entwined seriously. "Tell the Ranger to come through Pontoosa's Ludicrously Opportune Transdimensional Wormhole. It's not far from here."

"Doesn't that only lead from here to the Adventure Asteroid?" May asked.

"It's a transdimensional wormhole. It leads anywhere you want it to."

"But that's—" May began.

"Ludicrous? Yes, that's why they named it that."

"Who named it that?"

"Someday you'll understand," EkoDoDo said with a wink. "You're immortal now. The likelihood of understanding how everything works someday is extremely high. Tell him he must bring a shovel, a bottle of shermel, and a blue-scaled fish the length of his arm."

"What's the shermel and the fish for?"

"The fish is my payment. The shermel is for you. You believe your mouth to be full of dirt. The shermel will help you cope with that belief. Do you remember the key for your universe?"

"No," said May.

"Now you do," Ekododo said.

"Oh...yeah, I guess I do. How do I contact him?"

"Throw your consciousness. It isn't all that difficult."

"Then it should be easy for you to teach me how to do it," May said, almost growling the words in frustration.

A rustling sound, which seemingly came from the old woman, signified EkoDoDo's frustration. "Go walk into the ocean. Once your head is covered, you'll be able to see him, and I'll be free of your nettlesome mind."

"Thanks," May said, standing. EkoDoDo swatted at her as if swatting away a gnat, and May headed toward the cream sea, curiously eyeing the sculptures around her as she went. They were twice her height, all steel and copper twisting together, rising up out of the sand in arcs of frozen movement.

Not letting herself get distracted, she returned her gaze to the ocean line and walked into the water. She took a deep breath, though she wasn't quite sure how since she was still underground in reality, and then dipped her head under. Immediately, there was the Ranger. He wasn't where she had expected him to be, lying on the couch in his ship. Instead, she found him hunched over a campfire, pensively roasting something on a stick.

"Xan!" she shouted. He started and looked about, twisting around to find the source of the voice. He was looking in her general direction, but she soon realized she had no physical presence there because he couldn't figure out where to look.

Across the fire from Xan, May saw a large Panseen guy with broad shoulders and a neck as thick as a pine tree. He would do. She concentrated on re-positioning herself, visualizing the Ranger from the perspective of the guy across from him.

"Hey! Over here," May made the Panseen's heavy vocal cords vibrate. "It's me, May!"

The Ranger blinked a few times at her from behind the black eye mask. He squeezed his eyes shut, rubbed them with his palms, and looked at her again. "Sorry, sir, but did you say you were May?"

"Yes! I'm May, and I need your help."

He stood up, sweeping his hat politely off his head and holding it to his chest. "Anything, ma'am."

"Get to Pontoosa's Ludicrously Opportune Transdimensional Wormhole and give them this universe key: 89-Flummox5. Once you're in my universe, come to the Tree Museum. I got eaten by a sentient ravine, and I need you to dig me up. I'm twelve paces north of EkoDoDo."

"Okay...and you're alive?" he asked.

"Yes!"

"Underground?"

"Yes. Bring a large blue fish and some shermel and a shovel. Can you do that?"

"Yes, I've got it," said the Ranger, standing. "I will find you. You can count on me."

May coaxed the strong, fleshy lips of her host's body into an awkward smile. "Thanks."

And she was back in the darkness. Back in the dirt. Waiting. Feeding EkoDoDo.

TWENTY-EIGHT

PESTERING AS A FORM OF DIPLOMACY

* * * * *

A shovel to the ribs woke May from a pleasant dream about running for her life from a fast-moving wyrntensil. It was pleasant because any dream where she could breathe air and move her body was an improvement over her current waking predicament. She felt the dirt around her resonate with a thud, and then frantic fingers hauled handfuls of dirt off her until she was able to sit her stiff body up.

"Blitheon, it really is you," said the Ranger, squeezing May so tightly he denied her the first full breath of oxygen she tried to inhale. She pushed him off, coughing up a mouthful of dirt. "Are you alright?" asked the Ranger.

"Yeah, it's just...I'm not a dried wad of gum on the bottom of the universe's shoe, right?"

"I wasn't aware the universe had shoes."

"Right, yeah, that's silly." But she couldn't shake the feeling of being a helpless little lump attached to something much larger than herself, which would not stop squashing her against the concrete as it ambled ever forward.

She slapped her hands together and wiped her eyes, blinking tiny particles out of them until they teared up. Through blurred vision, she could see she'd been dragged deep below the forest floor. Standing, the Ranger's hat barely cleared the lip of the pit he'd dug.

"I brought the fish and the shermel," the Ranger said, holding up the items, one in each hand, illuminated by a blueish hover-orb which was trained on his left shoulder. "What are they for?"

May snatched the shermel bottle, pulled the cork with her teeth, and swished it in her mouth, spitting out the first mouthful to get the taste of mud out. Then she drank the rest of it to overcome the shock. Shermel wasn't the best liquor she'd had since leaving Earth, but it was a key ingredient in an old Tuhntian space flu remedy, and Xan had made a great deal of that for her when she had been sick back on Not-Tuhnt. The molasses-sweet syrupiness of the alcohol was comforting. And despite the eye-mask, seeing someone who looked and sounded exactly like Xan was comforting, too.

"What happened?" he asked, letting her lean against him as she continued to drink.

"Hungry ravine," she said simply.

"How long were you down there?"

May closed her eyes and tried to figure that out. "How long has it been since I manifested the dust ghost at you?"

"Oh, that? Why, that was nearly a season ago. Sorry it took so long to reach you. Old Silver's not in great shape without you to keep an eye on the mechanics. We had to make a few repair stops on our way to the museum."

"Silver?" May asked. "Oh...the *Audacity*. You called it Silver?" May blinked at him. "Did you re-paint it?"

He shook his head.

"So you've got an orange rocket, and you call it Silver?"

He nodded affirmatively.

"Okay," she said, not seeing any point in pressing the logic of that. Dislodging her legs from the pit, uncoiling the thick tree roots that had wrapped around her, she shakily stood.

"I'd wager being underground without food or air for a season is stranger than calling an orange rocket 'Silver,'" said the Ranger.

"I'm immortal," May said.

"Really, now? How did that happen?"

"Formless entity that governs the beginning and end of the universe did a bad job punishing a god, I think. Look, I need to find Xan," she told him. "My Xan, I mean. And...I guess I better recover Aimz, too."

The Ranger smiled, but it wasn't Xan's characteristic face-eating grin. It was far more subtle, and it mostly came through as a glint of excitement in his bemasked eyes. "I'd be honored to be a part of your rescue mission. Where did you last see them?"

"Also getting eaten by the ravine," May said, peering around in search of the ravine in question. The tree's roots had dragged her quite far from her original location. Xan and Aimz could be anywhere in the forest by now. "We'll ask another tree. Leave the fish in the pit. The tree wanted it."

She began trudging towards the nearest trunk, staring it down as if she could penetrate its bark with her very gaze and speak to it telepathically. She could not, of course, do this. The tree in question, whose name was Renauldon, blinked its many wooden eyes at her. Utterly silent. Utterly unimpressed. She touched its trunk with one hand, thinking perhaps that would improve their psychic link. And it might have done had they had a psychic link at all to begin with. She put another hand to it. Renauldon's many eyes rolled.

"Is this some kind of ritual?" The Ranger asked reverently. "You must have a special connection with the trees."

May shut her eyes and concentrated harder. After having fed one of them for a time, she bloody well ought to have a special connection with them. She did not, though. Eventually, she had to admit it. "Apparently not," she said. "We need to get back on the main path so I can find a spork. Any idea where camp is from here?"

The Ranger, like most versions of Xan, expressed a genetic predisposition towards being directionally challenged. But unlike May's Xan, the Ranger was self-deluded in regards to this fact. He looked up at the faux sun, which was always smack in the middle of the faux sky and only dimmed or brightened to simulate dusk and dawn. "That way," he said, pointing generally towards where he had come from.

"Alright," May said, brushing her hands off. Then, realizing that dirt had invaded so deeply under her fingernails that she might never be free of it, she gave up. "We can look for them the old-fashioned way while we walk." She said, searching the forest floor for a good stick.

"What's the old-fashioned way?" the Ranger asked, hoping that perhaps she was about to perform some ancient Earthling divination. She was, in actuality, only looking for a small stick or dried leaf to clean under her fingernails with. She found it and started to absently pick under her nails as she demonstrated the old-fashioned way.

"Xan! Aimz!" she called out to the forest.

"Oh, of course," said the Lone Ranger. And together they began the trek back to camp, headed about sixty degrees in the wrong direction. Fortunately, they wouldn't go far out of their way before they heard a familiar voice shouting May's name in the distance.

They discovered Xan, mostly entangled in the ropey roots of a tree that looked very much like a banyan tree, only with eyes. Tired, bloodshot eyes. Only Xan's mouth and nose were visible between the roots.

"Jesus, Xan! How did you get in there?" May asked, sprinting up to him. The Ranger followed nervously behind her, unsure he was ready to meet himself.

"Diplomacy!" he said as May tried to pull apart the roots that held him. They were impossibly strong. "Or perhaps pestering. Is pestering a form of diplomacy? Because I think I pestered the trees enough to want to help me out. This is Hugelnaught, by the way. It's trying to grow me out. Slowly. That takes some time, you know?

Trees...have a different perception of time than we do."

"Ranger, give me the shovel," May said. And the Ranger came into view behind her.

"Oh, is someone else with you?" Xan's eyes were still hidden behind a thick tree root.

"Pleasure to meet you," said the Ranger, tipping his hat.

"This is the Ranger. He's you, but instead of 'I Love Lucy,' he's obsessed with 'The Lone Ranger,'" May explained, taking the shovel from him.

"The show with all the guns?" Xan asked.

"Yep," May said.

"And the murder?!"

"That's the one," said May as she worked the shovel in between the tree roots, using it as a lever to pry the roots off him. Slowly, with a great deal of grunting and wriggling, Xan emerged from the trunk of Hugelnaught and landed with a thud on the dirt below.

"Zuut. That was massively horrible, right?" he said, shaking out his limbs and sitting up against the base of the tree. May hugged him tightly and then sat next to him while the Ranger stood aside, leaning awkwardly on his shovel.

"I don't think I've ever gone so long without talking," said Xan. "Almost, maybe. I did have some pretty low seasons on the *Audacity* after the, uh...incident with Tuhnt. But I guess that never happened now, did it? So, longest I've gone in this timeline without talking or seeing anyone. Or breathing! Weird, right? No breathing. What did you do to pass the time? I thought I'd compose a novel, but in all that time, you know, I never even got to deciding on the main character's name? Writing's tough. Me? I just ended up sleeping a lot. A LOT more than usual, I think. Maybe I needed it. Maybe I hadn't been sleeping enough, and now I'm all caught up! AND caught up. Ha! A joke. That's a joke for you. But you know, I did get in touch with this delightful tree. Its name was Mosamawa, and while I must say it wasn't terribly sympathetic to our situation, it did know a great deal about anthropological graffiti. May, you aren't talking— are you okay?"

"You haven't given me a chance to," May said.

"Right! Yes, of course. Okay, here's your chance, I am done, absolutely all talked out. Very ready to listen. Very ready to hear your voice again. Blitheon, I missed you. And I worried about you. Sorry, please go on!"

"Somehow, I found EkoDoDo," May said. "Or it found me, I'm not sure. It tried to help, I think. I went to another reality on purpose—that's how I found the Ranger—and I haven't accidentally jumped since."

"That's good!"

"And...we can't die. I had a lot of time to think about that," May said. "Don't you think that'll get sorta...awful? Eventually?"

Xan allowed a rare moment of silence to float between them, but not for too long. "I imagine it will be wonderful and awful in turns. Just like any life," he said. "Besides, what could be worse than being trapped underground? Nothing, I hope! Nothing, probably."

"Think of all the ways we could die...and remember it," May suggested.

"Getting buried was a fluke!" Xan insisted. "Getting brutally killed is probably really rare, right?"

"For us?" May asked pointedly. "You were impaled, I got stabbed, and we were both eaten by a sentient ravine already."

"So we're getting some of it out of the way early. Look, I've made peace with it. Mosamawa shared with me a lot of really inspiring graffiti from across the universe, and a lot of genitalia, of course, more variety out there than I ever imagined! I've decided to carpe diem. Genitalia varietals are endless, and I endeavor to pleasure them all. Call me for a good time. Kilroy was here."

"Please don't tell me I'm in for an eternity of bathroom stall quotes," May said. "Any idea where Aimz is?"

"Here," said Aimz.

And she was. On the other side of Hugelnaught's massive trunk, Aimz lay across the rooty ground like a dirty, deflated pool float. She wasn't trapped by anything heavier than her own soul.

"Aimz! How long have you been out?" Xan asked,

crawling closer to check her over.

"A while," she said. "It's rained like...ninety times maybe. I was making the trees depressed, so they kicked me out."

"You were so depressed, the trees kicked you out?" May asked.

"Yep."

"Oh, Mazelmez," Xan said. "I'm sorry I called you a horrible sister. You're not, you're just--"

"No, no. I am. I could've gotten us out of that ravine and I could've fought harder for Listay. I'm a horrible everything." Aimz wiggled into the rotting leaves on the forest floor as if she wanted to bury herself again.

"That's ridiculous," May said. "Sometimes you're horrible, but you can also be smart and fun and--" this wasn't working. May looked to Xan for ideas. He mouthed the word 'sexy' to her. She replied with a face of quiet disgust. He shrugged. She sighed, then said, "And you're sexy."

Aimz looked up. "You think I'm sexy?"

"Well, yeah. You've got those, um..." May started. "Ugh," she finished. She did not know what made Aimz sexy.

"Alright, I get it. You don't have to write me a poem, Earthmun." Aimz winked at her.

"Good. I suck at poetry," May said. "You want to help us steal the *Audacity* back?"

"Can you take me to Listay afterwards?"

"Sure can."

"Alright, I'm in."

"You can count on me, too, ma'am," said the Ranger, startling everyone. They had forgotten he was there.

"Thanks," said May. "Now we need to figure out how to get off this space station, track down the *Audacity*, board it, fight off our--"

"Can we shower first?" Xan interrupted, still picking leaves out of Aimz's hair.

"I don't need to shower," Aimz said.

"You might not need to shower, but I need you to shower," Xan said. "Come on." He helped her up, and they both stood shakily and headed back to the campsite.

TWENTY-NINE

FOOD SCIENCES

* * * * *

"I have a plan!" said May, grabbing Xan's arm excitedly. He had been picking food off the make-shift banquette some of the more generous campers had set up. She was still wet. She wasn't used to wet showers anymore, but that was all the campsite had to offer. She didn't have a towel, and there was no obvious way of drying off available. There was a non-obvious way, a switch in the shower that turned it into a full-body blow dryer, but she had been too eager to share her brilliant shower thought with Xan to look for it.

He turned around, his white cowboy hat in one hand and a broad, purple leaf full of food in the other.

"Oh--" she said. "You're not Xan." She shivered in the cool evening breeze.

This was only partially true. He was Xan, just not the version of Xan she was hoping he'd be. He swallowed. "Sorry, ma'am. He hasn't come back from the showers yet."

He hadn't come back from the showers yet because while he had washed all the dirt off himself already, it would take a while yet to wash the memory of the dirt off.

"You can tell me your plan, though," he said to encourage her.

"I guess I can..." May said. "Remember how I purposefully threw my consciousness to contact you?"

"Yep. That Panseen you possessed wasn't too happy about it."

"He cause you trouble?"

"Nothing I couldn't handle," said the Ranger.

May tilted her head at him. "You can handle trouble?"

Setting down his leaf-plate, he showed her the ray gun on his hip to demonstrate that he could, indeed, handle trouble.

"Wow, you really are nothing like my Xan," she said.

Strictly speaking, he was exactly like her Xan, but the circumstances of his life had been different. Different enough to lead to him purchasing a ray gun. He had never used it, though. It was mainly a deterrent. What he could use was the length of rope hanging off his other hip. He was mighty good at knots.

His mannerisms were also similar to her Xan's. She could tell she had disappointed him. She could tell he wished he was more like her Xan because that Xan still had a May.

"That's a good thing, in this case," she clarified. "So here's my plan. In another reality, I was a pirate. I think I can jump into that body and trick myself--the pirate me-- into helping us."

"Who's helping us?" Xan asked, coming up behind May and drying off his hair with a towel.

"Where'd you get a towel?" she asked.

"Borrowed it. I got a talking-to about how irresponsible it is not to have my own towel and a threat regarding what would happen to my neck if I didn't return it promptly, but overall, he was a nice guy. So who's helping us?" He began gently squeezing out May's dripping curls with the towel.

"Pirates. There's a version of us with a pirate ship. I think I can trick them into--"

"We're tricking people? Great!" Aimz said, appearing on

the other side of May.

"Why don't we grab a seat by the fire, and you can explain it from the start again?" offered the Ranger, grabbing his leaf of food.

"Spiced taubkin eggs?!" Xan asked, noticing what the Ranger had in his leaf.

"Yep. They've been sitting out, though. Not sure they're —"

"I'm immortal! I'll eat them if you're not going to," Xan said, slinging the towel over his shoulder and reaching for the plate of eggs.

"You could still get sick from them," May said.

"I don't care. I haven't eaten in two seasons. I'd happily get sick on these!"

"Alright, everyone, grab the most dubious-looking foods you can find, and we'll test whether we're still susceptible to food poisoning or not!" Aimz said cheerily, grabbing her own leaf and collecting a scoop of anything that looked like it had a dairy base.

They gathered around a faux fire pit with plates of food, May and Xan sharing an oversized nano-bot-pod-chair, the Ranger sinking forlornly into his own, and Aimz, freshly showered, sitting directly on the hard-packed dirt.

May set out her plan. "I'll intentionally possess the pirate version of myself and make her think there's treasure here at the Tree Museum. Once she's here, we tell her the treasure is on the *Audacity*, and we need her help to get it back. We take the ship; she gets the treasure. She's bound to go for it. She had nothing but jewelry and gold on her mind when I was in there."

"Gold?" Xan asked.

"It's an Earth metal everyone's obsessed with. I guess it's more intergalactically popular in her universe," May said.

"We don't have either of those things, though. We've got crystals. Not even that—we've got digital crystals! What happens if we don't have what we promised her?"

"Oh, I've got tons of gold," Aimz said. "And jewelry. The Crenalto crowd ate that trok up. Old-timey wealth, they called it. The ShuttleDisc is full of that junk, she can have it." Aimz waved her hand dismissively, rolling up her empty leaf-plate to eat it like a taquito. "Not the ShuttleDisc, the gold. I want the saucer," she clarified with her mouth full of leaf.

Finishing off her own food, May rolled up her leaf and tossed it in the fire, perturbed to find that this faux fire, though it did give off heat, had been intentionally designed to not burn anything at the request of the trees. The plate sat there unharmed, slowly unfurling in the dancing lights. "So we've got payment."

"Ma'am, if I might," the Ranger said, sitting forward in the nano-pod.

Everyone was silent; it wasn't like Xan to wait for permission to speak. The Ranger, in this respect, was not like Xan.

"Yes?" May nudged.

"I have a perfectly good rocket ship, and I've no need of it. Just drop me at the nearest habitable planet back in my universe, you can have the Silver, and I'll be on my way," said the Ranger.

"What will you do, though?" May asked

"Don't you worry about me, ma'am, I'll find my way. I could always go back to my old line of work."

"You were a sex worker, too?"

"Too?" The Ranger looked seriously at Xan, who only shrugged. "No, no, I've never done that, ma'am. I'm sure I wouldn't be too good at that. No, I used to train and herd ruffloo for pay. All I really need to do that is rope and an endless supply of treats," he said, hooking his thumbs into his belt.

"No, we can't let them get away with this," Aimz said. "I don't like the idea of another me faffing about out there. I can't share faffing privileges. There can only be one."

"Is that...is that like a rule of the universe, or are you just uncomfortable with there being two of you here?" Xan asked. "We're not in mortal danger if they don't leave, are we?"

"The gentleman at the PLOT hole was fairly clear on that," the Ranger said. "My visa to this universe is only good for two rotations. After that, he said there would be existential consequences."

"See!" said Aimz. "Existential consequences, I knew it. And they don't even have a visa!"

"So," May said. "If they're going to disappear anyway, we get the *Audacity* back when they do. As long as they don't crash it," May sat back in the nano-pod and pouted.

"Oh no, we're all in mortal danger," Aimz clarified. "Even the Ranger being here is a threat to Xan's existence. There's two other versions of him in this universe! That's gotta be tough. How you feeling, boha?" Aimz asked Xan, who was simply lounging, one arm slung around May's shoulders.

"Not amazing, but that's probably taubkin eggs," he said. "I'm feeling fine in an existential sense."

"Ugh, you're right. It's impossible to tell," Aimz said, lying back in the dirt with a hand on her stomach. "That's just bad science. Too many variables, zuut. We're going to have to try some perished foodstuffs after we kick those fakers out of our universe. What a waste of bad food."

"I could still bring you to them," the Ranger said.

"And how would we get in? They took our anchor buttons." May stared up at the glass bottom of the Tree Museum Lobby, which gently rocked high above them. Though it was night, several prignette sisters wandered the lobby floor, giving all the guests below a prime view of what was under their floor-length robes: tasteful, floor-length pants.

"We can hop out and break in through the manual access hatch! I'm pretty accomplished at breaking into things," Aimz said. "We won't need space suits, either. Immortality!" she said.

"Even if we did do that," Xan said, "And I don't want to do that because it sounds miserable, we would need propulsion! And opening the access hatch would suck the other versions of us out into space!"

"The alternative is murdering them by hand," Aimz said.

"Eugh," Xan groaned. He dropped his head back miserably, and a clump of nano-pod rose up to form a little pillow. "May, tell Aimz no, please."

"The EtherGalleon has matter-cannons," May said. "It

can beam us right into the ship, and we'll let the pirates take care of the alters."

"I can take them back to my universe," the Ranger said. "There's no Aimz and no May there; they'll be fine!"

"But there's a you there," May said.

"Well, I'll have to take that risk," said the Ranger. "I'll be sure to write back to you and let you know how it goes."

"How it goes is you'll die," Aimz told him. "And your alter will, too. Or...no, actually. Maybe the strongest survives. Maybe you combine?"

"Aimz, how much of what you say is shit you made up, and how much do you actually know?" May asked.

"I know everything I've made up," Aimz said. "Why?"

"Never mind. We're going to start with the pirates," May affirmed. "Maybe we can convince our alters to take themselves to a universe where they don't already exist. I don't know. We can wing it. First, I have to find out if I can convince the pirates to come at all. I haven't been as unstuck in space/time as I was."

"Can I help?" Xan asked.

"Maybe. I'm trying to go the EtherGalleon the Adventuresomeness. Take me there?"

"EtherGalleons...those were a really brief trend on Tuhnt. Horrible idea. They had wave simulators, right?"

"I think so," May said.

"Right, close your eyes!" Xan crawled out of the nano-pod and pushed into its side rhythmically to simulate the rocking of simulated waves. "Imagine you're on a boat--"

"It's a ship," she said.

"Imagine you're on a ship in the vast open space-sea."

"I think it's just space, Xan."

"Well, whatever it is, imagine you're there. The caws of ocean birds in the distance, caw-caw! Caw-caw!" he said.

"No ocean birds," May said, opening her eyes.

"Close your eyes!" he said. "The utter silence of open space." And then he was silent for a moment to demonstrate. "You're a fearsome pirate with no regard for anyone's needs but your own. Treasure's on your mind. You swirl a tankard of ale beneath your nose to waft the bouquet—"

"I don't think this is working." May tried to sit up, but as soon as she did, she was out.

THIRTY

FOREPLAY

* * * * *

It had been quite the battle. Agents of Clymasir lay strewn about the deck, each with an accompanying puddle of blood and some with attendant viscera. Finally, their assailants had been destroyed. Captain July smiled, bloody-faced, at Xanwell, who had fought bravely and only had a few minor flesh wounds to show for it.

"It seems we won," said Xanwell, leaning back against the banister and straightening his coat. "That was quite an adventure. Real high-budget stuff and a plot I, for one, never saw coming."

The captain nodded. "Aye, that it were," she agreed. "One thing never resolved though...who were those strange specters of ourselves what came to attack us? Then disappeared as if never they were?"

Xanwell scratched his ruddy beard, thinking. "Mayhaps our story's not yet at its end? But why oughtn't we celebrate anyway? Come to bed, love. If we are to be covered in bodily fluids, oughtn't that include each others?"

With a bellowing laugh, the captain agreed, grabbing

Xanwell's hand and pulling him down the stairs, down into the depths of her cabin where the air was so drenched with cannon smoke it gave the room a dream-like, eddying shimmer.

"Aye, but ye are a dirty dog!" said the captain, pushing Xanwell onto the bed.

"What be that, eh? A 'dog'?" Xanwell pushed her up by her shoulders, always curious about Earth phraseology.

"A scoundrel! A mutt! An insult, Xanwell. A right nasty one, at that." Captain July shut him up with a forceful kiss, pressing him into the crinkling, straw-filled mattress in her chambers. "Undress me, ye scallywag."

"Aye, Captain," he said, breathlessly peeling the blood-soaked coat from her shoulders, then rising up to lick a long line along her clavicle.

The saucy smile that had twisted her lips faded suddenly, replaced by a desperate confusion as her brain re-wired to its new dimensions. Captain July and her libido had gone nowhere, but now she was keenly aware of another presence within her. A presence that had not consented to this bedding.

Xanwell sensed her body stiffening under his tongue and paused, his tongue pressed against her as if she were a block of ice it had frozen to. "All's well?" he asked, though it sounded like "Ath wew?" because his tongue was otherwise occupied.

"I've sussed the meaning o' the doppelgängers," said Captain July, and then, "Sorry, I know this is weird, but could you uh...stop? That. I'm not myself right now."

Xanwell retracted his tongue. "Aye, an' ye sound off, I'll admit." He scooted up to get a better view of her, eyeing her face for signs of the space-sickness, but her dark skin hadn't gone transparent, and her eyes were still warm brown, not the tell-tale yellow/green. She didn't speak. "An' the meaning is?" Xanwell prompted her.

"Not sure," her face scrunched with effort. "Weird...brain...thing," her right eye winked a little too fast, her forehead ticked as if the internal struggles of her mind were playing ping-pong across her face.

"Let's get ye comfortable, eh?" He finished taking off her

coat and tried to help her lay down, but she grabbed his wrists.

"I've got it. I'm at the Tree Museum's campsite. It's cold, and I'm wet."

Xanwell's shoulders dropped; he was recalibrating. "Ah! Foreplay! That's it, mun. A lone and weary traveler bedding down at a hostel, eh?" His smile spread across his face like icing on a cake, and his eyes sparkled. "Got just the thing for that," he pulled away from her gentle hold and dug into a box under the bed, fishing out a length of rope, frayed at the ends. "I'll tie ye tight, ta keep ye from absconding in the night, an' then I'll warm yer body with my vigorous ministrations!"

"No!" Captain July hopped from the mattress, still shivering, unable to shake the chill. "Not foreplay. I need you to understand this: I am another version of myself from a different reality."

Xanwell, now thoroughly confused, dropped the ropes in his lap. "May..." he said, using his captain's first name because he sensed this was serious. "Think we ought to take port near a mind-healer, mun."

"My mind is fine! Please trust me on this. You're a pirate, for fuck's sake. You and I must've encountered weirder than this together. The Seam? Chaos goddess? All that happened in this reality, too, right?"

"The Seam? That ol' larvling tale? Why, that's fantasy, mun. We're space pirates. We're practical folk."

Captain July rubbed her forehead, re-thinking her plan. Xanwell not believing her was a mere annoyance. Not knowing how to get herself, much less an entire ship, to another reality was a problem. "I am your captain," she asserted, looking up. "And you will do as I say."

"Aye, captain," whispered Xanwell. "What be the plan?"

She sat on the edge of the straw mattress and tried to scrub her scalp, but found she couldn't on account of her locs. She rubbed her neck instead and, noticing this, Xanwell sat behind her and began to massage her shoulders for her.

"Shit, that feels good," she said. "I didn't know you could do that."

"I do it nigh on every rotation, captain."

"Maybe in this universe." She was warming up now, her consciousness fully acclimating to its new setting. Xanwell kept working on his captain's tense neck and shoulders, hoping maybe he'd work out a pinched nerve that was causing her strange behavior.

May stood and walked to the oval, patchy mirror hanging crookedly on the wooden panels that made up her chambers. She wasn't May. She was Captain July. She needed to start acting more like the captain in order to get the crew on board with her plan.

She fingered a dense loc, studying the various gold trinkets that had been woven into it. This one looked like a poorly rendered ch'stranda. Another, farther down, displayed some curling symbol she'd never seen. If she could access the pirate's mind without losing herself in it, she would know. But that was risky. The last time she was here, her own memories were lost. She resolved to hang on tightly to her identity.

She grabbed a feathered quill pen from her desk and, not finding anything to write on, wrote directly on the table. She drew a big circle, wrote 'PLOT hole. 89-Flummox5,' then she drew an arrow through it pointing to another circle, this one with some stick trees in it, labeled 'Tree Museum,' and then, below the Tree Museum, she drew an X. She was a pirate; she would know what the X stood for.

"Gather the crew," she told Xanwell. "This is a treasure map. Follow it. I probably won't remember drawing it in a moment, but you've got to convince me to follow it, alright?"

"Aye, Captain." Deflated in more ways than one, Xanwell stood and went to the sink, swiping up on the touchpad to start the flow of recycled water into the basin, washing the blood from his hands and face. If he was already clean by the time he got on deck, he'd have a perfect excuse for not helping the crew dispose of the bodies.

THIRTY-ONE

BEFRIENDING THE PREY

* * * * *

May slept peacefully as Xan climbed back into the nano-pod to watch her. It reminded him of their first few days together. She slept about twice as often as he did, and the time she spent asleep had made him nervous. He was nervous now as she contacted the pirates, and the rancid taubkin eggs trying to mutiny his digestive system weren't helping. Rolling over, he addressed Aimz, who was looking miserable on the ground.

"Why do I let you talk me into these things?" he asked her.

"Because you love me," Aimz said, eyes closed, with a goofy smile. "Gah," she said, wincing at the painful results of her science experiment. "Probably not the smartest decision, though. Carmnia has thousands of offspring. You really could've chosen a better sibling."

"That was on Kalumbits, not me," Xan said. "She picked you."

"About the last time anyone's ever done that." Aimz flipped onto her side, looking up at Xan. "You think Listay will forgive me?"

"For running off with Surg? Probably. She's a softie."

"Do you think she'd be right to forgive me?"

"I don't know. According to Plintharnius the Placid, right and wrong are just social constructs and don't really matter. She postulated that--" He stopped talking.

"Yes?" Aimz said.

"Oh. Weird. Usually, someone tells me to stop going on about ancient Tuhntian philosophers right about now. Anyway, she postulated that instead of asking whether we were right or wrong, we should be asking if we could be at peace with our decisions. So if Listay can be at peace with her decision to take you back, then she's right, according to Plintharnius. Now, the decision to eat those taubkin eggs was probably a wrong one because I cannot be at peace with that."

Aimz chuckled. "Ah, you'll burn it up eventually. It can't kill us, remember?"

"I'm not sure that's the comfort you seem to think it is."

"How did you lot become immortal?" asked the Ranger, startling Aimz and Xan, who had tried to forget he was still there.

As if it had been her fault entirely, Xan looked to Aimz to give the explanation. Slowly, she sat up. "No one knows for sure, but the prevailing theory is that when Xan and May summoned The Crack--"

"The Seam," Xan knew because he had been there.

"Whatever it's calling itself now. It banished Chaos from reality, and when she got unplugged, a bunch of universal synapses got short-circuited, and now everyone who knew Chaos is death-challenged. Surg said that most of the immortals were a result of The Seam seriously zuxing up the universe's base code. Seems like The Seam speaks the language of the universe, but not terribly fluently."

"Wait, just death-challenged?" Xan asked, sitting up. "So you're saying we can die now?"

"Failure to exist is always an option," Aimz continued. "There are worse things that could happen than failing to exist, though," she said seriously. "Don't sign any paperwork."

"So we've been told," Xan said. "Why not? Who wants us

to sign paperwork?"

"I don't know! I only know it's not good," Aimz said, shuddering. "I'm worried they got Listay."

"You're worried?!" Xan asked. If she was worried about something, it stood to reason that he ought to be, too. She never worried about anything.

"Surg accidentally signed away Crenaulto: Realm of the Gods, and it was seized faster than a ch'strandra on a mun," Aimz said. "You sign that paperwork, you sign your immortal life away."

"Paperwork?" May asked drowsily.

"Don't worry about it, starshine. Aimz was just explaining why everything's horrible and we can never relax ever," said Xan, readjusting himself in the nano-pod. "How were the pirates?"

Before she responded, May yawned and stretched. Tuhntians don't yawn because they receive most of their oxygen via their skin, but Xan had picked up the habit from May and yawned, too. "They're coming," May told them. And she was right in both senses of the word.

She was beginning to warm up and dry off now, and Xan seemed to be radiating heat. "You're really hot," she said, scooting closer to help her chase off the damp chill.

"Thanks, you too," said Xan.

"Heat-hot not, ugh." May shook her head at him. "That's an English double meaning, you know what I meant."

"I did," he said with a teasing grin. "Sorry, it's the taubkin eggs. Lots of horrible bacteria to burn off. Great idea, Aimz. Really excellent science."

"We've already established that I did science wrong," Aimz said.

"So how did you get the pirates to come?" he asked.

"I drew a treasure map. Once they get here, we need to tell them we know the location of the real treasure, but before we give it to them, we need to recover our ship," May said. This was answered by a buzzing sword at her throat.

"Aye, so we were summoned under false pretenses, is that it?" Captain July growled in May's ear.

"They don't have toothpaste in your universe, do they?"

May said, pulling away more from the rancid stench of the captain's breath than the sword.

Pirates surrounded them on all sides. Captain July's sword at May's throat, her first mate Xanwell held a whittling knife to Xan, Aimz was pinned under her even grimier pirate double and, it must be said, enjoying this a bit too much, and a one-eyed Listay held a laser gun to the Ranger's head.

"Start spilling yer guts afore I spill 'em for ye," said the captain. Though the camp was not deserted and several people saw they were all in imminent danger, no one did anything. They were so caught up in their own mystical journeys of enlightenment they forgot the cardinal rule of enlightenment: don't get caught up in anything.

Someone did approach them, though. A Pringnette sister strode up to Xanwell and held out her hand. "Whittling is strictly prohibited. It makes the trees uncomfortable," she said.

"Oh, uh, mighty sorry about that," said Xanwell with a nervous smile. He handed the knife over to the pringnette, and she walked away as he patted himself down in search of another tool of intimidation but couldn't find one. Xan raised his hands in surrender anyway.

"We're on a peaceful mission!" he said, hoping that was indeed true. "And I never realized we would look so handsome with a beard!" This aside was to Xanwell, whose mustache lifted in a pleased grin.

"We're quite charming clean-shaven, too, my friend!" Xanwell patted Xan on the shoulder.

"Oh, I don't shave. I had those genes switched off a long time ago. Might turn them back on now, though!" Xan said, rubbing his jawline and imagining the possibilities. The captain loudly re-sheathed her sword.

"Aye, and ye've gone and befriended our prey again. Out with it, then, for what have ye summoned my crew? And if that answer don't involve a reward, I'll make your limbs into garlands," she snarled.

"Could she do that, technically?" May asked Aimz.

"Technically, sure! Wouldn't kill us, but it would be nearly unbearable agony, I'd imagine," Aimz replied.

"There's a reward!" Xan said hastily, not keen on thinking about all the ways their immortal selves could be horrendously tortured. "If you help us collect our ship and send our doubles who stole it through the PLOT hole, you can have a saucerful of jewelry and gold!"

"But not the saucer itself," Aimz clarified.

"Right, minus the saucer. Plus all that gold, though!" Xan smiled tightly.

The captain, certain now that these doppelgängers were of no consequence, sat in the nano-pod she had coaxed May out of, leaning back as if it were a throne. Secretly, May wondered if she could ever be that cool and self-possessed.

"There's a wee problem there," said Captain July. "The PLOT hole suffered an unfortunate accident."

"Uh," Xanwell said. "What she means is the Adventuresomeness was a touch too large to fit through, according to the attendant, so we blew up the attendant and went through anyway. The Adventuresomeness is a wee bit smaller now, but she did fit! I'm afraid the PLOT hole didn't fare too well, though. It seems there was only one attendant. Destroying it in our universe destroyed it in every universe."

"So it will only go between our universe and yours now? How do we get our other duplicates out?" May asked.

"Two options!" Aimz piped up. "Either we destroy their DNA with fire or some nasty chemicals, or we get them to leave our universe using the tongue ring. So that's three options, I guess. Fire, chemicals, or the tongue rings."

"Let's aim for the tongue ring option, Aimz," Xan said.

"Aye," agreed the captain. "We'll cut their thieving tongues out!" She raised her sword, and her crew cheered. A few nearby campers glanced at the sudden noise but quickly re-focused on their arboreal contemplations.

THIRTY-TWO

SLAPPY HANDS

✳ ✳ ✳ ✳ ✳

The designers of the EtherGalleon The Adventuresomeness had no regard for the concept of circadian rhythm. There were no established daylight hours or UV lamps, so there was just one endless, candlelit night for the crew. And the crew were used to this. They knew about the store of supplemental vitamins and minerals in the cargo bay that, when delivered at just the right intervals, kept them from mimicking the sleep schedule of a heavily caffeinated bear in the dead of winter.

May, Xan, Aimz, and the Ranger had not been informed about the supplements, apart from a casual threat from the one-eyed Listay that if she saw them anywhere near the cargo bay doors, she'd make a necklace out of their teeth.

And this wouldn't have been a problem if the EtherGalleon had been even a quarter as fast as the *Audacity*. Warp technology in the pirate's universe was decades behind most others because so much time had been spent figuring out how to build a space-fairing wooden boat. Still, they were a great deal closer to inventing warp travel than any of the two-dimensional universes, which still struggled with differentiating 'up' and 'down.'

The Ranger, having had a busy day rescuing those in need, snored quietly on one of two dirty hammocks in the ship's hold. May, Xan, and Aimz, having had enough rest to last them a few months, were up and entertaining each other in the lamplight with various boredom-busting games May knew.

"It's the Trouflorian bhring pastry you overheated at that fuel station last season!" said Xan.

"Yes! Got it in two!" May confirmed another outstandingly quick 20 Questions win.

"You two are cheating," Aimz said. "Don't you know any games that don't rely on an intimate knowledge of each other's lives?"

May thought for a minute. "Give me your hands," she said, resting her hands atop his palm-to-palm. "Okay, now try to slap the backs of my hands," May said seriously.

He looked up at her through crunched eyebrows. "This is a game?" he asked.

She nodded. "Try it."

He tried, but she pulled her hands away long before he was able to slap them.

"Okay, try again—faster!" she said eagerly.

"Alright," he tried again, still too slow.

"You've got to catch me off guard!" she said.

"You're never off-guard," he whined, trying again.

"Ugh, you're not doing it right," Aimz said, shoving Xan out of the way and offering her hands to May as Xan resettled, leaning sideways on his elbow to watch them. Aimz held her hands steady. Steady. She locked eyes with May. Steady. She flinched, May tensed, but didn't pull her hands. Not yet.

"So the point is to not actually try to slap your opponent?" Xan asked, studying them.

"Well," May said, still watching Aimz. "Eventually, you have to break the tens—shit." Aimz had got her.

"I love that. I love this game, May," Aimz said, rolling with laughter. "Now do me!"

"We should play Bickowsker Bickbayer," Xan suggested.

"You'll short out your translation chip trying to play that across languages, you know," Aimz said.

Xan pulled a magnet from his pocket to scramble their translation chips, a simple hack ardent linguists had discovered for overcoming the universal translator implants. "It's more fun played with multiple languages! We used to do it all the time at university."

"Agh! My eyes!" they heard Bondoony wail from the lookout above deck.

"That's the *Audacity*!" May said, bouncing up and taking to the stairs. On deck, the one-eyed Listay was tending to Bondoony, who blubbered about the "blasted eye-scorching neon zuxers" and rubbed their eyes with their palms.

"What's this about?" Captain July demanded of anyone on deck who was brave enough to answer. Xanwell appeared behind her, getting dressed just as Xan appeared behind May.

"Bondoony found the ship we're after, Captain," said Listay. "Allegedly, it's nigh on as bright as a star. Blinded 'em."

"Is this a fact, Captain?" Captain July asked of May, who didn't realize she was capable of such ferocity.

"Aye," said May. "I mean...yes. It's bright. The trick is just not to look directly at it."

"That might make it a little hard to catch the beast, eh?" snarled the captain.

"We might use this to our advantage," said Xanwell, his hands bravely grabbing onto her shoulders. "You can't cloak a ship like that."

The captain's nose crinkled for a moment as she tried to rebutt him, but he was right. The *Audacity* stood out in the blackness of space like a ruby in a pile of gold. It would make an excellent addition to her fleet as a flashy distraction.

"Right. All hands to deck!" she called across the ship. "Prepare the energy-net! Xanwell, correct our course and full speed ahead!"

The deck boiled with movement as the crew scurried around May and Xan. The captain grabbed Xanwell by his coat lapels before he could run off and pulled him into a full twenty seconds of mouth-to-mouth recreation.

Xan and May watched, then Xan noticed May was watching, and May noticed that Xan had been watching, and they locked eyes. "Ugh, yeah, see?" May said. "This is the weird alternate reality I was telling you about in the shower."

"Right. About that shower we took together," he said. "Naked," he said. "You know, we'd never uh... In my lifetime, anyway, as far as I can recall, we didn't used to..." He froze, his jaw clenched tight against his will. May understood.

"Oh," she said. "We didn't used to shower together, did we? I must've remembered that from another reality. It felt natural. Damnit. How many of my memories aren't really my memories? And why are you so nervous?" she asked, her brow furrowing playfully. "Is it because you liked it?"

"Did you like it?"

She chuckled. "It was just a shower. Don't worry about it, blue. You can like it if you want to."

"Oh, good. Okay," he said.

The captain at last pushed Xanwell away with a sound like a suction cup unsticking.

"Ugh," said the captain to May and Xan. "That mushy talking about your feelings stuff makes me sick." She mimed gagging, then wiped the spit off her mouth with the back of her hand. "You either kiss or you don't. None of that measly hemming and hawing shit."

"Sorry, Captain," said Xan.

"Gather your crew, mate," the captain said, slinging her arm around May's shoulders. May could feel the warm dampness of her alter's sweat seeping into her suit and shuddered. Not only was the captain's face uncannily familiar, her body odor was the same, too. "Have them on deck in two beoops, armed and ready to board."

"My crew?" May had not thought of anyone as her crew. Ever. That implied some responsibility for them, and she was barely responsible for herself. "I thought you were going to take care of the doppelgängers."

The captain squinted at May. "If I'm risking my own crew to take the helm of your ship, it won't be your ship anymore. You understand me?"

May nodded. "We don't have weapons, though. We need something!"

"Not necessarily!" Xan offered. "We have a convincing argument. If they stay in this universe, we're all doomed, and they can't kill us, so logically, they would be better off finding another universe. I can talk them into leaving, I'm sure of it. And, just in case, we can bring along the Ranger. He seems like he knows what he's doing with that ray gun!"

"We'll bring Aimz, too. Aimz without a weapon is scarier than you with one," May told him.

"I shall take that as a compliment," said Xan.

"Alright, load them into the matter-cannons!" shouted the captain, seemingly to no one in particular, but two unnamed pirates appeared as if by magic beside them to do just that.

THIRTY-THREE

DON'T TOUCH YOURSELF

* * * * *

May, Xan, Aimz, and the Ranger's atoms hurtled across space, squeaked in between the atoms that made up the side of the *Audacity*'s hull, and, slightly disoriented, gathered themselves together again inside the ship. The telediscs in May's own universe were unpleasant, sure, but the matter-cannons far outpaced unpleasant. They were firmly in the territory of cruel and unusual.

None of the four were prepared for it. The whole lot crumpled to the shag carpet, momentarily catatonic with the pain of every nerve re-knitting itself—hopefully all in their proper places. There wasn't a lot of guarantee with the atom-cannons, as they relied on the body's natural desire to return to its previous state. If your body has no desire to return to its previous state for one reason or another, convincing it to do so can be quite tricky.

Aimz was the first up, a "borrowed" pirate machete raised. "Alright, let's make this easy!" she said to the wall because the rods and cones in her eyes hadn't quite settled in just yet. "You leave this universe, and we won't slice you to bits and pour caustic chemicals all over your mangled bodies."

"Blitheon, Aimz," Xan said, standing slowly. "Maybe you went too dark?"

The Ranger, once he had gotten his feet under himself, unclipped the rope from his belt, prepared to lasso anyone who needed a good lassoing. He was too late, though.

Mazelmez rushed Xan, a small pocket knife in her hand. She plunged it into his neck. "Oops," he said, pressing a hand into the wound and feeling it close up eerily fast. "You uh...didn't intend to do that, right? I'm afraid that won't work on us." Fortunately, he neglected to mention that it would work very well on the Ranger. "Can we talk? Or, failing that, could you just...leave, please?"

"Nowhere for us to go to," Mazelmez said, stepping back cautiously, licking the blood off the pocket knife to confirm that it was real. It was. She squinted at him.

"How did you escape?" asked otherMay, standing protectively in front of the control panel.

OtherXan hopped down to greet them. "Oh, wow, you made it! Good for you. See, May, I told you they weren't dead." OtherXan pat Xan on the back and then immediately regretted it.

As soon as he touched himself, something terrible happened, exonerating in one fell swoop every Catholic nun who ever warned us about the existential danger of such an act.

The price was not eternal damnation, however. What happened was this: The two Xans suddenly, with a sound like the universe breaking a bone and a flash of hot white light, merged into one.

All was silent, even Aimz and Mazelmez, as this new being went through the stages of coming to terms with his existence. Fortunately, since both Xans had already spent some time coming to terms with their own existences, this didn't take as long as one might expect.

"That was interesting," he said, studying his own hands. They looked like they always had. Part of him didn't remember that scar on his thumb, but the other part knew he had gotten it during the horrible crash that destroyed the *Ostentatious*.

"Which one are you?" both Mays asked simultaneously. They eyed each other warily in case either of them was about to consume the other.

"So..." Xan said as if preparing to launch into a long explanation of who, exactly, he was and how he could prove it. "Both," he said after some time. He shrugged.

"How are you both?" asked otherMay. "You can't be two people!"

"Only one way to check!" said Mazelmez, taking the ring out of her pocket, the slip of paper that explained the meaning of the various colors falling out onto the floor. She grabbed his hand and forced the ring onto his finger.

"Black," she confirmed. "No soul. He's not our Xan," she said to otherMay.

"Unpin it, Aimz. I am too your Xan! Look." He twisted the ring off and slipped it onto her finger, also black. "If I'm not real, you aren't, either."

May grabbed the instructions that had fallen out of Mazelmez's pocket. "That's a mood ring. It doesn't mean anything! It just reacts to temperature."

The composite Xan blinked at Mazelmez. "Is this so?" he asked.

"It did feel colder in this universe," Mazelmez mused.

Aimz piped up now. "Alright! So we know what happens if we overstay our welcome in another person's universe. Not too bad, honestly. So what do you say? Merge or leave?" she asked her alter.

"This is too much," muttered otherMay. She grabbed Xan's wrist and flicked the tongue ring, whisking the two of them away to another reality.

THIRTY-FOUR

THERE ARE SCARY CLOWNS IN THIS ONE, SORRY

✳ ✳ ✳ ✳ ✳

Though this information may unsettle you, it's important to know before we get into this next chapter. In an infinite multiverse where every possible combination of every possible thing (and several impossible things) exists, there is a universe in which you are best friends with a circus clown. There is, furthermore, a universe where you ARE a circus clown.

Xan, who was now double the amount of Xan he had been before, was suddenly faced with both of these troubling realities. The forcefully cheerful tones of a calliope banged on his eardrums, the smell of popcorn and large, musty animals followed quickly behind, and finally, he braved opening his eyes to find a crowded, smoke-filled backstage area full of half-dressed performers pinning on wigs, powdering their faces, and smoking cigarettes like their lives depended on them. Nearest to him, just next to the May who had taken him there, the angriest looking clown he'd ever seen, and he'd seen more than his share of angry clowns in his lifetimes.

"Xan, why the hell aren't you dressed? We're due at the miniature race in five minutes!" she shouted, smoke billowing out of her mouth in cartoonish pink ringlets, a variety of alarmingly colorful shapes decorating her face. Behind her, out of the smokey air, appeared another Xan, his face painted with equally alarming colorful shapes.

"I am dressed," he said, and the clown May turned around with a start. "That's not me."

"Fuck no," said the May who had brought them there and promptly took them away.

The next universe was worse, though, far worse. The DNA in the tongue ring was beginning to deteriorate. Important information about what a May should be had become lost, and some of that important information related to the type of symmetry a May ought to express.

Classic May, like most humanoids, was composed under the careful guidance of bilateral symmetry. With that important distinction missing, the tongue ring was free to bring May and Xan to a universe where radial symmetry was preferred in humanoids.

The radial May was moving quite fast, fortunately, cartwheeling away from them towards a radial Xan who cheered with at least twenty pom-poms. They quickly moved on.

The DNA had decayed further, though; this time, bilateral symmetry was in, but flesh was out, replaced instead with a clear film and a thick layer of mesoglea, revealing every aspect of their internal anatomy. May paused here, stunned, as she watched her own heart beat beneath her own ribcage. The clear Xan was nearby, as he had been in every universe, and she studied his unusual alien organs, her mouth hung open. Xan, the fleshy Xan, poked a finger into her mouth and flicked the tongue ring again, feeling a little too exposed.

A black whiteness surrounded them, as if the light of the universe had a short circuit. It wasn't gray, it was both black and white. Empty and full of light. They didn't appear to be standing on anything. There was no oxygen, but there also wasn't a sucking vacuum.

"Where are we now?" Xan tried to ask, but no sound could travel. May heard him anyway.

"I don't know," she failed to say.

There was one thing in the no-thing-ness. A helpful sign.

'Universe Out of Order' said the sign, which was either white with black print or black with white print and seemed to float exactly in the center of one's vision.

"Seems like an understatement," said Xan without a word.

"Arg, this is pointless!" May shouted into the present void. She crumbled to the down (for there existed no floor or ground) and hugged her knees. "I should've been erased along with my universe," she said.

Xan crouched beside her, catching glimpses of her in the light and instantaneously losing sight of her completely in the dark as he struggled to maintain persistence of vision. He put his arm around her. "Well, I should've died on Tuhnt, but I didn't," he said. "And for almost two hundred orbits, I thought that was a mistake. Until I met you. If I had died on Tuhnt, you wouldn't have made it off the Peacemaker, and if you hadn't done that--"

"Chaos might've eaten the universe," said May. She looked around again, the out-of-order sign following the center of her vision. "Maybe she did in this reality."

"And yet, here we are," said Xan. "Being."

May nodded. "Being..." she repeated quietly, leaning against him as they settled into a more comfortable nothing. "Are you really my Xan?"

He took a long time to think before answering that because, honestly, the question didn't make sense to him. "Yes...and no," he said. "You're my May, though. Both of you are. Actually, I think all of you are."

"Even clown May?!" asked May.

"Unfortunately, yes," said Xan with a laugh. "Don't you think it's strange that in every one of these universes, it's been the two of us together? Does that mean something?" he asked. "Aren't there versions of reality where we never met, I mean?"

"Must be," said May.

"Then why haven't we come across any of them?"

"I don't know," she said. And they went silent for a while, contemplating.

"If we can find a way back to your universe, I want to merge with the other me. If she'll let me," said May, at last. "I want to touch myself."

"Well, don't let me stop you!" said Xan, and they laughed together.

"Aha! Gotcha," said a voice from the beyond. A voice that sounded an awful lot like May.

"May?" said otherMay. "I'm ready to cooperate. Just get me out of here."

THIRTY-FIVE

PIRATES DOING PIRATE STUFF

* * * * *

"This is too much," otherMay had said before whisking Xan to a clown universe.

But nothing is ever too much. There is always more that can be piled atop.

In this case, the more came in the form of a piratical sneak attack. The pirates were a great deal more used to the matter-cannon, and they came in shooting.

"Mazelmez, take the helm!" shouted Captain July. "Xanwell, Wigglit, Listay, and Bondoony, secure the crew and lock 'em in the brig. I want this ship tethered to the Adventuresomeness and under our command with no fuss."

Still trying to comprehend what had just happened to Xan and where he and her alter had gone, May stood as if she were glued to the spot as the pirates descended upon them. Even if she had had the mental capacity to make a fuss at this point, she had brought no weaponry on board. This was the final straw, she thought as she watched the pirates descend on her wholly unprepared allies, the next opportunity she had to buy, make, or steal a flashy sci-fi weapon, she was going to do it. Xan wasn't around to tell her not to anymore.

Another flash of light blinded everyone, rousing May from her wide-eyed stupor.

"Mark me! What in Galtrooda's lacy undergarments was that?" asked Captain July, blinking to regain her vision, both pistols held aloft and ready to shoot at whatever was to blame.

Aimz was on the floor, at the epicenter of the flash of light, cackling gleefully. Just one Aimz, where before, there had been two. "Blitheon's stars," she choked. "That packs quite the punch, doesn't it?" No one else knew. No one else there had ever merged with an exact DNA duplicate of themselves before. "Whew!" she said as Xanwell continued tying her up.

"Search me, Captain," said Wigglit, who now no longer had a prisoner to tie up. "We was just lashing these two duplicates together when they turned into one!"

The Captain scratched her chin thoughtfully with the end of her pistol. "Turned into one, eh?" she eyed May as if worried she might take a running leap at her and suddenly merge bodies. "Be this a trick of light? Or actual fact?" she asked May, who was in no position to take a running leap at the captain on account of Bondoony tying up her legs.

"I guess," she said bitterly.

"And you." The captain gestured at Aimz with her pistol. "Are you more now than you were before?"

Aimz looked up into the corner of her vision as if searching her brain for new information. "I'd say so, yeah. I invented interdimensional personal travel! And I got a girlfriend. Then I lost that girlfriend. Why did we lose her?! Because we're not good at maintaining stable relationships, you know that," said Aimz, mostly to herself. "Maybe you're not, but zuut, if I had found someone as amazing as Listay, I would've--" Aimz stopped talking to herself because when she mentioned Listay, the one-eyed Listay looked up from her work tying down the Ranger and glared at her.

The captain knelt beside Aimz, pressing her pistol into

the soft space under Aimz's chin. She found she got better answers out of people when they feared for their lives. "Which one of you's in charge, eh?"

May perked up a little, hanging her attention on Aimz's answer. Aimz only shrugged. "Both, I guess."

"One of you must've been stronger, eh? Took over the other?" snarled the captain. May did not like where this was going. It was going towards the captain absorbing her. As long as she could be certain she was the stronger of the two personalities. May would like to see her try. No, actually. She wouldn't. She wasn't feeling terribly strong right now despite being immortal.

"There's not two of us, so lay off!" Aimz said. "I've got a few new memories now, that's all. I can't tell which memories are the new ones and which are the ones I've always had."

The captain scowled. Clearly, Aimz's answers had not been satisfactory to her.

"Right. Mazelmez, guard the rocket. The rest of you, put the prisoners in the brig until I decide what to do with them. And don't touch yourselves," she warned. "Not until we know how this one will turn out." She shoved the pistol into Aimz's jaw, making her cock her head awkwardly to the side, and then reversed the matter-cannons, plunging May, Aimz, and the Ranger into the brig of the Adventuresomeness where the crew made quick work of tying them up while they reeled from the horrific pain of the matter-cannons.

"May, what's the plan?" asked the Ranger, his arms tied to a metal pipe in the middle of the brig.

"I, for one, am going to join the crew!" said Aimz. "Did you see their Listay? She's perfect. And I haven't ruined anything with her yet! Fresh start! New me, new Listay. I love it. I love this plan."

"I asked May," said the Ranger. He had asked May because he figured whatever plan she had might involve somehow getting that tongue ring back from the May who had taken it and then him returning to his universe before he overstayed his welcome.

May was silent, her eyes closed. She was tied to herself

only, her legs folded up to her chest and her arms clasped behind her.

"May?" he tried again. "The plan?"

"You could always merge with their Xan. You could have a beard!" Aimz suggested.

"Both of you shut up," May snarled. "I'm trying to find...the other me. And Xan." She had been trying to accomplish this by shutting her eyes tightly and concentrating on the rage she felt for otherMay. The May who couldn't just accept her fate and disappear along with her reality. The one who had stolen her ship and her Xan.

But instead, her mind kept drifting to thoughts of the captain. What if the captain decided they should merge? She wouldn't be able to stop her, tied up as she was. And then who would she be? Would it not matter that her Xan was gone because the captain had Xanwell? Would she then have both the *Audacity* and the Adventuresomeness to command? Would it really be all that bad?

Maybe not.

She held her aching head with a pitiful groan. "I can't concentrate. This is pointless. I'm going to let the Captain absorb me." May had been sitting up against the brig wall, but she clumsily toppled herself over, thumping sadly against the wooden floorboards so that she would look exactly as miserable as she felt.

The silence following her declaration of defeat was punctuated with the manufactured sounds of squeaking planks, a faint whoosh of faux waves, and the rustling of Aimz fiddling with her restraints.

At last, the Ranger decided it was high time somebody said something. "You might look like my May, but you certainly don't have her spirit."

"Nope," said May, muffled, her face smooshed into the floorboard.

That wasn't the response he had been fishing for. Perhaps he could rile her up with another jab. "Maybe it is best if you merge with the captain; at least she has gumption," he said.

"Good point," she replied with all the conviction of an

asteroid bumping off a shuttle.

"Oh! I see where this is going," Aimz said, excited. "And you've made a glaring error, oh anachronistic one." Aimz winked at the Ranger. "Your Xan must've been an utter tchaag if you're giving him up this easily," she goaded May. "I mean, he's half of half of my brother, and if the other half is anything like the first half, I can see why you're so eager to try out a new model. And hey, this version of him is a pirate! That's got to be a trade-up from that 'I Love Lucy' obsessed precious butler you had. Probably, he even knows how to use a few weapons--"

"I get it, Aimz," May shouted. "Who the hell taught you reverse psychology? You're both awful at it."

"Aunt Kalumbits," said the Ranger and Aimz together.

"I tried to contact the other me, but I keep getting lost. I just can't focus. I don't know where she is. I don't know anything about her. I can't find her," May said, grunting as she rolled onto her side.

"Then focus on me instead," she heard.

"Ranger?"

"Yes, ma'am?" he replied with that transatlantic twang he'd picked up from watching far too much 'Lone Ranger.'

"I think I'm going crazy from all this reality hopping," she muttered. "Fine, I'll try it!" she shouted to the voice in her head. This is a beginner's mistake when one is going crazy. The key is to always respond to the voices inside your head with your inside-voice.

She shut her eyes again, and this time she sought Xan. Her particular Xan. She remembered his voice, different from the Ranger's, different from any otherXan she had encountered. She couldn't say how, exactly, but she could focus down on it. She'd certainly heard plenty of it over the years.

That's when she finally caught a glimpse. A smoky, velvet-hung dressing room, a cartwheeling conglomeration of limbs, a gelatinous clear finger that showed right through to the nerves and bone, then nothing. But she could hear something. They were there, alright. She mentally whirled around and found that she was very near to herself and Xan, indeed, though they didn't recognize her.

"Aha!" she shouted, both internally and externally. Fortunately, Aimz and the Ranger were getting used to her strange outbursts now. "Gotcha."

"May?" said otherMay. "I'm ready to cooperate. Just get me out of here."

"1 would love to do that, trust me," said May. "But I don't know how. I don't even know how I'm here! Where is this?" She tried to look around, but she had no form. The sounds she had been making at them only existed in their heads. It was all terribly disconcerting.

"Who on Patnu's knuckle is doing that?" shouted a form that appeared slowly from the void, coming together like magnetic sand pulled into place by a strong magnet. The form looked a great deal like Bezelbum because it was Bezelbum.

THIRTY-SIX
A FULL VOID

* * * * *

Bezelbum, the wrinkled old shopkeep, stood now in place of the Out of Order sign. Beside her, two other forms came into being, both Andolonian, with oil-slick skin and gnarled, curling horns, both twice as tall, both as old as anyone might reasonably look. They liked to look old. They found it helped to give them the illusion of authority.

"They've been mucking around in multiversality," said the one to Beezelbum's left. The one with unmentionable eyes. This one's name was Bretsy, but you, dear reader, will know her as Chaos.

"Oh no," said the one to her right. This one had mentionable eyes but an unmentionable name. Most people just called it The Seam, though there are many variations thereupon.

"You did this, didn't you?" Bretsy accused The Seam.

"I wouldn't have had to if you'd been more patient!" said The Seam. "Besides, I never gave them multiversality. I might've forgotten to plug them back into the recycling system. It happens."

"Happens too much, dearie, if you're asking me,"

muttered Bezelbum.

"If you didn't do this, how did it happen?" asked Bretsy.

"It's a long story," said May, who was still incorporeal and starting to get very annoyed by that. Her nose itched. She didn't have a nose nor a finger to scratch it with, but it itched anyway, and it really sucked. "Can you get us back?"

"We are not an interuniversal taxi service!" said The Seam, crossing its arms and looking down at them haughtily. "We shut that down eons ago. Too much trouble. You small-minds can't handle multiversality. You can barely handle one universe! You're just going to have to accept being here," it said.

"But this is nowhere!" shouted the corporeal May.

Xan stepped forward, hoping his diplomatic skills might work on these beings. It wouldn't, of course. Nothing works on them. They are the ones who work on things.

Before he could try, something caught Bretsy's unmentionable attention. "These forms are familiar to me," she said, holding a hand out. "Yes! Yes, they're my greatest devotees!" said Bretsy. "In several million universes, these two beings are absolutely obsessed with me."

"Excuse me," Xan said politely.

"Oh, yes," said The Seam to Bretsy, ignoring Xan completely. "They dragged me into one of their little games. That did happen this round, didn't it?"

"It's happened every round! It's just the same round, and you keep forgetting how to change things," said Bezelbum, her long, dry fingers flapping at the two flanking her. "You've gotten lazy, both of you!"

"May I speak?" Xan said, again politely.

"We've gotten lazy?" asked Bretsy, offended. "In how many iterations were you just puttering around that old junk shop? A shop! You're a being with infinite understanding, and you putter around a little dusty shop!"

"Ah, there's a good reason for that," said Bezelbum. "In the one universe where I'm not puttering around that dusty old shop, someone got their mitts on the invilitex!

That's the only explanation for what's happened here."

"So you've been using your infinite existence to guard a hunk of invilitex," said Bretsy. "How could you be so boring?"

"Enough!" said Xan, who had gotten quite tired of the bickering god-beings. He wasn't sure which part of him had gotten up the gall to do that, but the other part of him regretted it immediately as the six all-seeing eyes turned on him. "Enough," he said again, quieter, just to give him a little more time to think. "You don't want us in your void, do you?" he asked Bretsy.

"If you're in it, it's no longer a void," she agreed angrily.

"But you can't put us back where we belong?" he clarified.

Bretsy wiggled her shoulders, unwilling to answer.

"She can't," said Bezelbum. "Too scattered," she said, then demonstrated by appearing everywhere at once for a moment. "This is why I sit at the shop, you nitwit!"

"You can send us back," confirmed Xan to Bezelbum. "So what do you want in return?"

"Nothing," said the old lady. "Except...oh..." she wiggled her old little head. "Ten crystals?"

"Money?!" asked The Seam. "Why are you asking for money?"

"It's a fair exchange!" said Bezelbum defensively.

"Bezel, sending them back to their universe is worth a lot more than ten crystals! I'd say ask how much they're willing to pay. You could probably get their whole account," said Bretsy.

"Tsk! I don't NEED their whole account! I need ten crystals. That will do," she crossed her stick-like arms over her ample chest. "Ten crystals," she repeated. "Ten crystals to put you back where you were."

"Done!" said Xan.

A blue light flashed over his face, and a disembodied voice said, "Approved: Ten Crystals to Bezelbum's Baubles."

"Now you two," said Bezelbum, gesturing to May and somewhere near May. "The two who call yourselves May June July. Didn't EkoDoDo teach you anything, huh?"

"Huh?" asked the corporeal May, who had not met EkoDoDo and thus had learned nothing. The non-corporeal May HAD met EkoDodD and still wasn't sure she had learned anything.

"Make thine eye single!" said Bezelbum. "You're all scattered. Must take after Bretsy here. Bretsy, you're a scattered mess of a being, you know?" Bezelbum scolded her.

"I know," she agreed with a sigh.

Only Bezelbum could get Chaos to agree that she could be too chaotic at times.

"She wants us to merge, I think," said the non-corporeal May, her awareness now perched on her alter's shoulder. "You going to let me in?"

May looked at Xan, who was both her Xan and not her Xan, and decided it would be better if she was both her and not her. That way, they could be all four together. "Alright," said May, and then the two were one.

"That's it, dearie!" said Bezelbum, and then they were back in the brig.

THIRTY-SEVEN

OUR FAVORITE SHAWL

* * * * *

"We're back where we belong!" Xan said cheerfully. He then looked around. They were in the brig of the Adventuresomeness, and everyone but him was tied up. "Zeenz, maybe that's not a good thing. Alright, let's get you all untied, at least." He started untying May first. "Do you still have the laser sword?" he asked her quietly.

"What laser sword?"

"The one you got at the Tree Museum gift shop! We're going to need some kind of—"

"Xan, neither of us Mays went to the Tree Museum gift shop. We didn't even know there was one—you're not our Xan."

"Of course I am!" he said, his brow furrowing. "Who else would I be?"

"No," May closed her eyes tight. "This is too weird. I need to know where I am!"

"We're right here," she heard herself say.

"Where is here?!" And she found now that she couldn't open her eyes at all, the pressure was too great. All around her, it was nothing but pressure. She couldn't move, couldn't breathe. She was underground. Buried alive.

"EkoDoDo?!" she thought as loud as she could think. She wasn't sure if it was a plea for help or a cry of rage. "What's going on?" she asked. "Was any of that real?"

"It was all real," said EkoDoDo, in May's own voice, but older, deeper, crackling with time. Again, May found herself on the shore of the same beach, littered with rotting driftwood and massive metal sculptures.

She found her elderly self sitting on one of the dead trees, whittling threateningly. The wood shavings fell to the sand below and were washed away by the regular incoming waves. She found herself patting the branch next to herself where she joined herself. Sitting quietly. Pretending to breathe.

"What was all that for?" May asked. "What was the point?"

"Now you're asking better questions, at least. Here," and EkoDoDo handed the little chunk of wood she'd been working on over to May. May turned it in her hand. It was a tiny model of the *Audacity*.

"So what, you're saying the point of all that was the *Audacity*? A stupid ship? I don't care what happens to that ship!" she said, and as if to prove this, she tossed the wooden model out into the ocean, where it made a gentle plop. "I just want to know who I am again."

"Do you know who you are without it?" asked EkoDoDo.

May looked out over the water for some time, pondering. She knew who she had been before the *Audacity*, but having it had changed her. What would she be without it, now? The little wooden figure was back now; the waves had returned it to her. She looked down at the sad little lump of drenched wood.

"How long was I underground?"

EkoDoDo paused so that May would look up and see her own elderly eyes twinkling at her. "About the same length you are usually. Give or take a bit."

It was one of the very first things Xan had said to her, way back in book one. May shut her eyes tight, leaned into EkoDoDo's arms, and sobbed.

EkoDoDo said nothing, but the sounds of the beach kept her grounded in this particular reality while she processed what, exactly, had happened and what she had to do next.

That kind of thing can take time.

But once you know, you know. And May knew. She just needed one more piece of the puzzle, but there was nothing she could do to make it come any faster. There is nothing one can do to hurry along one's fate, for better or for worse.

General Listay, the knight to her damsel in distress, was digging as fast as she could.

The weight on May's body began to lift, and she quieted, wiping her face on EkoDoDo's shawl. She rubbed the shawl between her fingers, studying it. It was very old, thinned and faded by time, but she recognized the faint Murder Rail logo embedded in the greyed fabric.

"I thought we hated shawls," May said to her with a quiet laugh.

EkoDoDo smiled. "Why define yourself by what you hate? There's always one of us that proves an exception to any rule...and the exception to that rule is—"

The beach was gone. In its place was Xan pulling her into a filthy, damp hug.

"Blitheon's beard, I missed you," he said, and May knew it was real this time. This was her Xan.

"It's alright, I'm here," she said. "I need some shermel and a fish."

"A fish?" Xan asked, suddenly fearful that she was asking for the Big Mouth Billy Bass they had abandoned long ago due to its evilness. "What do you need a fish for?"

"It's for the tree. Nutrients," she said groggily.

"Come on, there'll be plenty of time for that once we're all cleaned up and fed," said Listay, helping May peel herself from the mud.

"How did you find us?" May asked.

"I put more than one tracker in Aimz," said Listay, ashamed.

They climbed a telescoping ladder out of May's former grave. On the forest floor, May was met by a gaggle of muttering prignettes and Rheans, some in white floor-length robes which were suspiciously unsoiled and others caked in mud up to their elbows, all illuminated by two massive floating orbs which May had thought at first were flood lights.

THIRTY-EIGHT

THE TIMELESS SELF

* * * * *

May, Xan, and Aimz were hosed off and escorted, dripping, into the back of an unfurnished crew transporter which glided over the knobbiest of raised tree roots with ease, ferrying them back to civilization as the three dripped steadily onto the metal floor.

"O'Zeno's glitter-encrusted liver, that was terrible," said Xan as soon as the transporter's double doors had shut them away out of sight of the trees who might take offense. "How long were we down there?!"

"About the same length we are now," May said, giving him a wry smile. She sat next to him on one side of the transport; Aimz had taken the opposite bench all to herself.

"Zuut, it's good to hear your voice," he said, wrapping her in another very wet hug.

"Half a season," said Aimz, who had curled her knees up to her chest and was pensively drip-drying.

"It felt like a half an orbit!" said Xan. "I've never been so bored. Never in my entire life. I had a lot of time to think down there. Too much, probably."

"Did you talk to any of the trees?" May asked, wondering if, in this version of reality, he still had nigh-unlimited knowledge of bathroom stall graffiti. Hoping he didn't.

"That was an option?" Xan asked, bereft. "Did you?!"

"I...think I spoke with EkoDoDo," now that she was saying it out loud, she wondered if that had just been another machination of her time-and-space-addled brain. "And then I got the Ranger to dig us up, and we convinced the pirates to help us take back the *Audacity* and—"

"Sorry, hold on, who's the Ranger?" Xan asked. "And the pirates?"

"The Ranger's a version of you who watched The Lone Ranger instead of I Love Lucy, and the pirates are...us but pirates, I guess," May said. She had the uncomfortable feeling that she'd just woken up in a sepia-toned farmhouse bedroom surrounded by goofy farmhands who had appeared in her fantastical hallucination. "Anyway, the pirates turned on us because they were pirates, so of course they did, and things generally went to shit in that reality. So let's not do that in this one," she said. "I guess I can just...let it go."

"The *Audacity*?" Xan asked. "Last time we didn't have it, you careened nose-first into a bubbling mud pit of depression," he reminded her.

"Yeah, well, I'm old now," she said.

"You said you were thirty-two orbits! You said that wasn't old in Earth-time!"

"She met her timeless self," said Aimz, as if that would be enough explanation.

"Go on," May said.

Unfurling with a wet slopping sound, Aimz leaned in closer to them. "That wasn't EkoDoDo. That was you. You just wanted to believe it was one of the trees, so you didn't have to take responsibility for whatever it said."

"How do you know?" May asked.

"I met my timeless self, too," said Aimz, looking up at the ceiling as if she could see right through it. "She was the baddest tchaag I've ever encountered."

"And what did you learn?" Xan probed.

Aimz gazed off into the corner, her eyes welling up, her teeth clenched, and Xan thought maybe, finally, she might have had some sort of revelation regarding how her lifestyle choices might be hurting the people she cared about. "Nothing." She shrugged and leaned back against the transporter wall.

"You know, your consistency is actually comforting right now. Good for you," Xan said. "So," he turned to May. "Just to be totally and utterly abundantly clear, you don't want to go looking for the *Audacity*?"

"You sound like you want to," May said, smiling. "You must've been really bored if you're up for death-defying rocket races again."

"I'm up for anything! As long as it isn't dark enclosed spaces," he said, looking around at the dark, enclosed transporter and wishing it had windows. "Zuut, there's so much out there to see, and we've got all the time in the universe to do it! We should hike the searing-hot crystal canyons of Fuggelhorm, explore the verdant caves under the acid lakes of Pertipolis, zuut, May, we could camp out in the wastelands on Tuhnt and weet-watch! Weets only affect dead things; they can't touch us!" said Xan with the same face-eatingly huge grin he usually reserved for activities like getting ice cream or watching a movie on the couch.

"You met your timeless self, too, then?" May asked.

"Oh. Zuut, maybe I did! You know what I learned?"

"Please don't tell us," Aimz said.

"Tell us," May countered.

"I learned that whatever we do, there's no point rushing through it. If you want to race, you're going to race until you can do it with your puherson pores closed."

"I don't think I have those," she said.

"Well, we've got plenty of time for you to get some installed! The tip of it is that we're doomed, or maybe destined, to experience every single possible iteration of existence. Right? That's infinity, isn't it?" he asked Aimz since she generally knew about these sorts of things.

"Eh," she wobbled her head. "In a way."

"So we get to do everything until we're so utterly,

thoroughly, brain-meltingly bored of it that we never need to do it again!" he finished triumphantly.

May laughed. "Maybe I don't feel like I need to be the fastest thing in the universe. Maybe I want to try taking it easy," said May.

"There will be no taking it easy, I'm afraid," said Listay as she opened the double doors to the transporter, releasing the wet trio on the world again. "You three get cleaned up and meet me in the cafeteria."

Aimz pouted. "We're in trouble," she said. Xan and May both silently assumed that she had meant to say "I'm" instead of "We're", and both were wrong.

THIRTY-NINE

THE ORGANIZATION AGAINST ORDER

* * * * *

May and her filthy cohorts were escorted by Tree Museum security to a luxury spa where they were given use of the showers, fluffy green bath robes, which they were assured were for sale at the right price, and their clothes taken to be laundered (several times, in the end, to get them reasonably clean).

Listay awaited them in the cafeteria, which wasn't so much a cafeteria as it was a grouping of benches and tables spread out under a canopy of trees genetically altered to provide single-fruit meals.

She was testing a round, purple, shiny palm-sized meal when May finally joined her, be-robed and scrubbed clean.

"Try this one," said Listay, pushing a basket full of yellow tube-like meals toward her. "These are the least heinously artificial tasting I've found so far." She then took a small bite out of the purple orb, which tore like meat, and ate it with a look of thoughtful horror.

Despite having been underground for three weeks, she wasn't hungry. She wasn't sure she'd ever eat again after that. "Catch me up," she said, sitting on the barstool across from her and taking one of the yellow tubes to study it. "What happened after Aimz—er we left you?"

"A great deal has happened. But first, the *Audacity* isn't in the parking bay. Do you know what happened to it? How did you get here?"

May sighed, peeling back the thin, leathery exterior of the tube to reveal a surprisingly banana-like fleshy interior. "Another version of myself stole it. I don't want to get into it. There's nothing I can do about it."

"Really?" Listay asked, taking a note down quickly on a little holoscreen that floated from her wrist. May assumed she was making note of her strange behavior, like a psychologist or something. In actuality, she was logging the flavor and texture of the purple orb for her personal records. "You don't want to try to stop them?"

May shook her head. "I've got an eternity to figure out what to do with my life. They don't. I'll let her keep it. You uh..." May cringed, realizing what she was about to say might come as a surprise. "You do know about being immortal now, right?"

"I know. That's what I needed to talk to you about. All of you. You should eat. You don't need to, but it'll make you feel better. You're a walking nutrient deficiency." Listay said, scanning May with a blue light from her BEAPER and reading the resultant text. "This is unnatural," she muttered, shaking her head at the readings, most of which were fatally low.

May broke off a chunk of the fruit and ate it, finding it distressingly like a banana made of a hearty stew.

"I won't let her strangle you," said Xan in the distance. May twisted the barstool around to find him nearly dragging Aimz to the table. Aimz's entire body seemed to be going in the opposite direction of her feet.

"You're not strong enough to stop her," whined Aimz.

"Come on, we're in a public place. How bad could it be?" he cajoled her.

Listay stood up. "Aimz, come here," she said, stern,

direct. Aimz shrunk back under the weight of her stare, and Xan got behind her, pushing her forward as she leaned back, her shoes squeaking across the polished glass floors.

"Uh...yes, larvling?" Aimz said with a weak smile.

"You knew we were immortal, and you didn't think to tell me? You know how many rotations I had to host those two Porgord Administrative Assistants while I read through the paperwork, only to find out that I'm immortal and they were trying to get me to sign over my life to some cornufaschten glotchbur-headed toe-ass dictator?" she said. Listay rarely cursed. She had found cursing didn't get her very far in the Rhean military, and so she had practiced restraining herself.

Restraining herself hadn't gotten her very far with Aimz, so now she was practicing wild abandon. She had a good hundred orbits of repressed insults, curses, and profanities built up now.

"This dictator's a toe-ass?" Aimz whispered, a sense of awe in her voice, trying to decide if this meant they had toes in their ass, if their ass was made of toes, or if their toes were, indeed, asses. Any of these options appealed to her.

"Metaphorically!" Listay shouted.

"What the hell was that paperwork about?" May asked.

"A job. All immortals are now legally required to have a job. They're assigned randomly, apparently. My contract was to be the Lesser Lesser God of Winged Insects, and it was a lifetime position. Now that I know how long a lifetime is going to be"—she glared at Aimz, who smiled sheepishly—"I had to decline, but they refused to take no for an answer." She rolled up her sleeve to show them a sticky, oozing gash in her arm. "The Porgord aren't immortal, but I didn't come away unscathed."

"How is that legal?!" asked May.

"How is that possible?" Aimz asked, poking at the wound curiously. Listay snatched her arm away and covered it again.

"Porgord venom is resilient. I can't wash it out with anything. And it's legal because they have enough power to enforce it," Listay said.

"That's true," Xan chimed in. "There's a whole monolith full of would-be laws on Bebaltion that make it illegal, across the universe, to have more than a single limb and three phalanges. For obvious reasons, they have a really hard time enforcing that one. Zuut, it took them a hundred orbits to figure out how to carve it!"

"If they only have one limb..." Aimz pondered out loud. "Is it a—"

"Sexual organs don't count as limbs, Aimz. You're allowed up to five sexual organs. That's why I know so much about the Bebaltions, actually. Great customers. A tad judgmental, but zuut they pay out the nose for services."

"Where did you pick up that idiom?" May asked, not remembering having taught him that one.

"It's not idiomatic; they literally evolved to pay out of their noses," Xan said.

"Huh. Life finds a way, I guess," said May. "So the big question now is...does the toe-ass dictator have the power to enforce the paperwork?"

"They might. But, while you three were cleaning up, I spoke to Maslow, Tree of Secret Organizations, who told me about the Organization Against Order. It then forgot about the organization because it was no longer secret, so I went to Mardy, Tree of Heretofore Secret Organizations, and I found out that the OAO is a coalition of immortals who refuse to sign the paperwork."

May gave up trying to eat the yellow tube thing, swallowed forcefully, and spoke. "So our options are to sign the paperwork or join this Organization Against Order?" May asked. "Is there a third option?"

"You could be on the run from the Administration and whatever other groups of immortal beings might be aware of your existence now. It seems now that we're immortal, we're in high demand."

Xan sighed, leaning his chin on his fist. "It's alright, I'm used to being in high demand. If you don't want to join the Organization Against Order, May, you don't have to."

"Do you want to?" May asked, incredulous.

He shrugged. "I'm pretty good at running away, but, zuut, with an immortal life, maybe there's time to learn a new skill."

"Or time to let all those idiots kill each other off while we stay far away from the action," May noted.

"They're immortal," Listay reminded her.

"Well...they'll get tired eventually, right? I say we wait it out."

"I had planned on you not wanting to get involved. If you stay within the The Organization Against Order's sensor range on Tzerbalba, they can protect you. I'll be checking in occasionally in case the situation changes."

"I think the situation has changed," Xan said, looking over Listay's shoulder to the main lobby beyond where he, May, and Aimz were all being hastily shoved into a room with clouded glass walls. There was something very much not quite right about them. Bits and pieces of their forms seemed to be missing, flickering in and out of place.

"I think that's a different situation altogether," Listay noted.

"Come on," May said to Xan, leading the group to their ailing, arrested alters.

FORTY

A GREAT SEA OF NOTHINGNESS

* * * * *

"What happened?" May asked as she stormed up to one of the guards who had paused, eyeing the duplicate before him suspiciously.

"They turned themselves in. I'll assume you're the actual owner of the *Audacity*?" he said.

"Yeah, but don't ask me for the title," May said.

"Fine with me," said the security guard, handing over May and Xan's stolen BEAPERs and anchor buttons. The Tree Museum wasn't in the business of upholding any law outside of the museum's interests. He'd help you hide a body, no questions asked, as long as nothing in the museum's public policy didn't contraindicate it.

"Oh! It's us!" the Xan who was struggling with existence said excitedly as May, Xan, Listay, and Aimz entered the small interrogation room. Half of his face was missing, along with a good-sized chunk of his shoulder.

"Zuut, does that hurt?" Xan asked, sitting across the table from himself as Aimz and May took their seats across from themselves. The security guard and Listay stood pillar-like at the door.

"N-n-n-" started otherXan. OtherMay jostled him, and his atoms shifted again. "You get used to it," he finished. "Look, I'm really sorry about the fleam and the killing you and stealing your ship. It's not like me to do that sort of thing, but having your universe destroyed kinda fu-fu-fu —"

"It fucks with you," otherMay said, the top quarter of her head flickering on and off and then skewing across the room. May's lip curled with disgust; she couldn't stop herself. It seemed neither of them had much control over what their faces were doing.

"Really, it's alright, I understand completely!" Xan said. "I mean, I don't understand, but I can imagine it must be tough. No harm done, really."

"Why did you want to talk to us?" May asked. "Change in heart?"

"Not just the heart, everything's been changing lately!" said Xan.

"We're not going to make it," said otherMay. "Xan insisted we should return the ship since we're not going to get any use out of it. He went into this whole thing about accepting our fate and clearing our consciences and how our weapons didn't work on you, and he promised to come back. I don't know. It was convincing, I guess," she grumbled.

"Thank you," said May.

"So what does it feel like?" Aimz asked, leaning in, eyes wide. She had been quietly observing for a while, to her credit, but she really wanted to know.

"Like I'm made of pop rocks," otherMay answered.

"That means nothing to me," Aimz said.

"It's like you're made of fizzer st-st-sticks," Mazelmez clarified.

"Ah, got it."

"I don't know. I think it kinda feels like you're on the edge of a great sea of nothingness with no inherent qualities whatsoever, and parts of you are jumping off one at a time, slowly, never to rejoin that thing which was once you," said otherXan, a melancholic acceptance in his far-off gaze.

"Well, yeah, existentially, it feels like that. Literally, it feels like fizzzzzzzz—" Mazelmez's image froze and became somehow lighter, as if the brightness had been turned up on the screen of her being.

"Alright, I have a proposition," May announced to the table. "Let them merge with us so they won't have to die. Not really, anyway."

"Merge with us? As in physically?" Xan asked, and May watched his shoulders rise a full inch as he tensed up. "Are you sure that's safe? Possible, even?" He quieted, leaning closer to her to whisper. "I mean, what would we be if we were half them?" his eyes flicked to their flickering foes.

"It should be possible. I did it in another reality, and it wasn't terrible. It was just like being me but with extra memories. They're not really that different from us," she said.

"We better do it quick because I don't think they've got more than a beoop left in them," Aimz said, appearing behind May and Xan's chair to join the whisper team.

They did seem to be getting worse by the moment. A huge section of May's chest was missing entirely now, but they couldn't quite tell how she felt about that because her face was heavily pixelated, as if she hadn't signed the likeness release form and was being blurred to protect her privacy.

"May," Listay said from the other end of the table, leaning in with concern. "You don't have to be the hero here."

May snorted a humorless laugh. "Now you tell me. I'm going to do it; you two don't have to," May said, looking at her own strange face with an expression that morphed from disgust to pity to compassion. "I'm going to do it," she repeated. And she reached across the table, closed her eyes, and gently touched her own shoulder.

There was no bang. No flash of light. And both Mays still existed, although one was a great deal better at existing than the other. Nothing seemed to have happened at all.

"Is that what was supposed to happen?" Aimz asked,

crouching behind an equally confused Xan.

"No. In one of the other universes...I guess the laws of physics are different in different realities," said May, defeated. "I don't know what to do."

"We should go to the *Audacity*," Xan said. "With them. If we take them through a teledisc with us, it'll merge us. It won't be able to tell the difference between us and them genetically. Right? That's right, isn't it?" he asked Aimz because this was really her field of expertise.

"Won't know until we try! It might just give us whatever universe-decaying disease they have. So at least we'll be suffering together!"

"No, you can't risk that," said otherXan. "It's alright, really. There's nothing wrong with dying," he said. Then otherMay, to show that she could hear him still, put a hand on his thigh. His thigh promptly disappeared. What was left of otherXan held what was left of otherMay tight to his left side and what was left of Mazelmez to his right. "Trying to-to-t- fight this turned us into monsters. I don't want to live like that, anyway."

"Christ, Xan, you're so dramatic when you're dying," said May. "Meet us at the *Audacity* in the parking bay," she said to Listay. "Come on," she said to her Xan, grabbing his arm. Then she reached across the table to take otherXan's hand and teleported them all back to the *Audacity*.

FORTY-ONE

AIMZ, AGAIN, IS THE ASSHOLE

* * * * *

Three individuals remerged in the *Audacity*'s living room, slowly opened their eyes, slowly looked around, slowly realized nothing catastrophic had happened.

Xan looked to May first and smiled brightly, then looked down at himself to be sure he was all there. "We're real! I mean, we've always been real, but the other us's are real. We're whole again!"

"More than whole," Aimz said, reading the teledisc's transfer report. "According to this, our atomic structure downloaded at 132%. Zeens! How does it feel to be 132% of a person?" she asked with a smirk, test-lifting her own arm in a wave-like motion. "Anyone else feel denser?"

"No denser than usual," Xan said. May stifled a laugh; double meanings didn't always translate, and she didn't want to have to explain that one to him.

"So, are we mortal now or not?" May asked Aimz.

"We're 100% immortal! And 32% mortal," Aimz said. "Getting killed would be unfun but not fatally unfun."

"And you're sure about that?"

"100% sure. And 32% unsure," Aimz said with an

unhinged grin. Then her eyes got wide, as if she'd just witnessed the horrible, many-eyed creature that devours space and time, its gnashing and blood-soaked fangs unwavering as they rend reality from reality. As if she'd just realized that this creature's face was her own. "There might be some unintended side effects," she told Xan and May quietly, gazing in horror at nothing.

"Like what?" Xan asked, looking around at the nothing Aimz was looking into and seeing, as you might imagine, nothing.

"I know things I shouldn't know. Things no one should know. I... Oh, Blitheon's tits, I'm a menace."

"Aw, May! Aimz has a conscious now! That's sweet," said Xan, his arm resting comfortably around May's shoulders.

It was not sweet. Aimz was entertaining her own personal worst nightmare: herself. It wasn't strictly true that she had learned nothing from her timeless self. She had learned that deep down, at her very core, she was a terrible, horrible thing. And that was unsettling news to Mazelmez, who was now half of her.

"We met ourself, an ageless and immortal version of ourself, and she wanted to consume the universe. That's a bad, bad sign!" Mazelmez said to herself.

"You weren't there!" Aimz retorted. "She wasn't exactly us. She's not real!"

"That thing lives in our brain!"

"Then she can die in it!" Aimz growled.

"What do we plan to do, ignore her?"

"We're excellent at ignoring things. Watch." Aimz flipped the hot water spigot on the *Audacity*'s coffee machine on and stuck her hand under the scalding water. She didn't flinch. Xan did, though. He rushed to the spigot and shut it off.

"Aimz! Unpin it, mun!"

"We can ignore whatever we want!" she said to herself, ignoring Xan.

"Even Listay?" she reminded herself.

"Not her. We can't ignore her."

"At least we agree on something," Mazelmez said.

"We don't even agree on our name!"

"The diminutive of Mazelmez is Zelma. Where did you even get Aimz?"

"You can't access my memories?" asked Aimz.

"You won't let me."

Aimz sighed, throwing herself over the back of the couch so she didn't have to continue holding her body up. "It was Xan's first word. Aunt Kalumbits thought it was hilarious. Everyone's called me Aimz ever since."

"Alright, we can be Aimz. But promise me you'll get my girlfriend back!"

"Our girlfriend," Aimz reminded herself.

"Should we do something about her?" May quietly asked Xan as he soaked up the spilled hot water on the counter with a rag.

"I think she can work through this by herselves," he said. "Okay, Aimz, we're going to go let Listay know what happened. Once you figure out the controls for your new personality, you can come join us!"

They headed for the teledisc, but Listay had already come to them. She knocked on the entrance hatch, hoping she would be greeted by anything but a terrifying flesh amalgam of all six of them. Xan opened the hatch and helped her in.

"Listay! We were just coming to get you," he said.

"Everyone alright?"

"We're great!" said Xan with a big smile. Although Aimz was still muttering to herself on the couch.

"Here are the coordinates for Tzerbalba," Listay said, watching Aimz warily as she printed out a thin slip of paper from her outdated BEAPER. "The OAO headquarters is in orbit on a space station there, so if any Porgords show up from the Administration and try to make you sign the paperwork again, you'll have back-up nearby."

"Can we still race?" May asked, accepting the slip of paper and reading over the docking bay instructions.

"I wouldn't recommend it until we have more information."

Aimz had gone silent, but now she popped up over the

back of the couch. "Listy, larvling!" she said, launching over to her and slinging an arm around Listay's waist. "I am at your disposal. Both of me. We're in cahoots now. We decided to be in cahoots. What do you need? You want an anti-venom for that?" She held Listay's hand and turned it over to look again at the gooey gash in her wrist. "I wager I can make an anti-venom."

Listay shrugged her off and stepped away. "Mazelmez, you're not coming with me."

Aimz laughed. "Sure I am! You brought the ShuttleDisc, right? Someone needs to fly the ShuttleDisc."

"I'm taking the saucer you stole back to the Organization Against Order's storage locker so they can locate and return it to its owner."

"Surg?" Aimz said, her grin beginning to falter. She saved it. "Surg has plenty of saucers; he doesn't need that one!"

"And you have plenty of love interests. You don't need this one," Listay said, crossing her arms over her bountiful chest. Her bountiful chest was Aimz's favorite.

"But—"

"Ooookay," said Xan, gently scooping Aimz away from Listay for both their sakes. "Aimz can stay with us until she figures herself out. And we'll stay on Tzerbalba until you can figure the Porgord issue out." He looked at May with a silent plea for sanity. "Never been to Tzerbalba. It could be fun! Right?"

May did not think it would be particularly fun to be on the run from venomous bureaucrats, but Xan was trying so hard to establish some harmony, she wouldn't dare sabotage him. "Yeah, blue. It might be fun. I need a break from racing, anyway. Maybe I'll take up a hobby." She smiled weakly, trying to imagine herself knitting, making pottery, gardening. Nothing hit quite like racing.

Aimz pushed Xan aside so she could get to Listay again. "Don't you want an anti-venom?"

"There are hundreds of other scientists in this universe whom I trust to invent a Porgord anti-venom before you. I've never actually seen you invent anything," said Listay calmly.

"I invented a cloche for your seedlings!" Aimz said, Xan holding her back by her shoulders since Listay clearly wasn't in the mood to be hung-upon.

"You cut a hole in the bottom of an old plastic fish barrel."

"It was a thick barrel," Aimz muttered in self-defense.

"That's enough," Xan told Aimz sternly. He was getting better at being stern. Not being anything for half a season because he was trapped underground had given him the energy to try being different things. "Leave Listay alone, Aimz."

Listay gave him a grateful nod. "I'll find you two on Tzerbalba after I meet with the OAO and brief you on the situation," Listay said, then started back down to the parking bay. She paused, hanging onto the ladder just outside the ship, eyeing the bright orange hull. "Try to be inconspicuous," she added. "Maybe look up a body shop on Tzerbalba and get the ship painted black."

"I'd rather die," said May, and Xan agreed empathically.

Listay shrugged. "You just might," she said, then closed the hatch.

Aimz flung herself back onto the couch. "You really zuxxed this, Aimz," she told herself. "Yeah," she agreed. "We did."

FORTY-TWO

MAKE THINE EYE SINGLE

* * * * *

May folded the coordinates up and stuck them in her pocket, her gaze shifting over to a languishing Aimz. "What are we going to do about her?" she whispered to Xan.

"Nothing we can do until she figures out who she wants to be," he said. "Speaking of! What hobby are you going to pick up when we get to the planet?" he asked, trying to redirect May from trying to do anything about Aimz.

"I was thinking...maybe..." May's speech drifted off, and her eyes became glassy, like she was about to sneeze.

Distantly, she heard, "Do you still have the laser sword?" and it sounded like Xan's voice. "Pirates! Find something to bash them with!" she thought she heard Aimz say. "Blitheon, is anyone here a medic?" said Xan. "It's alright. I'll go job hunting tomorrow," she heard herself say. All at about the same time, as if several hundred radios were playing at once, and somehow, she could tell what was being said on all frequencies.

"Damn," she muttered, pressing her palms into her eyes as if that would stop the noise.

"What's wrong?" asked Xan, but his voice was far away now. Under her palms, she could now see hundreds, perhaps millions, of distinct events, all playing in full color and sound at the same time.

She opened her left eye and looked up at Xan, but behind her closed right eye, she could still see a great overlay of the trillions of possible lives she was experiencing. Trillions upon trillions now. Most of them weren't even as a May.

Hesitantly, she sought out one specific reality... There she was. Wad of gum stuck to the universe's shoe. All was dark until the shoe lifted, and she raised up into the light, a long sticky string connecting her to her other half which was still stuck on the groundless ground. The shoe fell, she was squished, and all was darkness again.

She opened both her eyes wide as buttons.

"Holy hell, Xan! I think I'm partially infinite," she said, staring at the orange carpet, seeing only orange carpet. Here she was. She looked up at Xan and gave a crooked sort of smile which slowly grew as he watched her, confused. "Partially infinite," she laughed. "You can't be partially infinite!"

"You should maybe sit down? Maybe...lie down?" Xan asked, a steadying hand on her back.

"I'm fine, actually. I just...I just need to tie up some loose ends. Give me a minute." And she closed her right eye again.

✳ ✳ ✳ ✳ ✳

"Who else would I be?" Xan asked.

May was lying on her side in the pirate's brig again, her hands tied behind her back.

She remembered him now. This him, specifically.

"Oh, right! That laser sword. Of course," she said. "Sorry, I wasn't myself. Untie me?" He obliged, and once her hands were free, she pulled the pen-sized sword hilt from between her boobs and showed it to him, pressing the button which turned it on, her smile shimmering in the vibrating red light of the blade. "Let's get the *Audacity* back," she said to her Xan. Then, standing, she sliced the blade through the bonds that held the Ranger to the beam. "And then we're going to get you home, Ranger. And Aimz..."

Aimz tilted her head quizzically at her.

"You and Listay need to talk. That's happening next."

"Oh, May," Aimz said, breathless. "You really ought to order me around me more!"

* * * * *

Also, at the same time, May was in the underground lab, clean and clinical. She was slotting a screwdriver into the screws that held the interrogation chair clasps together because she didn't know the code that would unhinge them from the computer. "I'm getting you out of here," she said to previously unidentified extraterrestrial. "I don't care if I get fired; I'm not letting them dice you up and study you. Did they take your anchor button?"

"How...?" Xan tried to ask in English as she freed his wrist.

"Nod your head like this for yes." She demonstrated. "And this for no." She demonstrated again. "Did they take your anchor button?"

Yes.

"And your BEAPER?"

Yes.

"And is the *Audacity* within teledisc range?"

He wobbled his head side-to-side. He didn't know.

"Don't worry. I'll get you out of here, and then I'll explain everything. To you and my dad, I guess," said May. "I really hope I don't get fired for this."

* * * * *

And May was also laying on the cool, soft grass. Her skin was throwing off all kinds of pain signals, but she her self felt fine. Xan watched her from above with a look of utter terror.

"Hey, what's wrong, blue?" she asked.

The look of terror subsided slightly as it began to morph into joy. "You're alive?!"

"Yeah, I'm fine," she said. Then she noticed the clothes he was wearing. An open purple vest, a variety of colorful abstract tattoos, glowing jewelry, a headband. "Oh, I see. Fire." She noticed the many festive spectators bent over her crisped body, all aghast that she was still alive. "My skin hurts," she noted calmly.

"What skin?!" Xan asked. "No, don't answer that. I'm getting you to a hospital—just hang on!"

May smiled, but her face felt uncomfortably tight. "Will do. Sorry I scared you, blue."

"It's alright, I'm just glad you're okay! This will be one memorable Sun Begging for everyone!"

✳ ✳ ✳ ✳ ✳

"Arg! They be cursed with deathlessness!" shouted the captain, getting her ass absolutely handed to her as she shot round after round from the baulbeetor into her duplicate's chest to no avail.

"Captain, what are you orders?" asked Xanwell, cowering behind a barrel. The captain, though she wouldn't approve of this being written down, cowered beside him.

"I don't think we can hold 'em," she panted. "They can't be slain!"

"Aye, Captain, they be cursed to life, I'd say," said Xanwell. "Mayhaps it's time—"

"No," said the captain.

"Captain." Xanwell gave her a look she knew all too well. He was calling in a favor.

"Arg, I have a mighty, sucking wound in my heart for ye', Xanwell," she said to him, then gave him a tender kiss before climbing the barrel to announce her orders to the crew. "Retreat!! Back to our own universe! Leave the rocket!" she shouted, and the fighting stopped as suddenly as she did.

"You win this time, May June July," said the captain,

pointing her sword at her deathless duplicate. "But be warned: this shan't be the last you see of me!"

"I didn't expect it to be, Captain. I'll see you every time I look in the mirror!" said May, giving her a friendly wink. "Now, we'll need to use your matter-cannons one last time."

✳ ✳ ✳ ✳ ✳

"I'm a skilled mechanic, and I deserve this job," said May, standing in the open garage at her local mechanic and speaking to a perturbed white guy in a blue polo with a clipboard. His name tag read 'Josh – Manager.'

"Well..." He seemed to really, really want to say no, but he didn't. "We're too short staffed to refuse you. Be here tomorrow, first thing."

"That'll do," May said with a smile. Xan was waiting for her outside the shop.

"What happened?"

"I'm their new mechanic," she said with a proud grin.

"Excellent!" Xan said, relaxing as he looked out across the parking lot at the sun setting behind the distant trees and power lines. The clouds were pink and mesmerizing against the sunset's orange glow. "Earth can be really beautiful."

"Eh, it's fine," May said with a shrug as they began walking home. "Want to get some ice cream in celebration of soon being able to afford it?"

"Absolutely!"

✳ ✳ ✳ ✳ ✳

The Ranger had not vacuumed. She watched him as he lay on the orange carpet, staring up at the ceiling. From her dusty vantage point near the viewscreen, she could see that they were just floating in space, the engines off.

"You alright, blue?" she asked, pulling her particles together and making her dust-ghost appear to crouch beside him.

235

His eyes were closed behind the mask, but he smiled. "Dust-May?" he asked.

"It's me. Come on, get up," she cajoled. She attempted to get under his back and force him to sit up, but she didn't have nearly enough mass left to accomplish this.

"What for?" he asked, eyes still closed. He wasn't sure he wanted to see her as a dust-ghost anymore.

"Because"—May grunted with the effort of trying to make herself more substantial—"you have to do things."

"Why?"

"That's what people do! Things!" she insisted. "You can't lie here forever."

"May, I dug you out of the ground, helped you scare off those pirates, and we fixed the wormhole. Don't you think I've done enough today? I want to sleep."

She stopped trying to pick him up. He was right. He had done quite a lot and probably needed some time to process everything. She laid her dust body down beside him and watched him for a while.

"Don't you think you should be sleeping in a bed?" she asked finally.

He groaned. "Tired," he said.

She laughed. "Alright, blue. You rest. But I'm not going anywhere until we find you a job herding ruffloo, alright? And maybe a partner or two."

He opened one eye and looked at her side-ways. "You're trying to set me up?"

"I will succeed in setting you up. You've got to move on, Xan. My life is over; yours isn't."

He smiled at her. "You're going to stay?"

"As long as it takes for you to forget about me," she confirmed.

He closed his eyes, looking more peaceful than tired now. "You're going to be a dust-ghost for a long time, then, starshine."

* * * * *

The beach was stormy today, metal sculptures clanging gently in a rain which heralded wind. She sat wrapped in her faded shawl on a fallen tree, watching the storm clouds approach land, smelling the crisp change in the air. In her hands, she held another whittled figurine, a miniature of her next planned weld. It would be her biggest yet, a massive metal wheel within a wheel within a wheel which would spin in a strong wind like this.

She heard the porch door creak open from the house behind her and made a mental note to check the hinges for rust.

"Trying to get hit by lightning again?" asked Xan as he sat down beside her, handing her a chipped mug full of strong black coffee before taking a sip from his.

She was only a little surprised at his appearance. His orange hair was long and tied back, streaked with silver. His eyes, still bright and green, were framed with wrinkles.

"Shit, when did we get old?" she asked laughingly, scrutinizing her own leathery hands as if they weren't really hers.

"You remember, don't you? Fifty orbits, thirty-seven rotations back, you said you could 'feel the storm coming in your bones' and decided that you were old, so we got old!"

She could, actually, feel the oncoming storm in her bones.

She was old.

She cackled a nice, hearty, old-lady cackle and leaned against him to drink her coffee. As she stared up at the oncoming clouds, she sensed that there was something just beyond the atmosphere out there trying, subtly, to suck her in.

"Where does it end?" she asked.

Xan was silent for a while, leaving space for the sound of the clanging metal sculptures out there between them and the ocean on Taeloo VII to get louder as the wind picked up. "I don't know," he said at last. "Not here."

FORTY-THREE

ALL'S WELD THAT ENDS WELD

✳ ✳ ✳ ✳ ✳

"I think it's been a minute," Xan said, looking at his BEAPER, which only told the time in bloops, not minutes.

May was standing in the *Audacity*'s living room, her right eye covered with her hand, but her left eye open and totally aware of where she was now. "Xan, it's been maybe ten seconds. A minute is like a bloop and a half," she told him. "But it's fine. I've got the hang of it." Slowly, she lowered her hand and grinned at him.

"Being infinite?" he asked.

"Mhmm."

"What's it like?"

"It's like...I'm myself but more?"

"Unintended zuxing side effects," Aimz muttered from the couch.

"Am I the only one who's not going to have an existential re-zuxening?" Xan asked, a little disappointed.

Aimz and May both watched him silently for a moment as if a Trillosophiat of Blitheon might descend from the ether and whack him in the head with a personal epiphany at any moment.

Several seconds passed, and no such thing happened.

"It's alright, blue. Maybe you didn't have anything to re-zuxen." May patted him on the shoulder.

"Oh, wait!" He held up a hand and looked excited. "Wait!" He was smiling. "That's it!"

"What is?" May asked.

He laughed at his own internal realization, slapping a hand to his face, giddy. "My thing! That was my thing! There was nothing!"

May caught Aimz's eye, hoping she would be able to explain. Aimz caught May's eye, hoping she would. Neither could, of course. That's how personal epiphanies work, though. They're personal.

"Satisfied?" May asked him as his laughter petered off, and he wiped the mirthful tears from his eyes.

"Yep. Totally and utterly," he said. "So, what hobby are you going to take up to fill the great, swirling black hole in your heart left by racing?"

May laughed. "It's not a black hole. It's just a pothole. I think I'll take up sculpture welding."

"Sculpture welding?" Xan tilted his head.

"Yeah...I think I'm into giant metal sculptures now," May said with a shrug.

"Which one of you?"

"All of us," she said infinitely.

"Huh." Xan shook his head in confusion but smiled. "I like it! Sculpture welding. Maybe I'll actually write a book. I wager it'll be easier if I have something to write with!" He was right, it is, but not by much.

"Can you write me in and kill me off?" Aimz said. She had slithered off the couch and was now lying on the floor behind it, pulling apart split ends in her hair one by one.

"Mazelmez, mun, you know I can't do that," he said, pulling her braid out of her hands so she'd stop fiddling with it until he could give it a good trim.

May unfolded the thin slip of paper Listay had handed her and started inputing the coordinates for Tzerbalba. She thought that this time, Aimz could try coping with something more constructive that perception-altering substances, but again, she knew that would not help Xan in his effort to keep the peace, and so, she said nothing.

"Prepare to launch," she warned them. Xan, mostly, because she knew Aimz would not do anything to prepare. Xan joined her at the control panel and sat in the co-pilot's chair.

Before she hit the Button That Typically Made the Ship Go, May closed her eyes and caught glimpses of a trillion trillion other universes. In every one of them, she had the comforting sense that Xan was there with her. Even as a wad of gum on the underside of Universe's shoe, somehow that feeling of his presence remained.

She couldn't put it into words, but Xan was a linguist. He might be able to.

"Xan?" she started, planning to ask him if there was some hyper-specific Tuhntian word for that sensation.

"I'm here."

She smiled. "You always are."

GLOSSARY

Length

Qal: A wee bit.

Horbort: Slightly longer than a meter

* * * * *

Time

Blip: Slightly less than a second.

Bloop: About 50 seconds.

Beoop: About 45 minutes.

Rotation: Varies by planet, but lasts exactly twenty beoops in space (based on the rotations of the planet Estrichi).

Season: Varies by planet, but lasts exactly fifty rotations in space (based on the rotations of the planet Estrichi).

Orbit: Varies by planet, but lasts exactly six seasons in space (based on the rotations of the planet Estrichi).

Quilfraudoron: One infinity.

Quifeee: Infinity infinities.

* † * * *

Insults

Positor: "Dick". Short for "ovipositor".

Poslouian-slug-grass-eating-coward: Xan

Precious Butler: Prostitute (offensive). Also Xan.

Taagshlorph: A piece of slimy, wilted leafy green.

Tchagg: A jerk. Also the term for the musk gland of the common glotchbur.

Zoup-nog: Idiot.

Zingnat: Idiot (affectionate).

Ovi-booster: One who boosts another's ovipositor, a suck-up.

Jultido: A sucker, an easy mark. Common Anat term.

* † * * *

Endearments

Boha: Buddy, friend, mi amigo.

Mun: Comes from the cute fuzzy critters that like to chew up wires on spaceships.

Lav: Gender neutral pejorative term like "kid". Short for "larva".

Larvling: Another form of "larva", more respectful than "lav".

Zuxine: Sexy.

✶ ✶ ✶ ✶ ✶

Other

Splice in the duct: Like a "kick in the pants", referring to the oviduct.

Twa-don: Short for "Twagolohoontz dontargel" which essentially means "Twagolohoontz is leaving the building". Twagolohoontz was a famous Tuhntian comedian who would end every show with this phrase.

Trok: Casual term for the radioactive waste the Rhean government dumped on Tuhnt, creating the wastelands.

Unpin it: Relax. Referencing the physical restraint or "pins" used in cheap rocket races to make sure rockets don't start too early.

Porscinunct: A vow of truth. Invoking this word means you have to tell the absolute truth.

Serpentine palbeatus: Disease characterized by the compulsion and mysterious ability to slither.

Gloxalatal: Biology. Part of an A'Vilrial voicebox which produces clattering sounds which translate as either "Q" "Ch" "Ck" or "X." This is the reason May can't pronounce "Xan" and Xan can't pronounce "Fuck."

Zuut/Zux: Noun/verb. A sexual act specific to the A'Vilrial species.

✳ ✳ ✳ ✳ ✳

Species

Anat: Not actually humanoids! But they may appear to be. Anats are predatory creatures from Pan who have the ability to closely mimic their prey.

A'Viltrian: A'Vilrial race. Not extinct, but highly evolved. They don't play well with others, but they love to release futuristic technology into the galaxy and see how the lesser beings take it. Andolon was their planet of origin, but they are beyond the need of a planet as most of them live in a more subtle dimension.

Bewlahoo: Primoid race. Very large, feline-humanoids from the Primox system. Their language is Bewlahooon. Yes, there are three "o"s.

Filporthean Weet: Also not technically humanoid, though they may embody a humanoid. The weet is an entity that puppets corpses, keeping them partially alive. Most weets are beneficent, but all weets are deeply feared. Their natural form is as a pink sentient fog found in Tuhntian wastelands. The Filporthean Weet is a single weet, the most prolific one on Tuhnt.

Garveral: Primoid race. Large, tough-skinned, slow, and long-lived.

Panseen: Panen race. Characterized by reddish skin, typically five to seven feet tall, most similar, biologically, to Earthlings.

Pringnette: Primoid race. Tall and gazelle-like. Nearly extinct thanks to the Rheans. Ugh. Rheans.

Rhean: A'Vilrial race. Characterized by purple skin in a variety of shades and hues and blue-ish blood. Likes to think they're as evolved as the A'Viltrians; they are not. Have colonized several star systems, destroyed a few cultures, you know, just fun humanoid things.

Titian: A'Vilrial race. Nearly extinct and distantly related to the Rheans. Titians have dark purple-red skin and an extra set of arms (usually underdeveloped and vestigial nowadays). Most remaining Titians have found refuge on Estrichi, a previously uninhabited and neutral planet.

Tuhntian: A'Vilrial race. Blue to green skin tones of any shade, pale white blood that dries green, close cousins to the Rheans, but diverged in their evolution many centuries ago by colonizing Tuhnt. Started the trend of ear-lobe stretching, where the plugs are typically made of expensive metals. The larger the plug, the richer the family.

Udonian: Panen race. Typically short, green, and mustachioed. Their lip hair grows so fast, no one has ever seen one clean shaven.

* * * * *

Star Systems

Flotluex: Planets include Rhea I, Rhea II, Rhea IV, Tuhnt (scorched), Not-Tuhnt (aka Pontoosa or Rhea III).

Premerfherf System: Planets include Andolon (missing), A'Viltra (scorched), Estrichi, and Primox.

System 69F: Planets include Forn, Pan, and Udo.

THERE'S MORE WHERE THAT CAME FROM!

Visit CarmenLoup.com for updates and follow @Carmen_Loup42 on Instagram

The Audacity May's humdrum life is flung into hyperdrive when she's abducted and finds out that rocket racing is a quick, if life-threatening, way to make a living in space. Now, May has a career she loves and a friend to share her winnings with. Until a Chaos goddess decides to turn Earth into her personal sandbox and the Audacity is the only ship that can stop her.

The Audacity 2: Time Warp May and Xan are wildly successful rocket racers, but when a tea-sipping robot arrests Xan, and Chaos steals the Sphere of Time, May must team up with an adventure biologist and her undead girlfriend to save Xan, the Audacity, and Time Itself.

The Audacity 3: Be Kind, Rewind When Xan and Aimz succumb to the Carmnian Scourge, May must team up with old friends, enemies, and a haunted Big Mouth Billy Bass to find the cure before the goddess of Chaos enacts the final stage of her universe befuddling plan

The Audacity's Horrific Horrors: Sip In a haphazard grab at eternal life for the short-lived May, Xan gets reeled in by a killer pyramid scheme. Will either of them survive? No. The answer to that is no, they won't.

The Audacity's Horrific Horrors: Bite May, nostalgic for Earth carnivals, insists on visiting a shitty carnival on a distant asteroid, but when she and Xan get there, they find it abandoned. keen for an adventure, May breaks in to explore the empty park, which is exactly what the remains of the carnival staff want.

The Audacity's Horrific Horrors: Glug A vacation to the universe's most sinful city leaves May and Xan with an unholy mess.

Tarot in Space a 78-card Tarot deck set in the Audacity universe and based on the RWS Tarot.

Thank you for reading, starshine. You're the coffee in my fuel tank, the blueberry in my milkshake, and the good in my luck charm.